PRAISE FOR

"No one writes about the westering experience better than Win Blevins. He has a poet's way with words and imagery to match the wilderness reality."

— LUCIA ST. CLAIR ROBSON, BESTSELLING
AUTHOR OF *RIDE THE WIND*

"Fresh and rich."

— *KIRKUS REVIEWS* ON *DANCING WITH THE
GOLDEN BEAR*

"A rousing installment in a fine epic of the American Frontier."

— *PUBLISHER'S WEEKLY* ON *HEAVEN IS A LONG
WAY OFF*

"Blevins's sweeping vision of the American frontier is just plain irresistible."

— *NEW YORK TIMES* BESTSELLING AUTHORS W.
MICHAEL GEAR AND KATHLEEN O'NEAL GEAR

FITZ

FITZ

TOM FITZGERALD—AN EXTRAORDINARY MOUNTAIN LIFE

WIN BLEVINS

WOLFPACK
PUBLISHING
— EST 2013 —

AUTHOR'S NOTE

Tom Fitzpatrick didn't keep a journal of his life. That's a shame, because it's a fascinating life, from the years of growing up in Ireland through his three decades in the West as a trapper, co-owner of a fur-trading company, guide, Indian agent, and negotiator of treaties between the U.S. government and the Indians. Fortunately, a number of his friends and acquaintances in the West kept close track of him in their journals and books—Jedediah Smith, James Clyman, General William Ashley, John Frémont, and a number of others.

In this book, I've used the facts as known to create a biographical novel—an account of his life that expands to include why he went to the United States and to the mountains to begin with, how he felt about those magnificent mountains and the Indian peoples, and the adventurous life he chose. He himself speaks of how he felt about these matters in the voice I have created for him, one I think is true to his character and his upbringing in an Irish family.

I have also opened up the past understanding of his

life as the adopted father of the Arapaho boy he named Friday, how he made sure that Friday got educated, and the love they shared for all of Fitz's life.

Choosing to have Fitz tell his story in his own voice has meant creating the journal he didn't write and letting his manner of speaking, his feelings, and his personality emerge.

Here is Fitz for you, a jubilant man:

"When we get to Powder River, our camp feels like heaven. It's well protected against storms and full of buffalo. Our days are filled with raucous laughter, the crack of rifles making meat, the whoops of the Crow men when they bring a buffalo down, the shouts of triumph and rousing songs from trappers. I have this strong feeling: Yes, here in the mountains, death is ever-ready, but by God we're alive today. Most human beings never are."

So, this is a work of imagination based on a broad foundation of fact. Good reading to you!

FITZ

Tom Fitzpatrick Tells His Story

I hate pigs.

At this moment I'm breathing pig stink through my mouth, forming spit with it, and spitting it into the mud of the sty.

I've always hated pigs, but my father says slowly and with emphasis, a foot stomping down on each word, "The youngest son feeds the pigs." Unfortunately, the youngest son is me.

On our family farm the pigs eat everything—table scraps, garden greens my mother hasn't used, corn, soy meal, oats, and, I'm pretty sure, their own shite.

I'm stuck now feeding them before we have our evening meal.

Right now my mother, Mary, comes to the back door of the house and calls, "Dinner, Tom."

I breathe out in relief. I've just fed pigs for the last time. And the rest of the family is already inside, sitting down to a fine dinner of celebration. This is Midsummer's Day.

I go to the pump, strip, wash, and put on the clothes I've already laid out for myself. I go through this routine every evening, three hundred and sixty-five days a year, at my mother's insistence. Though I'm careful not to get splashed by the slops I throw to the pigs, my mother says ritually, "Clean clothes, clean clothes, nothing but clean clothes at my table."

Tonight, I'm glad to be clean, and starting tomorrow everything in my life will be different. I'm going to America.

Yes, yes, that decision will take me far away from my family, perhaps forever. And far from the pigs.

A lot of young Irishmen immigrate to America these days. The word is out and about. In the New World land is easily available, and a common man can get some. And unlike Ireland under the rule of Britain, no American gets his head cut off, or his body thrown in jail, for being a Catholic, as I am, or at least as the family and the priest say I am.

It's hard to be a common man in Ireland these days. The legacy of the cursed Cromwell is that landlords hold over 90 per cent of our land, and they're Protestants. My own Catholic family leases our farm from an absentee Protestant.

The pals I drink with at the pub, and play cards with, make mockery of it: Be a landlord, and you get to lord it over us Catholics.

The freedoms of America? No wonder a lot of young Irishmen set out over the sea for the New World. And never come back.

Going and not coming back is... maybe all right with me.

No one in my family except Ma knows I'm leaving. I've confided in her because, well, she is my mother. When I told her, she said she's always known I would be a roamer. I love reading stories of exploring the seven seas. The thought of adventure fires my imagination, and she knows that. She prepared her heart for losing her youngest child years ago.

I love my parents, my two brothers, and four sisters. I do. And at the same time, I feel apart from them, like I'm a stranger in the house.

They're people of the land. They love the land they live on and all of Ireland. They like making their land yield up good food to eat. They like milking the cows and even butchering the yearlings—what fine eating those calves make. They like gathering eggs in the henhouse and enjoy, when that time comes, using a hatchet to get a rooster ready for the dinner table. They're part of all of that, and it's part of them.

I feel very different, my mind more like Pa's. My father attended the local bluecoat school as a boy in Belfast, a charity school for lads of the middle and lower classes. He's proud of being able to read. He sits in his favorite chair in the evenings with the newspaper from Belfast, calling out bits to the family.

However, Pa did wed Mary, a beautiful girl from a farm near our little town of Cavan, which is not nearly so grand a town as Belfast. We have no bluecoat school. Aside from the priest, only a few people can read. Even in our family my mother, my two brothers, and my four sisters don't know how. They see no point in it. They say they don't care about the ways of people with a better-than-thou attitude.

People born and raised in County Cavan stay in

County Cavan. To me that's a strange loyalty. Are they trees, rooted to the earth?

At the age of six I started sitting on the floor next to Pa in the evenings after dinner, picking up the sheets of newspaper he discarded, and repeating some of his words—by listening to the words, not reading them. Pa took care of that in a hurry, plopping me onto his lap, teaching me the alphabet and then unlocking the secrets of how to make those letters into words. Before long I could read the first paragraphs of some newspaper articles to the family. Mostly my brothers and sisters just rolled their eyes.

But Pa and I went on reading together about great adventures. We escaped into Ma's sewing room for long evenings and read tales of miraculous navigations of this marvelous planet.

Also, Pa told me family stories I hadn't heard. I learned that our family once had status we've lost. We owned Castle Hamilton in Donegal, and lost it to that bastard Cromwell. How grand our life could have been.

My first big excitement was reading the explorations of Africa by Prince Henry the Navigator and Bartolomeu Dias. I started yearning to go on a big exploration of my own.

Starting tomorrow, my adventure will be America.

What a night, my last meal with my family for years to come. I tell myself to watch everyone and record their faces, I scrutinize them, and I repeat what they say to myself. I want to remember everything. I wish I was good at drawing, but this pencil and these words in my journal will have to serve me.

The pencil is in fact the recorder of my life. I've kept a journal faithfully since the first day of this year. It's a handsome book, bound in brown leather, with the date printed at the top of each page. With these tools I'll tell the story of my doings every day to the end. It will feel like celebrating the day, the week, the year, my life.

Though I'm not sleepy yet, I want to go to my room and write in this journal.

"Goodnight, everyone."

———

My nest egg for getting across the sea is deposited in the bottom of the bedroll that's packed and tucked under my bed. I let myself smile at the thought of one secret I've kept, my winnings at cards. I suppose I'll have to make my way in America by winning at cards again.

I wonder whether they play As Nas in Philadelphia, where the ship will beach me. I've heard they do. It's a simple game—drop out, cover, or raise. Then wait for each of the other players to do the same or drop out. Eventually, call—and either bluff them into folding or turn over your aces with a grin.

I think the name of the game is weird, As Nas. It should have been called Bluff. If you want to win, you have to learn to bluff and get away with it—simple as that.

But I win, because I stay sober and watch the other players down one beer after another. I've stayed sober by chanting four words to myself—I'm going to America.

————

I wake at first light, as I always do. I slip into the clothes I've laid out and slide my bedroll and a carry-on from under my bed. Everything is in the carry-on, my savings, two blankets, a butcher knife, flint and steel for making fires, a tin cup, two changes of clothes, and a brand-new invention, a Mackintosh, a coat that will keep off rain. Although America has nothing like Irish rain, I'm told. I hope that's true.

I reach under my bed—it won't be my bed any longer —tear out the last page of my journal, and center it on my pillow. I write.

> *I'VE GONE TO AMERICA*
> *GOODBYE*
> *I LOVE YOU*
> *TOM*

Beneath that note I tuck a longer letter I've written to my father:

Pa—Thank you, thank you for teaching me to read. You opened my eyes to the great stories of adventure in all of world history. Those stories are now the inspiration for sending me across the Atlantic Ocean to the New World. I'm sure you will understand, and I will send letters home from America.

Though I creep away at first light, I know you will wish me well on my big adventure.

Your loving son, Tom

————

I loop the rope on my bedroll over one shoulder and heft my carry-on. I pad very quietly down the hall past the other bedrooms and into the kitchen.

Ma is waiting. Half of her face is struggling toward a smile and half is about to cry. She hands me the string bag she's put together for me. In it is a wrap of today's food—bread, cheese, and left-over goose sitting on a piece of ice the size of her hand.

I tuck it under one arm. For sure I 'm carrying a full load.

She hugs me, kisses my cheek, and opens the kitchen door to the world. It smells of brisk, fresh air.

I follow the stone path around the house to the road. For the moment there's no rain.

Within ten minutes I get a ride on a hay wagon going into town.

There I'll catch the mail coach to Belfast, and from Belfast the ship to Philadelphia. I'll write in the pages of my journal every day.

December 1854—In A
Hospital Bed

Dear Reader,

The rest of this book is what I've recorded in two thick ledgers since I've known I don't have long to live. I'm only 54 years old, am happily married to a fine Arapaho woman named Margaret, and we have a two-year-old son, Andrew. But the doctors say I don't have much longer, and my lungs tell me the same.

That's why I'm in bed in this Washington D.C. hotel room, at government expense, waiting for the daily visit by my adopted Arapaho son, Friday. I'm proud of Friday. Because he learned fluent English while being with me for several years, the Arapaho people chose him as one of their representatives at the big Fort Laramie Peace Treaty.

I was there too, representing the United States government and heading up the negotiations.

Now I've come to D.C. with the other commissioners and a lot of representatives of the nine tribes. My son Friday is one of the Arapahos negotiating for his people.

I've been copying these words down since the last

time I was in St. Louis, months ago. I've kept copying since I got here, after I made my report on the Fort Laramie conference to the United States Senate and settled some issues.

We've come up with a new proposal that will be presented to the tribes, and I think they will accept it and sign the treaty.

Friday visits me here every day. When I pass away, he has promised me some good last services. He'll take these ledgers to William Clark for Margaret. He knows them well and knows where Margaret and our infant son live in Missouri. Friday and Margaret are Arapahoes from the same tribe.

Margaret and Clark will do what they can to have these ledgers published as a book. Why not? Kit Carson's adventures have been published, and he exaggerated wildly.

I hope she'll have money from them, plus my savings, to keep her and our small family strong.

November 1822

St. Louis, St. Louis! I stand up and peer ahead from the stern of the keelboat, excited. Ready. Mike says St. Louis is where beaver-trapping expeditions kick off for the West, and they'll be hiring.

I feel the current noodle the bottom of the boat. I take in a deep sniff t0 get the smell of the river, a rank mix of the stream, bottom mud, and marshy banks.

Mike Fink is a keelboat man on the Ohio River, and like me he's headed for St. Louy, as he calls it. Right now, he's steering us downstream toward Louisville.

Downstream is easy, according to Mike—you just follow the current. "Upstream, you fool, now that calls for a *man*, a half-horse, half-alligator of a man, liken to *me!*"

He explains: "That's because the boat, when we're going upstream, has to go forward where the current is least. Sometimes the Frenchies—French-Canadians hired for such work—force the boat upstream. Their poles dig deep into the mud bottom, and they push us by facing backward and treading on them thar boards."

He points to one side of the boat, where there's a tread of short lengths of wood reaching from bow to stern.

"*Damn* hard work."

"With the right wind," he goes on, "some of these same Frenchies will sail the big boat upstream. Or go ashore and pull the boat upstream with a rope called a cordelle. Isn't that the damndest? Sometimes they have to row it."

I figure they must be *brutish* strong.

My new friend Mike is bigger than me, six feet even and a hundred and eighty pounds, he says. Only a little bigger than me, except in attitude. In attitude he must be the whompingest man working the river.

When we're ashore, he likes to throw down his blanket and dare all comers to throw him. Naturally, he flips or knocks them all onto their backs and does a dance and crows a cockle-doodle-doo of victory after each one.

I've seen him do that when we were stopped at a town to unload freight.

If rumor and report are true, Mike also likes to put a tin cup on a man's head, march off twenty paces, level his rifle, and knock the cup for a spin without knocking the man off planet Earth.

Mike takes bets on this feat, splitting the spoils with the fellow beneath the cup. He's said to have an unblemished record. He says he even shot the scalplock off of an Indian's head once.

Nevertheless, I won't participate in this sport.

———

Now I get up and walk the length of the boat and back just to stretch my legs. You have to adjust your balance with every step, following the boat's sideways movements as in a dance.

I like to listen Mike jaw, but discount his tales by fifty percent.

When I get back to the stern, Mike has let go of the tiller so that the boat surrenders to the current. He's leaning backward, pissing into the Ohio River.

Over the *swooshing* sound of the river against the bottom of the boat, Mike says heartily, "This piss will be waiting for us right ready when we get to St. Louy. Give spice to the drinking water, it will."

"Oh, *Fotzenheimlich,*" I say. That's a word Mike and I made up from something we heard in a tavern. It means, as Americans say, "bullshit."

Mike has promised to show me around St. Louis when we get there. Now he adjusts his pants, sits down, and takes the tiller.

"Have a rootin'-tootin' time, we will."

"Rootin'-tootin'," I agree. I love that crazy Americanism. "If I can keep you from pissin' into the next man's beer."

"Keep me from it? Why?"

"Don't want a fight."

"But that's the fun of it!"

Mike is quite the fellow.

FEBRUARY 1823

When we get to St. Louis in early February, Mike shows
me the way to the home of a woman who rents rooms.
Then he leads the way by turn to every grog shop and
whorehouse he knows in town.

I can't keep up with all of that, and don't care to, but
I fake it.

Now I have my own program to follow. I go back, rent
one of those rooms, and stow everything I own.

The next morning I get dressed and eat breakfast with
Mike in a nearby restaurant. Then I kick off the day by
paying a visit to one of my heroes, William Clark, once a
co-leader of the Lewis and Clark expedition and now the
United States Superintendent of Indian Affairs.

At his secretary's invitation, I open the door to
Clark's inner office, stand in it, look across the small
room at him, and say with an eager smile, "Superintendent Clark, I've come all the way from Ireland to meet
you. I'm Tom Fitzpatrick."

I thrust out my right hand for a shake.

Clark grins, stands up, comes across the room, and

shakes my hand vigorously. Then he says, "Glad to meet you, Mr. Fitzpatrick. I knew you're Irish by your accent, clearly enough!"

The office reeks of the odor of tobacco and the of the colorfully painted hides hanging on the walls. A fine, rich smell.

"Sit down," Clark says, extending an open hand to the chair in front of his desk. I do, and he returns to his desk chair, facing me.

"I mean it, Superintendent. I'm a devotee of great explorers like Fernando Magellan and Sir Francis Drake, who circumnavigated the planet. You and Captain Lewis made a difficult and dangerous crossing of your continent, and I stand in awe of your accomplishments."

Now, looking dumbfounded, he says, "Call me Mr. Clark. And I didn't quite get your name."

"Tom Fitzpatrick," I answer, and add, "Call me Fitz."

"Mr. Fitzpatrick," says Clark, "I gather that you've heard a good deal about our expedition."

"Among the rivermen, Sir, those who work the Ohio and the Mississippi, there is talk, talk, talk about you and Captain Lewis, and all are in awe of what you accomplished."

Clark nods. "Mr. Fitzpatrick," he says—

"Call me Fitz," I put in.

"Fitz, I'm just going out to lunch. Will you join me?"

WI must be dreaming!

"I'm keen to do that, Sir, yes." I feel like gushing but think I've said enough.

"Call me Mr. Clark," the Superintendent repeats.

We walk to a restaurant he knows, no more than a cubicle, and at his insistence I let him order.

"The usual," says Clark. "Twice."

The waiter brings two ham omelets, two croissants,

and black coffee. Omelets for lunch—that tickles me, but it seems to be what Clark eats here every noon. And croissants are a new treat to me, a delicacy of Frenchified St. Louis.

Clark and I don't chat idly. I'm keen to hear details about the great expedition. In particular I ask about the Indian tribes they met along the way, and how the expedition managed to cross the territories of so many potential enemies with almost no conflict.

Clark is glad to talk about that. "The key," he says, "is to make gifts to the Indians in return for safety while on their lands. And you have to have the right gifts—tobacco, blankets, knives, kettles, and tin cups. Also beads, trinkets, and yards of colored cloth for the women."

Our conversation goes on and on. Which is my good fortune.

———

At length, over our final cups of coffee, Clark says, "You're an amiable young man, very intelligent, and the music of your Irish accent is enjoyable. Most people who come to visit the Superintendent of Indian Affairs come wanting something in particular. Is there anything I can do for you?"

With emphasis, I say, *"Thank you,* Mr. Clark. Sir, I want to travel to the West and go into those unexplored lands myself. I'm told that there are fur-trapping expeditions about to head up the Missouri River to Indian country. Do you know of a way I can go along?"

Pleased, Clark nods. "That's easy. Do you hunt?"

"No."

I don't want to say so, but I've never held a gun, much less fired one.

Clark nods again. "Do you trap?"

Again, "No."

A small smile from Clark. "Do you read and write?"

I let out a big breath of relief. "Both. I'm an avid reader, and I write in my journal every day."

"Good," says Clark. "So, you read and write, and you've learned to add and subtract, I assume."

"I haven't got my figures down, but I'm a quick learner."

Clark leans back and studies me. "The next upriver expedition, General Ashley's expedition, will need a clerk. Someone to record what happens each day in a ledger, and keep track of trades and expenditures, too. Next to Ashley, the clerk will be the key man of the expedition and the best paid. Two hundred and fifty bucks a year. That should appeal to you."

I'm sailing among the clouds. "Definitely, Sir."

He slides pen and paper out of a drawer and starts writing. "Here's a note of introduction to General William Ashley. He's one of the two partners of an aggressive new trapping expedition up the Missouri River. His next expedition is scheduled to leave St. Louis late next month. Go see him—Florence will give you the address—and hand him this note."

"Will do so!"

"And collect a book from Florence tomorrow. You must get ciphering down."

I wait until I'm outside his office to read the note. It says, "Ashley, this young man, Thomas Fitzpatrick, recently of Ireland, has made an excellent impression on me. He's educated, and I commend him to you as a clerk."

I yell "Hooray!" I jump into the air with both hands held high and come down on the edge of the wooden St. Louis sidewalk. The boards break, and my shoes slide into the mud of the street.

———

I collect the book from Florence the following morning and stick my head in to thank Clark again. I could come to love the rich smell of tobacco and animal hides in his office. Maybe I'll have an office of my own one day. Meanwhile, I decide to go back to Clark's lunch place for an omelet and a croissant.

I spend the afternoon reading the basics of adding and subtracting numbers. I spend the evening reading more about ciphering. I spend all the next day, working problems the authors have provided at the ends of chapters.

I give all the next day to re-reading the explanations of addition and subtraction and re-doing the problems. Fortunately, I arrive at the same answers, over and over.

On the weekend I enjoy myself by sitting in coffee houses, swilling coffee and munching muffins, until I've done all of that twice.

On Monday morning I go to see Florence and ask her to check my work.

"No," she says, "I don't know how to do that." She hesitates. "But if you'll come back to this office at 3:30 today, I'll have Arnie, my eldest, here for you. He's in the fifth form."

"I promise you that Arnie will go over all this learning with you." She hesitates. "Truth to tell, I've already asked him."

She hesitates again and adds, "He has a price."

"What price?" I ask. Actually, whatever the kid can think up is worth it many times over. I can almost feel that $250 American dollars in my pocket.

"You'll like his price," says Florence with a smile.

————

Arnie hands back my written answers and says, "Perfect."

"Great! Thanks!" I'm grinning big at him. "What's your price?

With a smile, he answers, "Vanilla ice cream."

To me, ice cream is just a rumor. I've never tasted it.

"Where do we get it?" I ask.

"The confectioner's," is the answer of the eleven-year-old.

I want to jump for joy, but I control myself. I actually know what a confectioner's is.

We walk to the ice cream shop, which is no more than five minutes away, and wait at the counter to order.

The clerk comes and asks, "What do you want, Arnie? Your usual, vanilla ice cream with chocolate sauce on it?"

To remember Arnie, the clerk must have an extraordinary memory.

"My usual," affirms Arnie.

The clerk writes down the order.

Arnie is grinning.

Excited myself, for reasons I don't know, I say, "I'll have the same."

I pay for our treats. The cost is one buck, as Americans call their dollars, plus a few coins.

We sit at a table with spoons and small dishes shaped

like flowers. I take my treat in small bites and savor each bite. I've never tasted anything so good.

When Arnie finishes his, we walk to his home, which is about ten minutes away. We go inside and sit at the kitchen table and I hand him the rest of my work sheets of addition and subtraction problems.

"Mr. Fitzpatrick," he says, "you've gotten every answer right. You're a whiz."

I smile and say, "Call me Tom."

———

Thrilled, I go back to Clark's office and stand in front of Florence's desk, and I give the math book back to her.

I give her a five-dollar bill and say, "For Arnie's time and effort."

She answers, "You're very good to Arnie. I think he'll come to thank you."

Smiling, I say, "I'll take him out again for vanilla ice cream with chocolate sauce on it."

"Mr. Fitzpatrick, he'll never forget you."

———

I find Mike Fink at our boarding house and get more good news: Mike has signed on with Ashley as a hunter and trapper and is happy about going to the mountains. I'm glad we'll be travelling together. We agree to celebrate with a fine supper.

Then I say, "After supper, my treat, let's have a drink at a tavern you like."

I'm sure Mike will frequent only taverns that appeal to drunks and ruffians.

At the tavern of Mike's choice, I get a fine surprise.

Do Americans play what we Irishman call As Nas?

No, they play a card game they call poker. And wonder of wonders, poker is exactly the same game of bluffing as As Nas, under a different name.

Tonight I'll win big.

———

As I play the cards, Mike stands behind me, legs spread, arms folded across his big chest, looking like a thundercloud about to strike. I think my friend diverts the other players' attention in a helpful way.

When it comes my turn to deal, I send Mike to the bar for another round of beers. When the round arrives, Mike distributes the glasses, and I give mine to him. This keeps my friend close by, gets my competitors a bit loopy, and keeps me sober.

I'm doing well at the table.

Loopy or not, I think, *Mike will protect me, his friend and the source of his beer.*

At one point a fair-haired fellow with a drawl I've come to recognize as Southern asks Mike, "Are you here as a bodyguard for the Irishman?"

Mike answers, "I'm just learning the game by watching."

Good, I think. *The suspicion is good, and the answer is good.*

When we leave, close to midnight, Mike still looking like he might erupt, I've paid for a fair amount of beer, and my wallet is thick with bucks.

March 15, 1823

I hurry to the river and spot Ashley's two keelboats, the *Rocky Mountains* upstream and the *Yellowstone Packet* behind it. They're the usual size, about fifty feet long, with tracks on each for the Frenchies who will pole the boat upstream, pull it from the shore with a long rope, or row it.

Now a brisk downstream wind makes my eyes moisten.

Ashley bustles his way through the gang of men going back and forth and spots me standing on the bank.

"Fitzpatrick! Let me show you around."

The two boats look identical. They have masts for sailing when the wind is right, deck space, and areas of covered deck for...?

"Come on," Ashley says, "I want you to see."

The general leads the way across the deck of the *Rocky Mountains* to a door and takes me into a room beneath the deck.

"These are my quarters," he says, "A single bed, a handsome desk with a can of tobacco, and several short, wooden pipes. Notice the two Hawken rifles angled upward on the wall, the two pistols facing each other flintlock to flintlock," he says, pointing with one finger. I also notice that an Indian ceremonial pipe is displayed, mounted next to the robe of an animal, I don't know what animal.

Considering that it's tucked below the deck, the room is spacious and handsome. It gleams from being oiled, and I'm sure Ashley didn't do the oiling.

There's a small, potbellied stove with a venting pipe sticking up and probably onto the deck. On top of the stove is a gray-speckled pot. The general must like his morning coffee.

Ashley sees me take notice of the stove. "Most of the men don't know about this," he says. "They're superstitious about fire on board, any fire at all. That's a sailor's superstition, but we're not at sea, and my fire is never more than coals at the bottom." The general smiles with relish. "*Hot* coffee," he says, filling a cup for each of us.

I take a cup from Ashley and suck in a deep sniff of the steaming brew, followed by a sip.

"This coffee is excellent," I tell him with a smile. I take another sip.

"Now I'll show you your quarters," says Ashley.

The general holds open a door I haven't noticed and leads me into another room.

"Work desk and bed," he says.

The space is about half of Ashley's. The desk is three rough-sawn planks pressed against a wall, with a wooden chair facing it. Two shelves are braced above it. While Ashley's walls display firearms, mine are plain wood.

I'll gladly supply my own firearms. Mike showed me the way to the Hawken shop in St. Louis. Having never fired a gun in my life, I am now equipped with a flintlock rifle and a pistol. I'll have to learn to shoot them. All I know now is to point the barrel away from myself.

Fortunately, Mike is an expert shot. Still, he's not about to get permission to blow a tin cup off my head, no matter how many bucks I could win that way.

I run my eyes over everything and count my blessings. Maybe the trappers, hunters, and Frenchies will have to sleep on deck in the wind and rain.

Having privacy and being inside from the elements—these are luxuries. Come to think about it, having shelter against the Indians may be a good idea too.

THE IDES OF MARCH 1823

This morning we set off upriver, headed into adventure. The crews of the two boats cast off their moorings, and we're underway by mid-morning, propelled upstream by Frenchies.

Mike Fink is the helmsman of the leading boat, the *Rocky Mountains*. He stands in the bow and steers us clear of sand bars and major obstacles in the river, especially the big logs that get stuck on the bottom in our path or come charging downstream angrily.

I stand near Mike. The wind whips into my face, bringing tears to the corners of my eyes. I try to smell the mountains and can't. I try to smell my future and can't.

I think, *the mountains are a thousand miles away.*

May 28, 1823

I've learned to wake up each morning, listen through the wall for signs of Ashley stirring, tap on the door between our rooms, and ask for permission to join the general for coffee.

He opens the door right off. "Good morning," each of us says at the same time and with big smiles.

The general hands me a cup full of brew and then hands me the coffee pot. It's heavy, but I can manage.

We take the stairs up onto the deck of the keelboat and sit in the chairs he keeps there. We've gotten into the habit of taking our cups and the pot of hot coffee up on the deck, enjoying the faint breeze. This morning it's blowing upstream, which is good fortune. It means we can use our sails.

So, I chance to be sitting with the general when a lone mountain man who is dressed like a trapper comes drifting along with the current, floating downstream in a dugout canoe.

I stand up to see better. "It's a trapper," I tell Ashley. "Alone." I'm stating the obvious because it's so odd. An

Indian in a dugout canoe by himself, sure, but a white man?

With a few economical strokes he crosses from the middle of river to the *Rocky Mountains*, which is anchored, and eases the canoe alongside. Mike Fink hurries to pull the fellow on board, and they heft the dugout canoe on board together.

The tall stranger looks around and spots the general and me, standing up to see him better.

He strides toward where Ashley and I stand on the deck above the general's cabin.

"Smith?" the general asks uncertainly.

"The same, Sir." He comes close and extends his right hand. They shake.

Then Ashley introduces us. "Fitz, this is Jedediah Smith. Jedediah, Tom Fitzpatrick."

We shake hands and say at the same time, "Good to meet you."

Ashley says, "Jedediah, Fitz here is our clerk, and he's doing a solid job. He'll record on today's page that you arrived in a dugout canoe, after paddling—how far? A couple hundred miles upriver from our fort at the mouth of the Yellowstone River."

Jedediah puts in, "General, I come with a message from Major Henry."

I've heard a lot about Henry, who's commanding our outfit of trappers and hunters a long way up.

What guts it takes to paddle that far by yourself.

I ask, "Did you sleep at night in a blanket on shore with the canoe pulled up on shore?"

Smith smiles and says, "I did."

"What did you eat?"

"Jerky, for breakfast, lunch, and dinner. I'm darn tired of it."

I think, *Seems like Smith doesn't cuss.*

Ashley says, "Jedediah, your dinner tonight will be damn good. Mike Fink will row us to the right bank, and we'll eat whatever game meat our hunters have brought in. If not buffalo, then deer or antelope, plenty of meat for all."

Jedediah smiles and says, "Can't think of anything better."

Then he delivers the message he's canoed two hundred miles, over three weeks, to deliver to Ashley, the big boss of all of us.

"General," Jedediah says, "for this mission to succeed we need a lot more horses."

———

The general and I listen to Smith's tale of his downriver trip. "No problems," he says. "I didn't build fires in the evenings because smoke from fires can be seen a long way off."

I'm wild with admiration for Jedediah's daring. Major Henry, who had our fort there built by his outfit, has sent Smith through all kinds of danger to deliver this message. And that message is, "Horses, we need more horses"?

Really?

Jedediah explains, "Trappers ride up creeks from the big rivers looking for beaver sign, working alone and riding one horse. They know the sign when they see it on the banks of the creeks. They dismount, hobble the horse, and set their traps."

"They spend the night wrapped in a blanket and wade into the water to get any beaver they've trapped. They wade back, carrying the drowned beaver and the trap."

Yes, Jedediah's account is getting long, but it needs to be. Neither Ashley nor I have stopped listening.

Smith goes on, "We load the pelts onto the horse we're leading upstream. Now we have to walk, and that's a problem. It's much slower than riding while leading the horse."

A clear and convincing explanation. The shortage of horses is slowing the trapper down. That costs Ashley money.

The general says tentatively, "I understand. I'll trade for the horses at the Arikara villages and take them onboard the keelboats for delivery at the fort."

"Are we approaching the villages?"

"They're a couple of days ahead, depending," Jedediah answers. "I slipped by them night before last."

Suddenly I think about Smith's travels. "Jedediah," I ask, "Have you had any breakfast? I could find us some."

Smith grins broadly and says, "I haven't had breakfast since I left Captain Henry four weeks ago."

"I'll see what I can do."

I jump up and go looking for Mike Fink. In ten minutes, I'm back with Mike and food.

They trade names and shake hands. Jedediah pays Mike the compliment of saying, "I know you by reputation."

Mike says, "After a journey as risky that one, you'll have a reputation, too."

He sticks out a big paw filled with roots. "You like prairie turnips?"

"Sure," says Jedediah. He takes both handfuls and then snaps off a bite with his front teeth. He chews enthusiastically.

He and Mike grin at each other. Jedediah says, "This is tasty business."

Mike's the boss of the Frenchie crew of this lead boat, it's time to get moving again, and he goes back to work.

Jedediah says to Ashley, "I didn't get much sleep. Where's a good spot?"

I pitch in, "Right through that door. You can use the bunk in my cabin. Welcome to it."

I get a nod of approval from Ashley. Maybe the general wouldn't be so quick to share his bunk with a man who's been sleeping on river banks for two weeks, but I don't mind. I want to make friends with Jedediah Smith.

He says, "Call me Diah. Everyone does. Sleeping indoors will be a treat for me."

I lead him below to my room and hold out a hand toward the bed.

Then I go back on deck and sit forward, next to Mike. We're moving upstream again.

Diah can sleep in my room again tonight. I won't mind sleeping ashore under a blanket.

———

Two days later Ashley and I stand on the deck of *The Rocky Mountains* while the crews anchor our two keelboats about ninety feet from the right bank of the Missouri River, all the way across the river from the two villages of the Ree Indians.

I've learned that the trappers have shortened the name of the Arikara Indians to Rees.

Diah, Ed Rose, and I row across the river for break-fast on the right bank. We're eating jerky and standing by the fire the trappers have built. If we'd thought to bring our cups, we could have hot coffee with them.

Diah says, "Look, the Rees have palisaded their villages."

I can see that the two villages are fortified with earth and trees, twelve or fifteen feet high. That must have been a project to build, since timber is scarce on these plains. They must have thinned out the cottonwoods along the river considerably to build it.

———

While Rose gnaws on jerky, Diah and I row to the boat where Ashley is drinking coffee on the deck of *The Rocky Mountains*. We finish the pot with some friendly chatter between swallows.

Ashley says, "Let's row on across the river to the other side and land on the sand bar. From there we'll have a clear view of those fortified villages. We'll take Rose along."

We get Ed Rose to help us load a lot of gifts and trade items for the Indians, then board and row.

———

Diah and I man the oars. We land on that sandbar, step onto the sand, and slide the rowboat onto the sand. Diah, Rose, and I unload the gifts and other items.

Ashley dives right in. With a nod of his head toward the villages, he asks Rose, "See that?"

I wonder why in hell we're bringing them so many gifts.

"Ever' coon of us done seen it when we'uns got here yesterday," says Rose. He speaks in the rough lingo of the mountain men, which I'm still getting used to. A trapper refers to himself as "this coon" or "this hoss" and otherwise speaks very oddly.

"What do you think the palisades mean?" asks Ashley.

"They done mean they're telling the Sioux, or us, or everybody underneath the sky to stay the hell away."

Ashley has said that the Sioux roam the plains all around these villages. For generations both tribes, Sioux and Rees, have tried to get rid of each other. Each has failed.

"Any way to tell whether they're mad at us or at the Sioux?"

"Not nohow," says Rose.

"All right," says Ashley. "Let's sound them out about trading. How do we start?"

"Just wait right'n here," says Rose.

———

The wait feels long to me, but at last a war party of young men and five Ree chiefs comes. They're led by a man who introduces himself as Chief Bear. He introduces us one by one to other chiefs, saying their names in the Ree language. They sit in a semi-circle facing us.

Their young warriors sit behind them on the sand, rifles in hand.

Of course, I don't understand a word Chief Bear says. Nor do I understand the signs Rose makes for us white guys.

We sit facing the chiefs. But then Ashley asks, "Jedediah and Fitz, will you please unload all the goods from the boat and put them in knee-high stacks in front of us?"

Diah and I do that. I don't know what's up.

I can't follow the conversation, which takes place with very fast movements of fingers, but Rose sums it up as the chiefs speak. "Chief Bear says the hearts of the Ree people are good toward white men. They will be grateful for whatever we want to give them. And they're ready to trade now."

Rose translates Chief Bear's words deliberately, like he's sucking each word for meaning as he speaks it. I wonder if he doubts what the chief is saying.

As Ashley names the gifts, he sets them down in front of the chiefs, and I write them in the big black ledger Ashley gave me for occasions like this:

- Six pounds of tobacco, which I know would cost a trapper nine dollars.
- A coat made from a red-and-white-striped Hudson Bay blanket, twenty dollars to a trapper.
- Four tin cups, worth four dollars. Two speckled coffee pots, worth six dollars. Two fire steels, worth four dollars.
- One string of blue beads, but I don't know the value of them. I make a note to ask Ashley later.
- A yard of scarlet cloth, also of unknown value.

Now Ashley takes a different approach. "Are you ready to trade?" he says. "I want horses."

Chief Bear looks at his people and nods. "Trade now," he signs. "We will trade only for powder and lead."

I can't tell whether Rose is frightened by this instruction. I am.

I have no idea how much a horse is worth this far

upriver from the settlements, and the chief doesn't know how many horses Ashley is after.

"I want twenty horses," says the general. Rose communicates that to the chiefs in signs.

Chief Bear turns to his comrades and speaks in the Ree language. At length he signs, "For each horse fifty pounds of gunpowder."

Outrageous! I think. That's a hundred bucks per horse.

"Twenty pounds of gunpowder," answers Ashley.

From there they finger-haggle. They settle at thirty pounds of powder for each horse.

That's a lot. What if they use the powder and lead we trade them to shoot at us tomorrow?

Abruptly, Rose says, "General, we gotta talk amongst ourselves."

Now Ashley holds up a hand to ask for a pause and gets a nod from Chief Bear. Rose stands in front of us, his comrades.

"General," says Rose, "you know I'm not afeared of no fight—no way, nohow. But feels to me like we're trading the Rees what they could use to shoot at us."

Ashley nods. "Yes, that bothers me too."

He interrupts himself. "What kind of rifles do the Rees have?" he asks Jedediah.

Jedediah says, "They're *fusils,* the smooth-bore muskets we know to be inaccurate. No self-respecting mountain man would carry one. We trappers know to trade for rifles with the most up-to-date technology, with rifling in the barrels. They're made at the Hawken shop in St. Louis."

"What's the range of a *fusil?*" asks Ashley.

"Eighty yards," says Diah.

"How far away is that nearest village, the one that's palisaded?"

"About a hundred yards," says Rose.

The general raises an eyebrow at Diah for confirmation.

"A hundred yards," says Diah.

"I'm thinking of holding the horses on this sand bar for the night," says Ashley. "The Rees wouldn't have any accuracy at that distance."

"None," confirms Diah.

"Even less accuracy at the distance of the keelboats?"

"Wouldn't reach nearly that far, Sir, not even close," answers Diah.

"But we would have accuracy firing back from the sand bar?" Ashley continues.

"Yessir, but they would probably shoot from behind the palisades and then duck down to reload. We'd have no targets."

"Let me think out loud," Ashley says. "If they fire at us from behind the palisades, they're pretty safe. But we're entirely out of range for them. Is that right?"

"Yessir."

"So safe both ways. Also," the general says, spreading his hands, "if they advance toward on us on the ground, they're vulnerable to our fire before we're vulnerable to theirs—right?"

"Yessir."

Ashley thinks it over. Finally he says, "A man of daring has to *dare*."

A moment of silence. I can see that he's sweating as he thinks. A drop of sweat falls from his chin.

The general turns back to the chiefs and keeps trading

until he has twenty horses and they have a lot of our powder and lead.

Then Ashley tells Chief Bear, "I'm finished trading."

Chief Bear gets the words from Rose's fingers and nods. He signs, "We'll bring the horses down to you here, just before dark."

Then the chiefs get friendly. Through Ed Rose's translations, one of them says, "You and all your men will be welcome in our village tonight. We're friends of white people. Bring gifts for our women."

Aside, I ask Diah, "Why does he say to bring presents for their women?"

"A lot of the women will be glad to trade vermilion, a yard of colored cloth, or beads for sex."

Ashley says, "All right, it's time to row back to our boat. Jedediah, you, Fitz, and Rose will stay here. I'll get seventeen more men to volunteer to sleep on this sandbar tonight. It should be safe for all of you."

I ask, "Will we have to go without supper?"

"No," says Ashley, "you can come across and eat with all of us. Get your blankets and your rifles. Later Mike Fink will row you back over to this sandbar. For twenty passengers, I'd guess that will require five round trips."

I have a rifle but don't even know how to load it. Mike can show me and teach me to shoot it later.

But right now, *OH, SHITE!*

July 1823—On A Date I Don't Remember

At dawn Rose charges onto the sandbar and wakes us up hollering, "Trouble! Trouble!"

He doesn't need to say that. I can hear guns firing from the upper Ree village.

We don't know what the hell to do. We can't turn into cowards and row back to the keelboats.

Most of the men load their rifles and shoot back. But the damn Rees are firing from in between the Vs made by the pickets at the top of their palisades and are only exposed for the moment it takes to aim and pull the trigger.

For a while, until a couple of horses go down, hurt, I don't realize that the damn Rees can actually hit us. And yes, with the powder and lead we traded to them.

General Ashley, damn you. You stuck us with the consequences of your decision.

Diah hollers, "Get down behind the fallen horses!"

I run to Diah and ask over the sound of the gunfire, "How can this happen?"

Diah shrugs. "Practice, I guess! They've figured out

how high to aim their rifles to lob the balls onto this sandbar. Maybe that's how they got low on powder and lead and had to trade their horses for our ammunition."

Sounds like a good guess.

I see men lying behind the three horses that are down. I crouch low, waiting to see another horse collapse, dash to it, and throw myself down behind it with my useless rifle in hand.

The men are grabbing spots behind the horses for cover, one by one. How many of our new horses will be killed before we can get them off this sand bar?

I take the risk of standing up. Mike Fink and a fellow I don't know are hauling the bow of a rowboat onto the sand. Other men run and clamber into the boat.

One gets shot and drops into the water. I dash to help him, but he's dead.

Mike says, "Fitz, we can take four more across."

I holler as loud as I can, "Four men run and jump aboard!"

But they're too scared to come out from behind the fallen horses.

I run, useless rifle still in hand, and flop down behind a horse. I'm staying here with my partners.

———

Still on the sandbar and under fire, Diah decided to drive the horses left alive into the water, swimming across to the keelboats. The Frenchies know to lower ramps so the horses can get aboard. If they don't, Ashley will tell them how to do it and make it an order.

Now there's Diah, me, and twelve other men left on the sandbar, all of us more or less safe behind dead horses.

But the Rees mount an attack on foot. Our men fire at them from behind the dead horses but must take time to reload. When they're ready to shoot again, the Rees are a lot closer, maybe sixty yards, and firing at our heads, which stick up above the horse carcasses.

The men dash madly into the river, carrying their rifles. They jump in and swim like hell for the keelboats.

I figure out how they're doing it. They've stuck their rifles up into their pants as far as the crotch.

Awkward, but…

Diah is the last man on the sandbar.

He checks on the Rees. They're getting too damn close.

He stands up, runs like hell into the river, stuffs his rifle down his pants, and starts swimming.

Out at *The Rocky Mountains*, Mike Fink pulls me aboard, then he grabs Diah.

"Thank God!" exclaims Ashley, and I let out a huge sigh of relief.

Now I count heads of the other survivors, both men and horses.

For some reason the totals are identical. Ten men and ten horses are alive and on board. Which means that ten other men and ten other horses are dead, their bodies on the sandbar or in the river.

———

The next morning Ashley orders the two keelboats to float down the river to an island with lots of trees. It looks defensible against another attack by the Rees.

But on the way two more men die of gunshot wounds.

The Frenchies dig graves for them, and Ashley asks Diah to say some words.

I watch as the two are dropped into their graves and dirt is shoveled onto them. A sad place to spend eternity.

Faces are waiting, filled with grief. Diah begins, "Lord of mercy, we know your love. Now we send to you the bodies and souls of John Gardner and Reed Gibson. They died fighting for the right. We ask you to show them your love. Please grant them eternal life in the heaven that awaits them.

"In the name of Jesus Christ, amen."

I look around. General Ashley's face, Diah's face, all the faces I can see and read, and I'm sure including my own, show quiet puzzlement and deep sadness. Life and death... Both come at us hard and abrupt sometimes.

About A Month Later
—August 1823

General Ashley begged and pleaded with his crew to continue our voyage, to go back and run the gauntlet of the Ree villages.

Most of them refused. They're French-Canadians and think getting shot at isn't what they signed up for.

The next morning, he pleaded with the crew again, but to no avail. He called for volunteers, and thirty responded, but the rest had had enough of Indian warfare. They want to go home.

Now the general resolved to ask the help of Colonel Henry Leavenworth at Fort Atkinson. Accordingly, he sent one of our two boats downstream, the *Yellowstone Packet,* carrying five of the wounded and such others as refused to stay, along with a message to Leavenworth.

He also sent two messengers across country to Major Henry at the mouth of the Yellowstone, asking him to come and bring with him such men as could be spared there.

Ashley moved his other keelboat, *The Rocky Mountains,*

down some seventy miles to the mouth of the Cheyenne River, awaiting reinforcements.

Colonel Henry arrived at our camp in late June, bringing bad news: He had suffered a defeat at the hands of the Blackfeet Indians for trying to invade their territory. Four of his men got killed, and the others retreated to his fort at the mouth of the Yellowstone. Leaving twenty men at this fort, he showed up at our camp with the other handful.

———

News of us getting our asses kicked at the Ree villages somehow reached Colonel Leavenworth in the middle of June. A few days later, with about 250 soldiers and two six-pound cannons, Leavenworth brought his soldiers north, some by land and some by water.

In the last week of June, a big outfit caught up with them. Joshua Pilcher, head of the Missouri Company, was bringing about sixty men and a howitzer. Later on, several bands of Sioux warriors joined Pilcher's big force. They were chafing to be part of the war against their ancient enemies, the Rees. Now about 400 whites and 700 Indians had united and were warming up for a fight.

Ashley divided those of his men into two companies. One was captained by a man I didn't know, Hiram Scott, and the other by Jedediah.

On August 9 our little army got close to the two Ree villages. The Rees came out to fight. Our mounted Sioux attacked them. When the rest of us pitched in, the Rees fled back behind their palisades, leaving a lot of dead warriors behind.

Very strangely, to my eyes, the Sioux seemed to take

pleasure in mangling and cutting up the bodies of the dead.

Now Colonel Leavenworth arrived with keelboats of men and cannons.

———

The rest of this affair was a disaster and a farce.

The Sioux soon got tired of fighting. They raided the Ree cornfield for ears of corn, stole some Ree horses and mules, and rode back to their villages.

In a peace conference the Rees promised to restore Ashley's property and to keep the peace.

That night they abandoned their villages and disappeared.

Leavenworth and Joshua Pilcher left for home with their big forces. Pilcher thought the disaster was entirely Leavenworth's fault. He soon wrote the Colonel, "You came to open and make good this great road, instead of which you have, by the imbecility of your conduct and operations, created and left impassable barriers."

Strong words, but true.

The whole affair was also a disaster for General Ashley. Frustrated, he started back to St. Louis. But he still had a lot of fine men in his employ as trappers. Twenty of them were at the fort at the mouth of the Yellowstone, and if reinforced, they might accomplish something.

He dropped down to the trading post at Fort Kiowa and reconsidered. He owed a lot of money, and his credit was damaged. Travel up the Missouri River was now blocked. To get out of this dilemma, he would have to do something decisive. So he did.

Ashley asked Jedediah to take command of a brigade

that would ride west, join the Crow village on the upper Yellowstone River for the winter, discover South Pass, cross it, and trap on the headwaters of the Green River. We had heard that beaver were so plentiful on the head-waters of the Green that they walked the banks and could be beaten to death with clubs.

Still, our assignment, to discover South Pass and trap the headwaters of the Green River—that was a whomper. Jedediah asked Ed Rose, me, my good friend the Virginian Jim Clyman, and a dozen other men to join his outfit. All of us said, "Sure."

We traded for horses at the fort. A guide led us up White Clay Creek. It ran thick with white sediment and tasted pungently sweet. Though the guide warned us that the creek water would bind our bowels tight, we had no other water and so drank it greedily.

On the third day out our guide said, "Everyone! Carry all the water you can!" Then he led us across a big bend in the creek, and our next water was 24 hours away.

We came to the next water hole before noon the following day. It was baked dry, so dry that digging made no sense. We rested and walked on. It was fifteen more miles to a river.

That afternoon our brigade straggled all over the countryside. Our eyes stung from the alkali dust. Our tongues swelled in our mouths until we couldn't speak. Our minds wandered into fantasy.

Our guide goaded his horse faster than the rest of us and rode out of sight. We strayed off to the left and right in half-conscious hopes of finding water. Our brigade spread out over a mile.

Jim Clyman found his pack horse more cooperative than the others. He pushed hard in the direction he had last seen the guide. Looking over his shoulder from time to time, he wondered whether the outfit would ever get back together again, or whether some of the men might wander off into the sagebrush, sink down, and die.

He swung off to the right of the guide's path. And there—providential sight—he stumbled onto a water hole.

As Clyman and I dashed toward the water, he fired his rifle. We even outran our horses. Standing shoulder deep, Jim soaked it up with his whole body, gulped it down, dunked his head, and wallowed in it.

After a bit he clambered out and fired his rifle again. He saw another man and horse. This time the horse outsprinted the man and dashed in first. As soon as the man had wet his throat enough, he hallooed.

One by one they wandered in, dunked, and shouted. By dark all had gotten to the hole except for Jedediah and two others. Diah had been bringing the rear to herd wanderers in the right direction.

Young and slender, Diah walked in through falling dusk. He waded in the water and took his ease for a moment. Then he told us, "Two others have given out, and I buried them up to their heads in the sand. To keep them from drying out," he added. He looked around and said, "Since I feel like I can still walk, I'll go back after them."

He took a kettle, a horse, and headed back.

———

Diah brought the men in during the night. The next morning, they walked four or five miles on to the river, carrying their saddles. Our guide was sitting calmly on the bank, waiting for them.

High up in the valley of White Clay Creek, we came

onto a brigade of Sioux. Our guide turned back, leading the horses we'd borrowed at Fort Kiowa. We traded for two horses, so that our entire brigade would be mounted.

We rode on to the Cheyenne River in a misty rain and came to its badlands. The soil was loose and grayish. It stuck to the horses' hooves in great globs. It was hard going—not a foot of level land in sight, a bewildering maze of ravines and canyons crossing everywhere, and all of it moving toward the Missouri River as fast as rain could carry it.

Finally, we got into the Black Hills. They seemed delightfully alpine after the dusty plains, and we found some hazel nuts and plums.

As we labored down the ravines and ridges of the Black Hills, our horses started failing.

JUNE 1824

This is a letter home I wrote on the last Christmas day. Fortunately, I didn't tear it out and mail it to my family in Ireland. Although, I was sure they were wondering where I was and what I was doing.

Dear Pa,

I'm writing to you because only you can read, and I ask you to read my words aloud to the family.

It's Christmas day and I wish I could be at home with my family for Christmas dinner.

I miss my family, all of you. You, Ma, and each of my sisters, Elizabeth, Mary, Katherine, and Bridget, and brothers Patrick and Francis.

I wish I were with you. There's nowhere on this planet I'd rather be than with you today.

I realize that I'm being more emotional than I intended, and now I'll take a different tone.

With an expedition of two big boats and employed as a clerk for $250 American dollars a year, I sailed on a keelboat *with a hundred other men up the Missouri River to two villages of the Arikara Indians. When we got to their villages, we made generous gifts to them, but they turned to treachery and fired on twenty of us, guarding our horses on a sandbar next to the river.*

Though I was under heavy fire on that sandbar, I'm glad happy to say that I emerged unscathed.

Love,
Tom

WINTER 1824—IN THE
VILLAGE OF THE CROWS

The trappers of our brigade had a good winter, as Ed Rose promised we would. We have stayed warm and eat well. We've learned some sign language, learned how to handle the sacred pipe properly when smoking it, and we've heard a lot more about the plentitude of beaver just across the mountains on the upper Green River.

We've also learned a lot more about our Crow hosts. The men are so intent on bathing that they chop holes in the ice of the Wind River for winter cleanliness. Also, they're determined to make their children good riders. They strap even two and three-year-old kids to the saddles of mounts so they can learn balance on a horse.

Some of our men may have fathered Crow children during this winter. Perhaps they've promised to come back to take care of these families. Maybe they will.

During the middle of the winter a brigade of other Ashley-Henry men rode into camp. Major Henry sent them from the post on the Yellowstone, and they had a long ride up the Big Horn River under the command of a Captain Weber.

More lodges were sewn, and more men made welcome.

Life was good.

FEBRUARY 12, 1824

Diah has announced that our outfit will move out tomorrow morning. The Crows have told us how to find the pass over the Rockies, and though the Crow leaders tell him it's too early, the captain wants to get a head start.

We head west into the Wind River range and soon find that it's much too clogged with snow. Whipped, we make our way back to the Crow village and rest.

In early March we make a start that lines up better with what the Crows are telling us. We ride and lead our horses south around the bottom of the Wind River Mountains and into the face of an enemy as wicked as deep snow—violent winds. Even the game has fled to lower elevations.

In a few days we're weak from hunger—we can't get a clean shot at an animal—and we're losing sleep to the vicious winds. Jim Clyman and Bill Sublette get angry at being cold and hungry and ride off in search of buffalo. I decide I damn well should go along.

As the sun sets, we see three bulls at a distance. Since

our horses are too worn out for a chase, we crawl on hands and knees within range. Sublette shoots at one of the bulls and hits it, but the others run off.

We crawl closer. There's nothing more miserable than holding your face about eight inches above the ground while the wind makes the snow spit straight up into your face.

Each of us takes another shot, and the bull finally falls. Not my bullet, for certain. I still don't know what I'm doing with a fire arm, not really.

We walk to it, break up some sagebrush, and defy the wind with enough determination to get a fire going. We cut off the meat most available, cook it over the sagebrush fire, and gobble it up.

Then we discover that we have only two buffalo robes betwixt the three of us. In my rush to come along, I didn't bring one. Sublette and Clyman generously insist that I take one robe. They pull the other one over the both of them. They try to sleep back to front, touching—no luck. I try to sleep alone—no luck. I figure I'm colder than they are. The wind comes harder and a frosty snow falls. We spend a numbed and sleepless night, watched over by our numbed and sleepless horses.

In the morning we try to get a sagebrush fire going. The wind says NO WAY. We ride about four miles to a timbered hill, carrying all the meat possible, and try again. We find dry wood and—LUCK!—get a blaze going. We share a steak and smile big. Our outsides are freezing but our insides are warm.

We ride back to our companions. They already have a fire, and they throw on more wood to cook the meat we've brought.

———

When everyone has eaten, they're ready to ride and maybe get out of this wind. The three of us are less ready, but we go with them over a low divide and down to a river. Off to one side Diah and I talk things over.

"I think this is the Sweetwater River," says Diah. "Its placement fits the description of the Crows."

Though reluctant to get our hopes up, I agree. "It's in the right place and the right travelling distance from camp, all right. If we go up the river..."

I hesitate to say it.

"If we go up the river and a bit beyond," he says, "we'll find ourselves on top of South Pass."

I let breath out and grin. It's the first of the big goals Ashley laid out for us—find the Southern Pass and then the Green River, with its plews aplenty. Send a *big* catch downriver to the general. I just say, "Let's go find South Pass, Diah."

While we're wrapping up to sleep, one of the men new to the mountains comes to me with his head hanging. "There's something I don't get it. 'Plews' are mentioned a lot. But I can't figure out what a plew is."

I clap him on the shoulder. "Beaver hides," I explain. "The hide we cut off a beaver is called a plew."

He gives me a wry smile. "I guess," he says, and goes back to his blankets. I don't add that the word *plew* is our adaption of the term the Frenchies use for it, in French '*plus*,' which sounds just like *plew*.

———

That night the wind blows so hard we all have to stay awake and clutch our blankets tight to keep them from blowing away. The same all the next day and night.

The following morning, desperate, some of us wrap

ourselves as warmly as possible and set out down the Sweetwater into a canyon. Deep between these walls the wind is better-mannered.

Cliff Branch sees a mountain sheep high on the precipice above us and tries a long shot at it. The sheep jumps on impact, loses its footing, comes tumbling down, and lands—KERPLOP!—right at our feet.

"Faith and begorrah!" I exclaim, "damn fine of the sheep." Not understanding my first words, my two companions just pounce on the animal. We make meat and carry it to camp, share and share alike.

But the wind is so damnable here that we can't cook the meat. We hide in our blankets and buffalo robes, lie down, each downwind of another, and try to keep breathing.

In the middle of the night comes a blessing—the wind softens and gentles. We get up, start a big fire, cook, and eat until dawn.

In the light of day, and with the softer wind, the whole crew packs everything up and moves on down into the canyon. The further we go, the quieter the wind. Four or five miles down, the canyon opens up, the wind is easy, and we see plenty of mountain sheep on the slopes above us. We stay here for several days, getting warm, and we shoot sheep until they figure out what's happening and make themselves scarce. We eat a lot of mutton, happily.

Soon we're saying silent prayers for the arrival of April. In this canyon we dig a cache and deposit powder, lead, and other things we won't need until after the spring hunt.

When the cache is secure, Diah calls us all together. "Our time here has been good. As of today, we're moving along. Further on, when we get to the Green

River, we'll split up, half of us going upriver, half downriver.

"Then"—he pauses for emphasis— "we'll all meet here by June the first. We'll open the cache, get our belongings, float downriver, and send General Ashley his furs."

Another pause for emphasis. "No matter what happens, be here by June 1st. If the outfit isn't here, go to the first navigable point downriver. We'll be there.

"All right?! Now pack up and let's go—up the Sweetwater."

Diah leads the way, as usual, and I ride last, watching everything. The days are cold, but March winds will bring April breezes. We're riding upward but into a region of hills, not mountains. There are no creeks, so we melt water for drinking.

On and on.

One morning I look carefully at the gullies. From above us they slant down. What water there is trickles down ahead of us. The earth stretches out ahead, all of it lower than we are.

From the last position I kick my mount up alongside Diah's, in the lead.

"Diah," I say, "the whole landscape—all these hills, all of this prairie—it's angling down."

"I know," says Diah, looking at me sideways with a smile.

"We've done it," I say. "We've found South Pass."

Dish reaches out to shake my hand. He says, "We are the discoverers of the Southern Pass. In fact, we've already crossed it and are on the downhill side."

A big grin and a couple of nods from him. "Yes, we've already crossed it. From here all water flows to the Pacific Ocean."

"You can put it on your map," I tell him.

"I'll put it on *the* maps," he says.

Then, quietly, happily, he goes on. "We've found South Pass and filled in the maps. Mark the date down in your journal."

"I will—March 22, 1824."

Shining times.

APRIL 1, 1824

Diah and I wake up beside each other, each rolled in his own blankets against the chill of the first week of April in the mountains.

I sit up and look across the Green River. It's clear why the Spanish named it Rio Verde. Yes, the water is green. Sleeping on its banks feels good. Getting to this river is the big goal Ashley set for us, next to trapping its beaver.

Right now, though, the river is ice on the surface. And for sure no beaver are walking around on the banks. We knew that was a silly tale to please us. Still, it's just an exaggeration—there will be plenty of beaver, we hope.

"I'll get the coffee," Diah says. "Just stay here."

I roll out, roll up my blankets, tie them, and sit on them, wondering what's on his mind.

He comes back with brew in each hand and extends a cup to me. I breathe in the rich aroma before I savor the taste. Sorry, Ma, you love tea and won't let coffee in the house. In America I've come to love my black morning brew.

"Fitz," says Diah, "time for the spring hunt. I want to

divide the brigade, half to the north and its tributaries, half to the south. Will you take command of the outfit going north?"

"Certainly."

"Trap the main river, trap the tributaries, wherever beaver sign leads you. We have about six weeks of trapping and then a march back to our cache on the Sweetwater."

"Yes."

"All decisions I leave to your judgment. You're a good hand—I have complete confidence in you. Watch your horses, be careful around Indians, and get back to the cache by June 1st. We'll go a half dozen men in each party, north and south. Who do you want?"

"Sublette and Clyman. Good men, good friends. The rest you choose."

The next day I lead my men up the river. We'll ride upstream for a while, waiting for the ice to break up. Then we'll work the creeks upstream from their mouths. I don't know which will be better trapping, Green River or the creeks that feed it.

Soon the men are bringing plenty of beaver carcasses back to camp to skin. We make packs of the plews and eat the beaver tails.

One afternoon, in a valley near us, we see a band of Shoshones, about twenty warriors and a bunch of women and children. Because of the number of women, I make presents of beads, cloth, and vermilion to the leaders. They seem delighted with these gifts, and each evening I give them the beaver tails that are more than we want to eat. They think the beaver tails are a treat. I'm glad about our comfortable relationship. We trap upstream and downstream from them.

Then, one morning, the Shoshones are gone, and all

of our horses have disappeared. Every single one. We can't ride, and we can't take our plews anywhere. Stuck. Since they've taken the horses over stony ground, we have no trail to follow.

Some leader I am. First effort and I jank it up.

I tell the men to keep trapping. We have to stack the plews high—we have no way to take them anywhere. I'm looking for a miracle. Maybe some Indians will come by and trade us their horses. Maybe Diah will appear suddenly with his outfit. Maybe...

I wish I believed in a saint to ask for intervention.

May 1, 1824

Neither Saint Jedediah nor other miraculous help arrives.

It's time to start for the cache. We have a June 1st deadline, and we're forced to walk.

I give the order. "Dig a cache. Hide our traps and furs in it. Put our saddles up in trees. We have to walk, so we'll carry our guns and our knives, nothing else."

We've been stripped clean, and we're going back with nothing to contribute.

We walk a little downstream and turn up into the valley where the Shoshones were camped. Bad memories.

Several days further on we come face to face with six mounted Shoshones, and every man of us recognizes the horses they're riding—*our* horses.

The men ready their rifles before I tell them to.

I speak to the Indians in signs.

Dismount.

Looking nervously at our rifles, they do.

Now lead us to your village.

They start walking. As we walk, tension grips my whole body, neck to feet.

When we see the village, I tell the Shoshones in signs, *Go get the rest of our horses.*

They bring all our horses but one. Now the tension seizes my feet too.

"Not good enough," I tell them. "Bring the other horse."

It's Bill Sublette's riding mount.

They don't respond at all.

I'm wild with inner urgency—*Take action or give up,* I tell myself.

No choice. I tell Sublette, "Go forward, take the one on the left—he seems to be a leader—put a rope around his upper body, pull him off his horse, and walk him over to my feet."

Bill is damn well as stricken with tension and fear as I am, but he does it.

I give the other Indians my fiercest look and sign them: *"Unless you bring the other horse—now! —I will shoot this man."*

Inside myself I scream, *Will I really? Another human being?* First inner answer, *I have to.* Second inner answer: *Doesn't matter. They believe I will.*

Two of the Indians ride to their herd and are back quickly with the horse.

Sublette takes its lead rope.

I say to my men, "Reach into your possible sacks and get a fire steel, a tin cup, maybe a knife, a bit of foofuraw —any small present—and put it on the ground in front of them."

The men understand, and they do it.

When they finish, I sign, "These are gifts to you. We are your friends. Let us remain friends."

As we ride the recovered horses back toward our cache, bareback, I turn my head several times to look at the Shoshones. First, they're picking up the gifts. Then, still picking up gifts. Finally they ride into their village.

I relax. It's like something was screeching inside me. Now that's stopped.

At last, we get to our cache, raise it, and put the plews on the horses. I look at the beasts loaded with beaver pelts. We have a bumper crop.

I call for the men to get mounted and swing up onto my horse,

Just then Bill Sublette walks alongside me, looks up, and says, "That was good leadership."

"Thanks," I say, and nod to him.

Sublette lets a moment go by. "But I have a question. You threatened to shoot those Shoshones. But has your Irish ass ever fired that rifle?"

I grin. "Only at paper targets."

We laugh together and head for the meeting place at the cache on the Sweetwater River.

JUNE 1

When we get there, right on time, we see no sign of Diah or any man in his crew. None.

Late. I hope they're only late.

We raise the cache. All's well with everything except our powder. It's damp. Damp powder is as useless as a limp pecker.

We set the powder out to dry and wait. And wait. When most of June is gone, we're out of coffee, *and* I'm out of tobacco for my pipe, Jedediah and his outfit come riding in, smiling like nothing is out of whack. I don't ask the captain why he said, "DON'T BE LATE. BACK HERE AT THE CACHE BY JUNE 1st."

But he and his men are jovial. Part of the reason is that their horses are piled high with plews, a haul like none of us has seen before.

That means we have to find a way to get the whole lot down the river and into the waiting hands of General Ashley.

I send Jim Clyman downstream to spot the first place this river has enough water to float a bullboat.

What's a bullboat? It's shaped like what we Irishmen know as a brolly, what Americans call an umbrella. Imagine an umbrella without a handle set afloat on a local creek. That's what a bullboat is. Of course, they're impossible to steer and may bang into anything. We carry long poles to fend off the boulders in the river.

We build these boats by sticking the butts of willow branches into the ground, arching them over, lashing them together, and tying buffalo hides on tight. This craft floats high, drawing only a few inches of water.

Now we wait again, this time for Jim Clyman to come back. Wait and wait. Again. No sign of him for two more weeks.

Jedediah and I ride downstream, just the two of us, looking for Jim. Never mind how valuable he is. I can't stand the thought of losing my friend.

But inspection reveals the worst. We find Jim's camping places easily—the remains of his fires are sign enough.

At the last of his camps, though, the ashes tell a grim tale. Above one of Jim's fires, but all too close, is certain sure evidence of the camp of a couple dozen Indians. The hoof prints and ashes are eloquent. Jim camped right down there. These Indians must have made their camp after he came. Maybe he tried to bluff his way through by offering presents. But they wanted more—his rifle, his horse, and his life.

On our way back to camp my spirits droop.

But action turns sorrow away. The morning after we get back, we see that the river is running a little faster and a little fuller. Maybe the sun is finally melting the snows upstream of us.

With volunteers named Branch and Stone—I don't think I ever learned their Christian names—I set out downriver in two bullboats, steering badly. We pole our way off the rocks that challenge us. In that clumsy fashion we bump and spin our way down as far as a huge rock that looks like a giant turtle on the plain, which later will be called Independence Rock.

About five miles before that landmark, we thrash through the roughest water we've seen yet, waves that toss our bullboats around like pennies pitched into the air by betting boys. In no time all three boats are upside down and all three men are swimming in icy water for our lives.

If we were betting, we'd bet against survival.

But all three of us somehow manage to struggle onto the shore, shivering, and look at the damage. Our boats have been turned into sticks by the rocks, and our furs are on the bottom of the river—along with our rifles and the lead we've carried to make into bullets.

No choice. "We'll have to dive for our stuff," I tell Stone and Branch.

Branch, the lippier of the two says, "Our rifles?"

"Our rifles, our bullets, and our furs," I answer. *In for a dime, in for a dollar.*

We shed our buckskins—they would only weigh us down—and brave the waters in the nude.

We dive and dive in water just barely melted from snow. No need to explain about that.

When we have one of the guns and most of the furs, I call a halt. "I'm so frozen my arse is blocked with ice," I complain. "I couldn't even take a shite."

We walk to Independence Rock, wet, dripping furs on our shoulders. Since the boats are turned to splinters, we cache the furs there and face our only alternative: Now we'll have to walk to Fort Atkinson, and it's probably four hundred miles downriver.

At first I think we'll have to make a starvation march. But Branch and Stone show real ingenuity. They knock the brass mountings off our rifles and hammer the brass into bullets.

"Boys," I say, though they are men aplenty, "you may have just saved our lives. Now we have a chance to shoot a buffalo or two on the long, long walk."

Though one buffalo divided between three men over several hundred miles is damned little to eat.

I try to keep track mentally of what happens as we trek the days away, but my journals are soaking wet—I can't write in either of them.

Sometime in September we walk into Fort Atkinson and get a huge surprise.

There's Jim Clyman to welcome us.

Stone and Branch holler at the same time, "Coon! Ye're above ground!"

Clyman embraces them and says, "Glad to see ye've still got your hair." Then Clyman clasps both of their hands and says, "Sight for sore eyes."

I say, "Amazed to see you, and even more than glad."

Unbelievably, he has gotten here only ten days earlier. He had a rough time of it because Indians took his rifle. He got captured and escaped with his life only because his two hosts sneaked him out of camp. Approaching the fort before he saw it, he fell down on the trail and passed out. When he woke up, he saw Old Glory hoisted in the distance, realized what that meant, and shouted "Hallelujah!"

He loves telling that story.

The next morning Clyman shows me what he's written in his journal about this whole crazy business: Straggling across the same plains just over a week later, we've gotten to the fort, in Clyman's words, "in a more pitiable state, if possible, than myself." From his journal I now know what the date is.

The Sweetwater River, and the Platte to follow, make a friendly highway for us mountain men. As long as Indians don't kill us.

September 10

Here now I get to one of the most miserable episodes of my life. I'm left-handed, like both of my brothers. It's strange—our parents are right and left—father right and mother left—yet all three boys are left-handed and all six girls right-handed.

Father has a saying for when one of us janks up a task. He quips, "Are ye thinking kerblink today?" Meaning thinking crooked or muddled. Sometimes, when life really gets sidewise, he says that the Almighty must have been thinking kerblink to let such-and-such happen.

And he likes to say that Jehovah must have been kerblink to make all three of his boys left-handed and all six girls right-handed.

Never mind. Here's that miserable episode:

Jim Clyman asks how my skills with firearms are coming along.

"Rotten," I tell him truthfully. So he takes time to go over the basics of firing a flintlock pistol or rifle with me again. Make sure the weapon is unloaded. Measure your powder and pour it down the barrel. Put a lead ball and cloth patch in the top of the barrel. Use the ramrod to push them all the way down. Make sure the ball is seated on the powder charge. Clear the vent with a pick. Pour powder into the pan and close the frizzen. Cock the flint, aim, and fire.

The flint is supposed to strike a spark, the powder in the pan to catch fire, the fire to race down the barrel, and BOOM!

This process applies to both pistols and rifles.

Jim leads me a short distance away from the fort and lays my pistol, rifle, and the other elements on a blanket. Then he tears a page out of my ledger, sets it on a sagebrush not far away, and motions to the pistol.

"I admit," he says, "it's harder to hold steady with one arm than two, but we have to start somewhere."

He stands across the blanket from me and nods. Carefully, I do everything he's said. At every step he nods and murmurs his approval.

Thinking of the pictures I've seen of duelers, I take a stance—sideways, with the left foot and left arm and hand forward. I aim at the wretched piece of paper. I pull the trigger and—

The pistol blows up in my hand.

Pain rages throughout my body, bone to bone. I never knew that pain could be a universe entire unto itself.

I can't tell who is screaming louder, me or Clyman.

He's knocking the pistol out of my hand, or the twisted remains of what was my pistol. In a flash he has his shirt off and my hand—what's left of my hand—my hand is in a crude bandage.

Then he's hefting me back toward the fort, *hefting* because he's supporting the weight my legs can't take.

I can hardly make out what's happening in the midst of my own bellowing.

Now I feel Clyman taking my weight in his arms and the bumpety-bump of his footrace toward help.

––––––

Time passes on a trestle of pain. Later I will have broken images of help from the fort's surgeon, words spoken about easing the pain, and a jumble of... I don't know what. Everything.

When I come to, it's morning. The surgeon—we call him the "sawbones"—is hovering over me, asking questions I can't make out. My hand is bandaged until it's invisible, but the pain tells me where the devil it is.

It stays that way for days, which seem like eternities. The sawbones says the skin and tendons (or whatever they're called) and muscles on the hand are growing back. It will look almost normal, he says.

All I know is that right now I can't pick up a pen and write "boo."

Clyman is sitting next to my bed. I sleep off and on for several days, and every time I wake up, he's sitting there.

I'm incredibly glad to see him. I hope never to see a pistol again.

––––––

I decide to teach myself to write with my other hand. After all, what General Ashley has hired me for is to keep a record of what we do, what we trade, for how much, and so on. Even when I'm the boss of the outfit, I'm also the record keeper.

Before long I can write a date in my log. October something.

The left hand has turned into a claw. Yes, when it's relaxed, it looks very much like a claw. I can make a fist, but I can't flex it to where it lies flat. Apparently, for the rest of my life I'll be able to close it but not open it.

At the moment I wouldn't go near a pistol for anything. Rifle? Probably not.

For everything else? I count on my friend Jim Clyman.

———

Soon I get up and walk around the fort, being careful not to bang the hand on anything. Before long life is half-normal. But I think God, if there be a God, must have been thinking kerblink. He sure enough let me get hurt.

And our job isn't done. We've made it to the fort, but our furs haven't. We can't let Ashley think the first outfit to trap the beaver paradise of the upper Green River has let him down. Or that Jedediah Smith and I have let him down.

I write to him immediately, using my right hand. I tell him that his catch of furs is a good one and that it's cached on the river at the giant rock that looks like a turtle. And I dispatch the letter downriver to his comfortable life in St. Louis.

Then I get my arse going. I acquire horses from Lucien Fontenelle, who happens to be at the fort. Fontenelle is a veteran leader of mountain-man brigades. He agrees to supply the horses I need to haul our beaver on one condition: In return I must buy the horses from him, paying in plews when we get back with them.

General Ashley, I'm sorry, your beaver catch won't be

as bountiful as I said. Some of the plews are still drowning at the bottom of the river. But we'll dig up the furs hidden in a hole dug at the foot of the giant turtle-rock, and you can sell those in fancy St. Louis.

Branch, Stone, and I now spend Ashley's money re-supplying ourselves with rifles and lead. We've just walked several hundred miles on starvation rations, and we haven't the slightest desire to repeat that trick. In fact, we gorge ourselves on the way there and back, to regain the weight we lost on our hunger march.

October 26

Today we get back to Fort Atkinson with the furs and, wonder of wonders, General Ashley is already here, waiting. He got word from Major Henry of the success of our party led by Jedediah Smith and led another packtrain up from St. Louis. He has brought enough supplies to keep us trappers in the mountains for another year.

So everyone of us—Ashley's crew, this cripple, my small crew, and Clyman—head back upstream. Though I can't do much with one hand, the general puts me in command of fifty pack horses and a miscellany of men. I know none of the men except Clyman, Branch, and Stone. I soon get to know Jim Beckwourth, like Rose a mulatto.

From the start I set down Beckwourth in my mind as a man who will make his mark. He's handsome, has a commanding presence, and is a great storyteller.

Right off Jim Clyman has a gift for me—he gives me a new name, usable by mountain man and Indian alike— Broken Hand.

As it turns out, Ashley makes a mistake when we set

out. He's counting on getting food from the Pawnees
when we get to their villages, and that seems reasonable.
When we get to where those villages usually are, though,
the Pawnees have moved south to wintering grounds in
warmer climes.

Any clime to the south would be an improvement.
But as we march up the Platte River, November brings
deep snow and cold so intense that our horses freeze to
death at night. The meat of the horses adds a little to
what we have to eat. Otherwise our pittance is half a pint
of flour a day, which everyone makes into a gruel. Sometimes a man shoots a duck or goose—I'm not doing any
shooting—and we share those as evenly as possible.

But the camps are miserable. We eat in grim silence—
no jokes, no banter, no stories, no fun. We shiver
through each night and get up grumpy. Then we build
fires and wolf down our gruel unhappily, wordless, and
plod on. We've lost so many horses we have to walk and
carry the animals' loads on our own backs.

Pushing on, in the fifth week we find some game and
add meat to our ration of gruel. In the sixth week we
come to a camp of Grand Pawnees still on the Platte.
These Indians warn us against pressing further up the
river. If we do, they say, we risk losing all our men and
our horses.

Bullheaded, Ashley insists on barging on. After a few
miles we have great luck—we fall in with a band of Loup
Pawnees and travel with them in bitter weather up to the
forks of the river. Before these Indians go on, we trade
with them for twenty-three horses, some buffalo robes,
and dried meat. The men who get the buffalo robes are
truly grateful for the warmth.

While we camp on that spot, December takes hold.
Surprisingly, though, the weather then actually moder-

ates, and some herds of buffalo turn up. The meat is very welcome. Even better, the paths forged by the buffalo hooves coming downstream make roads for our horses going upstream. Except for the grass exposed by those hooves, a lot more of our horses would die.

By this time, as second in command, I've started to assert myself and my mountain experience to General Ashley. He listens some of the time, and the outfit is better for it.

Also, I'm getting a blessing. My clawed left hand is making something of a comeback. I can grip knife, fork, and the like pretty well. I'm getting better and better motion of my fingers. Now I can write words with my left hand as well as my right, though not well with either. But my claw can hold things.

Clyman insists on something new. Before my injury, when throwing a knife as a weapon, I naturally used my left hand. That's working again now—I can grip a knife well enough to throw it hard into a tree.

Jim has some counsel. "If an Indian charges you," he says, "don't take a chance with that hand. Instead of throwing your knife with the left hand, save it for stabbing with your right."

Right-o—got that.

Still, I practice throwing the knife with my clawed hand. After all, the hand only holds the knife. The arm controls the speed and the accuracy.

For the thousandth time I study this hand. It's never going to look all right. It will always look withered and crabbed. But God has let me have it back part of the way. Maybe He's sorry for thinking kerblink when He let my pistol explode.

At the general's insistence we forge our way on up the south fork of the Platte. On January 1st, according to my log, we happen into a grove of sweet cottonwoods. Horses are very fond of the inner bark of that tree. And since their health is improving on the bark diet, we stay here for ten days. Then we trek on up the river and come by luck onto another grove of cottonwoods. From here we get the men's first view of mountains rising high at a distance I guess to be sixty miles. Even from this distance they look like home to me. Yes, the mountains are cold, but the wide, open plains, with their unblocked winds, can be even worse.

When we get to the foot of the Rockies, we stop for more than two weeks to hunt. The meat raises the morale around our campfires considerably. Then we head northwest toward the Laramie Plains, passing through what will be prime beaver country in the right season, and then across a treeless stretch we call the Red Desert.

Months Pass

By now January, February, and March have passed, and April is making her promises. Just at this time a band of Crows runs off seventeen of our most fit horses and mules.

I tell General Ashley I'll go after the thieves and pick Jim Clyman to go with me. Riding hard, we follow the Crows all the way to the Sweetwater River but never catch up with them.

After this failure our men have to stagger along with even more of the loads of the pack animals on their own backs. In that fashion we come finally on April 20th to the Green River. Finally—hoorah!—trapping country, in fact the richest country for beaver we've discovered to date. And right at the height of the spring season. It's been so long since we trapped that I'd almost forgotten why we marched into the West.

One problem now is that we have a gang of beginners who don't know anything about trapping beaver. Or as the mountain men put it, don't know what way the stick floats. You may ask, What way does it float? The expression is a standing joke among old hands, used to expose the inexperienced. Needless to say, it floats downstream.

We split up in different directions, each outfit led by a man of experience in the mountains. I take six men southwest into the Uinta Mountains, Clyman leads six up the Green to the north, and a good hand named Zach Ham leads seven out to the west.

The fourth outfit is commanded by General Ashley with a different goal—to explore the Green River. For this mission Ashley has us build two bullboats that no river can overturn, or so he hopes. He sends out nine hunters to get enough buffalo hides while the rest of us cut willows and shape them to the general's great expectations.

The boats are very different in design, nothing like umbrella shapes. Their frames are seven feet wide and sixteen feet long. When the hunters bring back the hides, we stretch them and tie them tight across these willow structures. These giants truly make our usual size bullboat, five or six feet around, look like a teacup. And unlike our teacups, these rectangular boats won't tilt or tip. Or so we hope.

MAY 28, 1824

Now, in our last evening before splitting up, Ashley calls all of us together and with the flare and timing of a showman springs his big, fine surprise.

He announces, "Friends, trappers, brave men of the Rocky Mountains, HEROES!, on the backs of these horses we've minded all the way from Fort Atkinson I've brought the supplies needed to keep all you mountain men living in the mountains, as you love to do… Keep you out here year around. No longer will you have to ride all the way to one of the trading posts on the Missouri, or down to Taos or Santa Fe to get what you need, or at least what you long for—whiskey to lubricate your blowouts, coffee to wake you up next morning and sugar to sweeten it, lead to make bullets, pistols and rifles to replace those you've broken or lost to Indians, Green River knives, tobacco for your pipes, more tobacco as presents to the Indians, tin cups, pots for cooking, knives, wool blankets, and all the things Indian women long for—vermillion for the parts in their hair or for their cheeks, colored cloth and scissors to cut it with, beads, and every kind of foofuraw."

At this point some of the men cheer out loud. We're thinking that hauling all those loads from Fort Atkinson to this spot may have been worth the trouble.

"Here's the best part," Ashley sails on. "I will float down this river a ways and mark a spot. I'll peel the bark off the trees or build a big mound of earth, or both, so you won't be able to miss it. And there"—he pauses dramatically and goes on in what is almost song— "there we will have a grand rendezvous, a get-together for every man who loves to live far from city doings and in these grand mountains. This rendezvous may go on for weeks—I don't know how long. I'll trade all these fine supplies to you for your beaver hides. Those are worth nothing to you here, but I'll transport them to St. Louis where they can be sold to make fancy hats for the gentlemen of Washington goddamn D.C., New by God York, London, and Paris."

Now he shouts—"We know how they love their hats of BEAVER FELT!"

He pauses and then calls out. "I've saved the best for last. We will repeat this rendezvous in the middle of each summer when you're not trapping. We will also invite cordial Indians to trade. In that way, we'll keep you supplied with everything you need, every single thing you want, from back in the settlements!"

Now the roar from the men rivals thunder from the clouds in the flashiest of storms.

Ashley rumbles on. "Now, until about the tenth day of July, we part ways. You will hunt beaver, and I will explore the river downstream. Then we will meet at the place along the river that I will mark. Starting on July 10th we will have a party to end all parties."

Ashley roars on, but he doesn't need to. Our spirits are soaring.

————

The next morning the general sets out downstream in his big boats. Clyman, Ham, and I lead our outfits off in different directions to catch the wily beaver—with greater enthusiasm now that the general has promised us big rewards for bringing back a lot of plews.

JULY 10, 1824—RENDEZVOUS

Ashley's adventures on the river turn out to be wilder than he wants. His two boats thread their way through deep, narrow canyons and down treacherous waterfalls. In fact, he reports that he had to haul the boats out of the river and make portages around waterfalls sixteen different times.

Finally, Ashley quits the river, trades with Indians for horses, and heads back. On the way he and his men run into Etienne Provost and his twelve trappers, working north from Taos.

This Provost is quite a character. He was born a French-Canadian but emigrated to St. Louis and soon joined a fur-trading expedition. When he and his men got arrested by Mexicans, he made peace with his captors by making Santa Fe his home. In this year, 1824, he's led a trapping expedition to the upper Green River country, met General Ashley, and fallen in with his outfit. Knowing the country well, Provost eases the way with local Indians, and his outfit comes in with Ashley to the appointed place for rendezvous on July 10th.

Now we're all re-assembled on the spot. In fact, even more of us turn up than Ashley hoped for. Word has gotten around.

————

This first rendezvous turns out to be everything Ashley promised except in one way. He hasn't brought any whiskey—he didn't think of it—and our throats are mighty dry. Our word for booze in mountain-man is *awerdenty*. We've borrowed that word from the trappers who've come up from Taos. And I might mention that neither Mexican brandy nor American whiskey can hold a candle to Irish whiskey.

Otherwise, rendezvous is a ball of fun. Mainly, we have the sport of competitions—foot races, horse races, shooting at targets, throwing knives at marks on trees, gambling, wrestling—you name a way of having fun and we d0 it.

Also, I get to see Mike Fink for the first time in a long while. I'm glad to get back with my fine friend.

Mike sets out to have some of his particular kind of fun. He puts a blanket down on the ground and challenges every man in camp to come whup his arse. To win, in Mike's way of playing, a fellow only has to stay on his feet. First man to land on his back is the loser. My friend is the half-horse, half-alligator of the rivers, and now he's looking to claim that title for the mountains.

But maybe not. Mike is six feet and about two hundred pounds, more than me both ways. But some of those Frenchies are really over-sized brutes.

The first one to take Mike up on his challenge is a fellow named Depwee—I don't know how it's spelled in

French, but that's how it sounds. Every crowd has a bully like this one.

Depwee looks like he has half a foot and fifty pounds on Mike, and he wants to bet a blanket worth twenty dollars that he can throw Mike on his arse.

Mike covers that bet with a smile.

Then a half dozen other Frenchies want to make bets a bit bigger.

Mike waves them off. "Wait till you see what happens on this one," he says.

Then he says to Depwee, "When you're ready."

Before the word "ready" is out there, Depwee makes a bull-like charge, arms waving wide and voice a-roaring.

Mike waits. Then, just as Depwee is about to knock him down, Mike ducks low, sets his feet, drives a shoulder into Depwee's belly hard, stands up fast, and flips the brute high into the air.

The Frenchie lands ten feet behind Mike—flat on his back. WHUMPF! Air explodes from him in a bark.

Mike walks back casually, whaps a foot onto Depwee's chest, and raises his fists high in triumph.

The American trappers cheer, but the Frenchies are dead silent. I raise a fist for my friend.

After that display, amazingly, Mike still has a dozen or so challengers. Some men just can't resist a dare.

Mike throws each one onto his back, collects the loot he wins, and displays it on the blanket he got from Depwee—several plugs of tobacco, a fur hat, two Green River knives, and I don't remember what else.

I do count the number of challengers Mike whips—seventeen. He's undefeated for the day. I swear it's true.

From that moment forward that first rendezvous, even without whiskey, is a hootin'-and-hollerin', rip-roarin' good time. For myself, I don't get into the competition of playing cards, whist they call it, I have no need to make enemies. Nor I do try my luck at shooting either rifle or pistol. My luck with firearms is less than none, and my left hand, the hand my pistol crippled, the thought of using it gives me the willies.

Although I won't try to shoot with my left hand, I have developed some skill in throwing my knife. We line up and take aim at a heart scratched into the trunk of a tree.

Jim Clyman sets the standard early on by splitting the heart right in two, so center that we leave his blade in the trunk as the mark to beat and the other blades get pulled out of the tree, losers.

A bunch of men then send their blades into the tree trunk without hitting even the heart, and their knives are handed back to their owners.

Finally, it's my turn, and I'm confident: I've had *lots* of practice, in fact practice every day against Jim himself.

I go into a quiet palaver with Jim, and we agree on a wager: The loser will buy the winner a capote, a winter coat sewn from a heavy woolen blanket made by the Hudson's Bay Company. That coat will cost thirty dollars from Ashley.

Satisfied, I walk to the tree and outline a *broken* heart above the one we've been aiming at. I scratch it into the bark torn down the middle, the way most of our hearts get from time to time.

By agreement Jim takes the first throw. His blade sinks directly into one of the two ragged lines I've scratched down the middle, the one on the left. Excellent throw.

But I have a plan. I boast, "Now I'm going to show my love that my heart is true."

I give the knife a good, clean, seven rotations between

me and the tree, and get just what I wanted. My blade barely glances off Jim's and deflects into the space *between* the two ragged lines—the exact center of the heart.

The whole crowd cheers.

Jim says, "You got me."

I answer, "With that coat and a blanket I'll sleep so very warm this winter."

———

To jump well ahead in my story, the rendezvous after the one of 1824 are even better. As the word spreads, one Indian tribe after another joins in, and they're glad to trade—rifles, pistols, powder, lead, blankets, they want everything. And their women often trade their favors for all the finery used to decorate themselves. That brings a kind of satisfaction you can imagine to a bunch of rough-and-tumble men who have spent too many nights alone in their blankets.

I don't speak of myself—that's none of anyone's business.

———

Speaking of business. Back at the first rendezvous General Ashley checks each one of the trapping parties in. My outfit hands over 140 pelts, Clyman's 164, Ham's 461. I'm embarrassed. My men can't have been that far behind the others, regardless of their inexperience. I prefer to believe our creeks just weren't as full of beaver.

At the second rendezvous the men get straight to trading with Ashley, and they learn a quick lesson. The general is adding the price of transportation from St.

Louis to the original cost of the goods. That way he arrives at a mountain price for each item.

I tell the men that's only fair. He paid a lot in wages to the men who hauled that merchandise out here. What he bought in St. Louis for five dollars has cost him that much more to transport to rendezvous.

At any rate, life isn't cheap in the mountains. Coffee and sugar are $1.50 a pound from Ashley, tobacco $2.00, scissors $2.00, knives $2.50, and cloth $6.00 a yard. Indian women are crazy about that colored cloth.

In the end, for one beaver hide the general gives two and a half pounds of tobacco, which may last a month. To get his smokes for a year a trapper has to hand over twelve hides. Two pounds of coffee and enough sugar to sweeten it will require one hide each.

If the general weren't paying me a salary as brigade leader, I might not be able to stay out in the mountains. Where, by God, I'm determined to be.

———

One evening when the rendezvous is winding down, Jedediah comes over and tosses his blankets on the ground. With all these big doin's, we haven't had much time together. This evening, though we've both eaten, I get out the coffee pot I've traded Ashley for, put grounds in it, and make us a full one. My Methodist friend doesn't drink liquor.

After one sip of steaming brew, Diah says, "The general has offered me a full partnership in his fur-trading business, and I've accepted. I'll ride back to St. Louis with him, carrying the furs. This winter we'll buy supplies for next summer's rendezvous."

"Don't forget the whiskey this time," I say.

"We'll remember from now on," says my friend. Though he doesn't drink, he's smiling.

I let that sit a little and then say, reflecting as I go, "So you'll switch from catching beaver to trading for plews. You'll supply this big crowd of trappers. Good deal for both you and Ashley."

"You think so?"

"Diah, every man out here is crazy about this new system—you and Ashley bringing supplies and us staying in the mountains year 'round—that's great."

"Yes?"

"Quite sure, so."

"Ashley plans to get married when he gets back and wants to spend more time with his new bride."

I study my friend. "You'll be in St. Louis for months."

"Right."

"And then you'll bring the goods for next summer's party."

He grins. "That's about it."

———

Next summer? Not just that one. As it turns out, rendezvous is our annual jubilee. We mountain men like it so much we'll repeat it for fifteen more summers in a row. YEE-HAW!

December 1826

After the fall trapping season, when my outfit takes a lot of furs, we mountain men assemble in the Cache Valley, a beautiful spot above the Great Salt Lake. Soon, though, it is disagreeably snowy and we move down into the valley of the big lake, where there's less snow and there are even buffalo grazing. Various Indians join us here at the mouth of the Weber River, and soon we have a community of six or seven hundred people, nearly half women and children.

In short order we're raided by Bannocks one night and they make off with about eighty horses. The next day a gang of us sets out after them on foot, Jim Bridger and I commanding. On the fifth day we get to one of their villages and see our horses in with their herd.

Now we split up into outfits led by me and Jim. The plan: I will lead my men against the village and provide cover for Jim's men. They will stampede all the horses possible.

Charge! I love charges—they're thrilling. The wild clatter of hooves, the straining of the horse between my legs, the shouts we send up to frighten the enemy, the shots we fire into the air. It's exhilarating.

There are three or four hundred Bannocks, and my men and I keep them busy while Jim and crew rout two or three hundred horses. After a chase, the Bannocks get more than half the horses back, but we still have the eighty they stole and about forty more.

Back in camp our fellows greet us enthusiastically. We've come back with a lot of very fine animals.

A big village of Shoshone Indians joins us here, and we spend a comfortable and amiable winter with them.

One mishap... Digging a cache for the furs we catch, two of our diggers get buried in a cave-in and suffocate.

And then another accident. One of our trappers, while out hunting, shoots what he takes to be an antelope. When he gets up to it, he sees that it's a Shoshone hunter using an antelope's head and skin as a decoy.

I say to Clyman, "Trouble. The Shoshones will be angry."

Jim says, "Let's go see the chief. Together, the three of us."

I reach for my rifle, and Jim grabs his. The hunter who made the mistake, Andrew, walks unarmed.

There's no telling, after all.

Taking the body draped across a horse, we ride through the circle of lodges, calling the chief's name. Women follow us, wailing.

Out of his lodge the chief comes, looking uncertain.

He sees the body, goes around the horse to the far side, and embraces a woman. She's wailing and scarifying her forearms, a gesture of mourning.

Jim and I look at Andrew. "Must be his wife." Andrew circles that way.

Afraid Andrew doesn't know better than to touch her

to show his sympathy, I follow him close. He stops two or three steps from the widow.

Clyman is talking to the chief, explaining.

The chief says to Jim, "You and the Shoshones are brothers. We are all friends. We can't always guard against accidents. You lost two of your warriors in the cave-in. We Shoshones have just lost one. Give me some red cloth to wrap up the body. We will bury our fallen relative."

I give him a red blanket. Several men, I suppose the dead man's relatives, come, take the body, and lay it across a horse. Then the Shoshones get mounted and ride toward the nearest trees. There they build a platform across some branches and lift the wrapped body onto it. Finally, the Indians circle the tree and sing some songs of farewell. Later I'm told these are honor songs.

Most of the whites and Indians stay at our camp in Cache Valley, undisturbed.

———

For our spring hunt I lead an outfit across a divide and onto the Portneuf, a tributary of the Snake River. We make a good catch, but at the mouth of the river we come onto a band of Blackfeet. We call these Indians Bug's Boys, which means children of the devil. They come forward with their usual trick—they feign friendship. But I know this ruse when I see it and put a heavy guard on our horses for the night.

In spite of our watchfulness, the Blackfeet cut some tether ropes that night and try to drive our horses off.

Night-time battle is indescribably chaotic. My men and I are ready, and they fire at moving shadows. I see one Indian get hit and crawl to the river. When he gets there, he slithers in, and I watch him get swept away by the waters.

Signal fires on the hills tell me that a lot of other Blackfeet are advancing on us. Right off I tell our outfit to pack up and head back up the Portneuf, even in the dark. We get to the rendezvous of 1826 in our favored spot, Cache Valley, with no more troubles.

July 5, 1826

This rendezvous is another big party. Ashley has brought whiskey this time, and that helps. The presence of a large number of Shoshones helps just as much, because their men want to compete in the various sports of rendezvous, and their women want to trade their embraces for bells, beads, and the like.

At the end of rendezvous comes a sea change. The general sells his half share of Ashley-Smith to Jedediah, Bill Sublette, and Davey Jackson. Those three will be running the show now, setting up the hunts, bringing the supplies out from St. Louis, doing the trading, everything. Good men.

At first, I'm a little hurt by this arrangement—I'm surprised Diah didn't choose me as one of his partners. He and I have been comrades for most of the last three years, and I helped him through his healing after that bear tore his ear off.

On the other hand, Jackson was the clerk for Ashley's fur expedition of 1822, a year before I was the general's clerk. He's been in the mountains a year longer and has more experience as a leader of brigades. And Diah apparently wants him on board, so I reconcile myself to the situation.

Yes, I know that the big dollars in the fur business are in supplying rendezvous, not in trapping beaver. But I'm out here for the adventure, the excitement of mountain life, not for the money.

In farewell, General Ashley makes a big speech to the mountain men gathered here, thanking us for our efforts on his behalf. I think his mind is all the way on being in Missouri, living in the house with his new wife in St. Louis, and running for governor. And in fact we never see him in the mountains again.

———

As it turns out, that rendezvous of 1826 is a turning point in the mountains. Ashley goes back to St. Louis to stay. Jedediah sets out to the southwest. *I* think he's going to California. But Diah says he's just looking for new beaver territory to the Southwest of the Salt Lake. California is a long way further to the southwest.

Yearning for adventure, I want to go to California with my friend Diah. But he asks me to stay in the mountains as clerk to Sublette and Jackson. I'm a little puzzled, but then consider that maybe my friend is making sure his new partnership succeeds. After all, he may find nothing where he's going, and he's depending on his partners to bring in the beaver.

The new partnership must also send a mid-winter express to General Ashley in St. Louis, asking him to send out next year's supplies and telling him where the rendezvous will be.

I accept Jedediah's decision and his reasoning. My

friend keeps his own confidence sometimes. I'm not sure what he's thinking.

Our fall travels, which are partly explorations, take us to the Snake River and up it. The damn Blackfeet harass us every day. Since we can't drive them off, we keep going until we cross the mountains we call the Tetons, which I'm told means "breasts" in French. They do have suggestive shapes for lonely men.

Then we ride up the main Snake River to its source and over a divide to a miracle—a lake of truly wondrous beauty and spectacular ornaments. Daniel Potts, one of the men who keeps a journal and writes well, has described the lake, so I'll copy his description:

> On the South border of this lake is a number of hot and boiling springs, some of water, and others of most beautiful fine clay, resembling a mush pot, and throwing particles to the immense height of from twenty to thirty feet. The clay is of a white and pink color, and the water appears fathomless, as it seems to be entirely hollow underneath. There are also a number of places where pure sulphur is sent forth in abundance. One of our men visited one of these while taking his recreation—there, at an instant, the earth began a tremendous trembling, and he with difficulty made his escape, when an explosion took place, resembling thunder. During our stay in that quarter I heard it every day.

————

I can confirm every word Potts wrote. Altogether this big lake is a wonder like nothing I have seen before or since. To come upon it? That's why we go adventuring.

I predict confidently that this lake will eventually

draw many, many Americans to exclaim at its marvels. This awesome region is a treasure.

————

Now our brigade circles to the north and west, and then on south back to Cache Valley, where we settle in for the winter.

This is the time for Jedediah's partners, Davey Jackson and Bill Sublette, to make a decision. Their agreement with General Ashley is that, if their prospects look good now, they will send an express to the general asking for supplies for the 4th rendezvous, the one of 1827. In that express they will list for Ashley any needs that he doesn't already know about. They know he won't forget whiskey again.

The problem is, who can do the job of carrying the message? And who will?

Bill and Davey spread the word—they want volunteers, and they're paying a bonus in trade goods.

Seems to me no one will be crazy enough to set out in winter weather.

But Black Harris, a rugged fellow if ever there was one, is eager to go. I mark that down as madness. But Harris roars, "I'll eat them mountains alive. I'll out-howl the winds. I'll *whup* them temperatures." Now he hollers at the skies. "Come at me! Bring your worst! Black Harris conquers all!"

He likes to talk like that.

Harris's first name is Moses. When talking to him, we mountain men call him Moses, but out of his hearing he's always Black Harris. Maybe it's because his cheeks look like gunpowder.

Bill Sublette brings his breakfast coffee next to me at

the big fire and sits. Bill and I have ridden many a mile together, and I know his moods. This one is reflective. For a bit he sits, all the way quiet. After a while he says, "I'm going with Harris. When I took the partnership, I put myself in this spot. I have to go."

For sure he'd rather stay. Cache Valley has sweet, gentle winters compared to the mountains and the plains he'll have to cross.

I bring my coffee cup up to my face and enjoy the warmth of the steam. I look through it at Bill. "You and I went through that kind of harshness going up the Sweetwater to South Pass. I think you can do it."

"I can," he says. He takes a long swig from his cup. "I just hate to."

I'd feel the same way. I say, "You'll be all right."

"While I'm gone," he says, "Davey will be the only partner here. So back him up, will you?"

"Sure."

He stands up. "See you at rendezvous."

———

That night I actually have nightmares about the weather ahead for Bill and Black Harris. South Pass will be howling with winds. I remember trying to stay warm with a blanket and a buffalo robe up there and wondering if I would wake up—ever. Over South Pass and down to the Sweetwater River may be the worst of it, or may not. Crossing the plains to the Missouri River—a huge reach of land with nothing at all to block the winds—that will be one hell of a trial.

Do they have a chance? Harris has already made the trip alone in the middle of winter once and claims that he actually likes doing it.

MARCH 4, 1827

Sublette and Harris actually arrive in St. Louis early in March. Ashley's happy with all the furs he's going to get. Sublette and Harris go around town with the general's money, buying supplies to take back to rendezvous and horses to carry them. Late in March they head back to the mountains with an outfit of 44 men. They're going to need the sweet weather of April.

What counts is that they ride into rendezvous in the middle of June. It's at Bear Lake this summer, a beautiful piece of the earth circled by hills. This time the Shoshones are back to trade again, and a lot of Utes come in as well.

The trading is vigorous. Two of the brigades of the new partnership have had good hunts, and the trappers are big spenders, particularly the free trappers.

The fur business is different now. When we first came to the mountains with Ashley, we worked for a monthly salary and the beaver we caught belonged to Ashley. Since the first rendezvous we're free trappers. That is, we're not hirelings. Ashley's booshways lead the hunts, and we go along, or don't, as we please. Ashley will end up with our furs when we trade with him at rendezvous. So he's happy with the new system, and so are we. It even sounds good—we're *free* trappers.

————

But now Davey Jackson and Bill Sublette are worried. Where's Jedediah? And where's his share of the furs that should be here for the long haul back to St. Louis? Have he and his men all been killed? We're frightened for them.

As we wait and wait, hope dwindles.

Then, all of a sudden, Diah rides in on July 3rd, but with only two men of the fifteen he left with and no furs at all.

His brigade is fine, Jedediah explains. They found good beaver country in California. They've caught plenty and will catch more while they're out there waiting for him to come back and lead them on.

We celebrate. We're so thrilled to see Diah alive, and hear that his men are doing well, that we fire the four-pound cannon Ashley sent with the pack train, quite a roll out here from St. Louis.

Jedediah's story is a long one and is mixed news. He had a hard journey and had to cross a terrible desert but ended up in California. I *knew* he'd end up there, his wayfaring heart demanded it. He rode all the way to the West Coast without seeing a single beaver. The authorities in California didn't welcome him. They suspected that he and his men were an advance party of Americans checking out California for a possible American invasion. Under pressure, he escaped northward with his men, pushing along the east side of a high range of mountains.

They found plenty of beaver in the creeks rolling out of those mountains.

When Jedediah thought the melting mountain snows might allow passage, he left most of his men behind and promised to come back for them later. In the meantime they were to keep trapping. Then he took two men and forced a difficult crossing.

Here at rendezvous, he tells his partners, "When I bring in the furs I left with those men, that haul will make our year's take a good one." Any other man would say "a damn good one," but Diah doesn't cuss.

Now Sublette and Jackson are satisfied. And Jedediah will go back to California to finish the job.

Even without Diah's share, the other two partners tell me that their catch for this year has been good for the partnership. It's 7,400 pounds of beaver, plus some money for otter skins. Ashley will give $3.00 a pound for the plews here at rendezvous and sell them for $6.00 a pound in St. Louis. The difference in price covers his cost for transporting the supplies out to rendezvous and hauling the furs back to St. Louis. The partners calculate their total take at $22,690. They're happy, and Ashley will be happy.

I'm a little envious at being left out of the partnership. They're making quite a profit.

1827-29

The next couple of years are havoc in the mountains. Jedediah and his men miss the rendezvous of 1828 completely, because they get surprised by a band of Umpqua Indians on a river in Oregon. Fifteen trappers get killed. Only the three out of camp at the time survive, and Jedediah is one of those.

I spend the next year clerking for Davey Jackson. Since Robert Campbell has done well trapping and trading with the Flathead Indians, far to the northwest in the Oregon country, we go all the way to Flathead Lake doing likewise. I'll be glad to see Campbell, who is not only an Irishman my age but from Ulster, a county near mine. He's a good friend.

And when we find Campbell, we get a terrific surprise: Jedediah Smith walks into camp with one other survivor of the massacre on the Umpqua.

I'm delighted and excited to see my friend. And then I begin to see the change in him.

At first, I think it's because he feels guilty about his performance for the firm of Smith, Jackson, and Sublette.

Davey Jackson and Bill Sublette have brought in hundreds of pounds of plews. The three partners have a bank account in St. Louis that's fat and getting fatter. But Diah's contribution to that has been small. He said he was going toward California to find new beaver territory. In two years he's found only some creeks flowing out of what he calls Mount Joseph, a long range of high mountains in central California. He's established that American trappers are not a bit welcome in California. If we go, we'll get tossed out. Meanwhile, his catch in furs won't match the accomplishments of his partners.

The truth my friend is keener on exploring than trapping. He became the first to lead an outfit across the deserts to California, the first to cross that big mountain range, and the first to make the very difficult crossing of the deserts from west to east, back to the Rockies.

His heart is wayward, more attracted to exploration than profit. Like my heart.

The result is that he feels like he hasn't done his share. Worse, he's lost about two dozen men under his command. The partnership will have to pay the estates of those men.

But it's not the loss of money that haunts Diah. It's the lives of the men who were his responsibility.

———

The rendezvous of 1829 is in Pierre's Hole, an extraordinarily beautiful valley on the west side of the Tetons. But Diah seems untouched by this beauty. He's strange, remote, and hard to fathom. One evening when we're having coffee next to my fire, he stands up and says, "I'm going to turn in."

"Sweet dreams," I say.

Turning away, he says, "Now my dreams are drenched in death."

I don't know how to reach him.

———

For the fall hunt of that year I go with Bill Sublette north onto the Madison Fork of the Missouri. As usual in that country, the Blackfeet harass us all the way. Damn Bug's Boys.

One morning as we're turning the horses and mules out to graze, the Blackfeet cut in and try to run them off. They've miscalculated, though, and only a few of our animals are out on grass yet. When the Indians charge, a lot of horses and mules run back into camp.

I jump on my horse, holler at all our men to follow, and gallop out to help drive the other horses back. Right then, though, my horse gets shot out from under me. I roll across the ground and get to my hands and knees unhurt. Other trappers gallop by me on the chase. As fast as possible I get a rope on another mount, swing up onto him, and join the fight.

Then the damnedest thing happens. *This* horse gets shot and goes down rolling. I jump clear, get another mount, take some shots at the fleeing Blackfeet, and herd some of our horses back toward the camp.

Now the Blackfeet take refuge in a ravine. There, protected by rocks, they're hard to hit. It takes us hours to drive them off, until the sun is saying it's noon. We have a few men wounded, none mortally.

———

We trap our way over to the Yellowstone, getting a good catch of beaver, make our way through a region of sulphur springs and stinking odors, and push on south to the Wind River, where we've previously spent winters with the Crows. It makes a good winter camp.

But not good for Jedediah. One evening I sit with him through one of his moods.

He says, "I miss life back in the settlements, around people who speak better English, have better morals, and go to church. I want to be on God's side of the Missouri River."

"But people back there," I respond, "they don't get it. They still think the Great American Desert on their maps is uninhabitable. They don't know that buffalo run all over those plains, meat on the hoof. They think the Rocky Mountains can't be crossed, yet we mountain men have danced the fandango back and forth over those mountains and even rolled a wagon across South Pass. Folks back in the settlements can't read sign to save their scalps, which they will therefore lose if they come here."

I'm getting up a head of steam now: "Read sign? Bill Sublette or Jim Bridger can come on an Indian trail and tell you how many men were on it, from what tribe, whether they were peaceable or warlike, how long ago they passed here, and where they were going. Yet people on the wrong side of the Missouri think parsing letters into words and sentences is a big deal."

Now I can't stop. "Back there they have preachers to tell you how wrong you are about everything and quote Bible verses to prove it. Out here you aren't judged by your color or whether you can read and write, what kind of family you come from, or how much money you have, but only by your mountain skills and your willingness to stand by your partner.

"Back there they have sheriffs who boss people around and lawyers to trick you into jail or out of money. People stay in line, especially the churchy line. They're not wild, not free. No one goes just whatever direction he feels like. No one knows what it feels like to ride a horse in the middle of a huge herd of buffalo, hooves thundering-thundering-thundering and turf flying past your head."

I conclude, "Who wants to live in such a place?"

Jedediah sips his coffee and says, "I miss the comfort of a Christian church." Then he gets up and walks into the night, headed for his blankets and his loneliness.

I sure don't miss the priests I met in Ireland, with all their thou-shalt-nots. The preachers on this side of the ocean are just as bad.

———

Back in Ireland, when I had read stories of the great explorers, I got that yen to see the world. Now I look around me and feel the call of the wild. If I see a mountain peak, I want to stand on it and look into country virgin to human eyes. When I see a beautiful river, I want to paddle it. When I imagine a far shore, like California's, I want to walk until I get there and look across the ocean into infinity. I want to go, go, go.

I respect the skills of the men who live out here. They shoot center, and that shot will save your life from an enemy or bring meat for the fire. They know how to make friends with Indians and trade with them instead of fighting them. They know how to make a beaver come to medicine. They will stick by you and stick by you for good.

These men are true and trusted companions.

———

When we wrap up the fall hunt, Jedediah leads the brigade east toward the Yellowstone River. But the Blackfeet can't let us trappers march into their territory and come out unscathed. They mount a full-scale attack.

Though none of our men is killed, we get scattered all over the country.

Joe Meek gets cut off entirely. Stranded with just his mule, blanket, and gun, he decides to make straight for the winter camp agreed on, along the Wind River. Leaving the mule, he sets out southeast and thereby wanders into the hot springs region of the Yellowstone country.

The whole area is sending up smoke from boiling springs—he can feel the heat and smell the burning gases. The place reminds him, by God, of Pittsburgh.

Before long Diah sends two trappers out to hunt for Joe, and they bring him back to the brigade. He allows as how he'd thought maybe he'd been near the back door to hell, but "If it war hell, it war a more agreeable place than I'd been in for some time."

Now we trap our way up the Big Horn to where that river changes its name to the Wind River.

Winter camp. We build lodges. Shoot buffalo and dry the meat. Lounge around. Learn more sign language from the Crows. Some of us learn to speak some Crow. Trade with women for shirts of hide instead of cloth. Trade blankets for buffalo hides. Make friends. Flirt. Tell stories. Exaggerate the stories. Enjoy our *free*dom.

December 24, 1829

My journal says tonight is Christmas eve. My mind flies like a bird across North America and the North Atlantic to the family farm in County Cavan in Ireland. In imagination I see my brothers and sisters gathered around the table to enjoy the Christmas goose. I can't help remembering the similar night when I ran away from home, and then from my country, the beginning of my great adventure in America.

Feeling lonely, I seek out Diah, who always sleeps alone in a lean-to.

At first I just sit down, light my pipe, puff, and wait. He pours me a cup of coffee but doesn't speak. He's using the light of his fire to write in one of his own journals. I know he keeps a log of daily activities in there, and more precious to him, keeps his sketches of maps of country none but he has seen. Always the explorer, often the mapmaker.

After a while I ask what he's writing.

"A letter to my parents," he says.

"Hear much back from them?"

"Not a word," he says. "I've gotten two letters back from my brothers, but nothing from Ma or Pa."

Though he says nothing about his feelings, loneliness echoes through his voice.

———

I don't tell him what my record on correspondence is. Every Christmas I've written to my entire family, but since leaving home I haven't heard a word either. I tell myself that's because only my father can read or write.

But my father? He could write me. But I was the son who did the chores, especially feeding the pigs, and I ran off. I smile at the thought that he may still be miffed at having to feed the pigs himself. In each letter I've given him my address—in care of General Ashley in St. Louis, Missouri—but after these long years I have no hope of a letter from home.

Ma understood that I had wanderlust, and she knew where I got it—from reading the books by the great explorers, or about them, tales of their adventures all over the globe.

By the time I was old enough to run off, the vast reaches of the globe were mostly known. From what I could tell, the biggest adventures left were in America.

The only fellow with an urge to go and see as strong and wild as mine is Jedediah. First man across South Pass, first to cross the desert to California, first across the California mountains and the deserts beyond and back to the Salt Lake, first north California to Oregon—he never quits. I'm just sorry I didn't always get to walk with him.

———

Here and now, next to the fire in front of his solitary lean-to, Jedediah is still writing in his journal. Though I notice that he spends more time staring at the page than in actual writing.

I'm waiting to tell him something. It's a sort of confession. I'm doing something that can bind me to the mountains forever.

First, I've gotten envious of Jim Bridger, who is sharing a lodge with a woman named Willow. Me, I sleep on a buffalo robe and wrapped up alone in blankets, with three other trappers in the lodge we've traded for. Jim's sleeping a lot warmer than I am.

Before long, though, Willow introduces me to her younger sister, called Curly by the family. I notice right away that Willow, Curly, and the rest of their family look at me with the kind of smiles that say something is going on between the two of us. At first that isn't true, but it changes soon enough. Soon Curly and I have our own bed of buffalo hides and blankets in the lodge with Jim and Willow.

Usually, I'd have to pay the family a bride price of several horses to get Curly, but it seems that they consider hooking up with a trapper a guarantee of wealth to come. And I will give Curly goods aplenty when rendezvous arrives, foofuraw for herself, cooking utensils for her mother, and cloth and blankets for the entire family.

Meanwhile I'm enjoying indulgence in sensual pleasures. This is sort of my first time, at the advanced age of 30. I did have a trial run one night in St. Louis half a dozen years ago when Mike Fink pointed me at a woman of the taverns in St. Louis. But we were both drunk, and it was a misadventure I'd prefer to forget.

I felt so rotten about it at the time that I went to

confession, the only time since leaving home that I've darkened the door of a church. Result—a duty of "Hail, Marys" and that's all.

Now I'm lying with a woman without sanction of marriage every night and have no priest to confess to. "Forgive me, Jedediah, for I am a sinner."

It's surprising how little I miss the church. Actually, I feel set free from it.

We mountain men are set free from a lot. But I think the bonds of the Catholic Church are tighter than those of Diah's Methodists, the Baptists, and other American Protestants. Out here *free* is breath itself.

But freedom also has consequences. I wonder whether next autumn will bring into the world a son or daughter of Jim Bridger, half-Crow. And I'm haunted by the thought that nine months may bring forth a son or daughter of mine, and whether I will have a part in the rearing of my own child. I even wonder whether that child will speak English, much less English with an Irish accent. For sure he or she will grow up speaking Crow.

––––––

Jedediah's still composing that letter in the pages of his journal. Judging from the amount of time he spends biting on his pen, the letter is hard for him to write.

I take a deep breath, look around, and decide to make another pot of coffee for this long evening. After nine years here in the wilds, he's writing his family. I've been in the mountains for eight years now, writing each Christmas and getting no letters in return. Diah's record isn't any better.

Whoops! He's talking to me.

"Fitz, will you help me with the spelling?"

I smile and say "Sure." Though he's educated, Diah can be wayward with spelling and punctuation. I've helped him in the past.

His letter begins:

Christmas eve, 1829

Your unworthy Son once more undertakes to address his much-slighted parents.

Diah goes on to say he's sorry that, although he's written to his family before, he has heard only from his brothers, and seldom from them.

He continues,

It is a long time since I left home & many times I have been ready to bring my business to a close & endeavor to come home—but have been hindered hitherto—as our business is at present it would be the height of impolicy to set a time to come home. However, I will endeavor, by the assistance of Divine Providence, to come home as soon as possible. The greatest pleasure I could enjoy would be to accompany or be in company with my friends, but whether I shall ever be allowed the privilege, God only knows. I feel the need of the watch and care of a Christian Church. You may well suppose that our society is of the roughest kind—men of good morals seldom enter into a business of this kind. I hope you will remember me before a Throne of grace.

Then he says that he'll give his family the details of his adventures in the mountains when he sees them face to face, and asks them to write him in care of William Sublette in St. Louis.

He concludes,

May God in his infinite mercy allow me soon to join my
parents is the prayer of your undutiful

Son, Jedediah S. Smith

I add a hyphen in one spot, change a capitalization in another, and hand the journal back to Diah. "Your spelling is fine," I tell him.

He hands the journal back, saying, "Here's another letter."

It's to his brother Ralph. Diah gives a general account of his adventures, going across the continent from St. Louis to the Oregon country, always being on the watch for hostile Indians.

Then he gets particular about his losses:

In August, 1827, ten men who were in company with me
lost their lives by the Mojave Indians on the Colorado River;
and in July, 1828, fifteen men who were in company with me
lost their lives by the Umpqua Indians, by the river of the
same name… Many others lost their lives in different parts of
the country—my brother, believe me we have many dangers
to face & many difficulties to encounter, but if I am spared, I
am not anxious with regard to difficulties—for particulars
you must await a meeting.

Now I can see that my friend is punishing himself when no punishment is deserved. No one thinks less of him for those misadventures. The first time he was tricked by "friendly" Indians, and the second time he was scouting ahead and the man he left in charge foolishly let the Indians into camp.

I know, though, that Protestants and Catholics alike

blacken themselves with the label *sinner*. It's the curse of the white man. One of them.

The little fire is down to coals. I add some sticks to it and fan it with my hat until it lifts into a flame. Then I finish reading Diah's letter:

> *As respects my Spiritual welfare, when shall I be in the care of a Christian church? I have need of your prayers. I wish our Society to bear me up before a Throne of Grace. I find myself one of the most ungrateful, unthankful creatures imaginable. Oh, when shall I be once more in a community of believers?*
>
> *I cannot speak to my friends with regard to my coming home. I have set so many times & have always found myself unable to perform that it is better to omit it.*
>
> *Give my love to my father, mother, brothers, sisters, nephews, & nieces, none excepted.*
>
> *I remain, as ever, your affectionate son and brother,*
> *Jedediah S. Smith*

On the back side of one of the pages of this confessional Diah has written a note giving his brother Ralph two thousand dollars, a lot of money, and promising more, which is to be given to family and friends anonymously. Since Diah is co-owner of the business that supplies rendezvous, he's flush.

I say to myself, but not to Diah, 'guilt, guilt, and guilt.' I hand the letter back to him with the words, "An eloquent expression of your feelings."

I don't add that I'm sorry he is afflicted with such feelings.

But I wonder: With these feelings, how much longer can my friend stay in the mountains? How long before I lose him to the strait-laced settlements and the cursed Christian church? Will he follow his heart, which loves wilderness and freedom, or his religion, which condemns the mountain life as sin?

I don't know, and I don't think he knows.

———

The Wind River usually makes a good winter camp. This winter of 1829-30, though, is so cold that the game is driven to lower elevations. Even the Crows say they can't remember a winter here that's so cold.

We trappers pack up in early January to move northeast to the Powder River, hoping for warmer weather and counting on groves of cottonwoods with the bark that nourishes our horses. And counting on buffalo, which also like cottonwood bark in the winter. We look forward to some good hunting and good eating.

Since the Crows come along for the cottonwoods and the buffalo, Jim Bridger and I get to keep our winter wives for a while longer. Mine, actually, has me well persuaded of the advantages of marriage, or at least marriage to my darling Curly.

And if she brings forth a child next summer, so much the better. I'll stay to help raise the children. I'm attached to her.

When we get to Powder River, our camp feels like heaven. It's well protected against storms and full of buffalo. Our days are filled with raucous laughter, the crack of rifles making meat, the whoops of the Crow men when they bring a buffalo down, the shouts of triumph and rousing songs from trappers. I have this strong feeling: Yes, here in the mountains death is ever-ready, but by God we're *alive* today. Most human beings never are.

April 1, 1830

Come April we break up this happy camp and get started on the spring hunt. Davey Jackson asks me to go west with his brigade to trap along the Snake River, and I agree. I'd be inclined to go with Jedediah's outfit toward Blackfeet territory, but he doesn't ask. Also, Snake River country will yield as many beaver with a lot less danger. To hell with Bug's Boys.

Soon comes rendezvous 1830 on the Wind River, joined by our friends the Crows. I am glad to see Diah— he and his men made a good catch of beaver even on Blackfeet lands. However, I'm also worried. He has learned that his mother has died. That letter he wrote last Christmas already said he was missing his family very much and that he longs for what he called the comfort of a Christian church. I'm afraid he's going to give up the mountain life and go back to the settlements to stay.

I'm afraid of losing my friend. I'm also concerned about him. I think he doesn't know his own heart. He loves life in wilds, he loves risk, and he loves exploring. I can't imagine him cooped up in St. Louis or on a farm somewhere.

I also get the news that I'm losing my Crow wife Curly. Turns out she's not pregnant. She and the family think I'm inadequate, and she's already moved in with a new husband, a Crow fellow she's known all her life.

I'm downhearted. I wanted a son.

Early in August news runs through camp like a wildfire. It comes in a deceptive form—Smith, Jackson, and Sublette want to sell out. The partners are finished with trapping.

This bad news comes to me first in disguise. Davey Jackson asks, "Would you like to join with the new partners who will take over from Smith, Jackson, and Sublette?"

"What partners?"

"You, Bridger, and Milton Sublette. Under the name the Rocky Mountain Fur Company."

I'm excited. Ever since supplying rendezvous became a separate business from trapping, I've wanted in on it. After all, that's the money end of the business. In just two or three years Diah has banked seven or eight thousand dollars, so he tells me. Meanwhile, we trappers, enjoying our lives as much as we may, spend all of our earnings each year in buying supplies for the next year.

Partner or not, I'm going to keep leading brigades through the mountains. Dangerous, yes. But for me that's where the juice is.

Suddenly my excitement is struck with a dagger. This proposal seems to mean that Diah is leaving the mountains. For his family, his church, and for money.

I go straight to him and ask: "Diah, I know part of you wants to live back in the settlements, near a church and near your family. Is this it? Are you committed to going back and staying?"

"Yes."

Simple answer, no elaboration. Just like my friend.

My mind whirls with what to say next. I pass up saying "I'll miss you" and try instead, "I hope that's the right decision."

But I want to tell him to know himself better.

He gives me a fine smile. "You're going to be a partner now," he says. "It's what you've earned. And you'll be the brains of this outfit."

"I suppose so, but... But Diah?"

————

Before the pack train leaves for St. Louis, taking Jedediah along, I learn more about our Rocky Mountain Fur Company. We have two more partners, Henry Fraeb and Jean Baptiste Gervais. It's good—all of us are old hands in the mountains.

Also, I find out in full what the deal is: We're obliged to keep whatever goods Smith, Jackson, and Sublette have left at the end of this rendezvous and pay for them at next summer's rendezvous. Diah says this amount will be about $15,000. Considering what he has earned in his partnership with Jackson and Sublette, he says our intake will cover the debt easily.

Unfortunately, Sublette also has scary news. John Jacob Astor is headed to the mountains with his gigantic American Fur Company to compete with us. Astor is a damned monopolist who has huge amounts of capital and is absolutely ruthless. Just when I've agreed to be a partner in the fledgling Rocky Mountain Fur company, Goliath is about to stomp on us.

I go straight to Jedediah. He's busy adding and subtracting figures. I ask him what he thinks about Astor.

He has a clear answer. "Astor doesn't know the mountains. He'll do what he's done in the past—follow your brigades to learn the best way around, staying several days behind. So lead him into Blackfeet country and feed him to Bug's Boys. You know how to deal with them, and he doesn't. They'll destroy him."

Understood.

Competition has no heart. It's not supposed to. We have to compete.

Now I'm a partner in the business of trapping and supplying trappers at rendezvous. That will be good. I think.

September 1830

With Diah's advice in mind, Jim Bridger, Milton Sublette and I set out for the center of Blackfeet country, the Three Forks, taking a big force of 81 men—there's safety in numbers. We have a good hunt there, pack up, and head back to the Yellowstone.

We hear about an outfit of Astor's but never do see it. I wish them good and bad luck—a minimum of men killed and damn few beaver caught. We've cleaned out the creeks behind us pretty well, leaving them damn few beaver.

We hear later that the Astor men got their tails kicked by the Blackfeet and then followed us to Crow country. There our Crow friends robbed them of 57 horses, but the Astor men got them back.

Let them follow us all they want. They'll find slim pickings where we've already trapped.

Meanwhile I have a job to do—make sure supplies are sent to the rendezvous of 1831. Our new partnership will be putting on that rendezvous for all the trappers and

Indians who want or need tobacco, coffee, whiskey, blankets, knives, and a lot more.

Getting a late start, it's already April 1st, I set out down the Yellowstone with one companion in a bullboat to make sure we get supplies. The two of us float down that river to the Missouri and on down the big river to Lexington, Missouri.

The ferry there is the first big sign of the westward growth of the U.S. population, a so-called improvement.

And trouble. It's already the first week of May, and I'm very late to let Jedediah, Bill Sublette, and Davey Jackson know we definitely want a pack train to take supplies to the rendezvous of 1831.

In St. Louis I get bad news. Jedediah has left town with Davey Jackson and Bill Sublette to go to Santa Fe on a trading expedition.

Part of me is miserable. I'm going to have to catch up with those three partners and beg for them to supply our rendezvous. Maybe they'll let me have some of the goods they've planned to trade in Santa Fe.

But part of me is exhilarated. After making inquiries all over St. Louis, particularly from General Ashley and William Clark, I'm excited. My friend Diah has already surrendered life in the settlements for the adventures of the mountains.

There's plenty of sign that he intends to become a civilized man. He's bought a fine house on First Avenue and is apparently setting himself up as a prosperous man of business, not a creature of the mountains, where I think his heart is.

On the other hand, he is heading back west, isn't he?

I'll find him.

June 12, 1831

At the end of a long, hard day's ride I catch up with their outfit at Lexington, where they've stopped to cut axles for their wagons. The plains ahead will be treeless.

The three partners jump up from their evening fire and pound me on the back.

"Great to see you, Pard!"

"Have some coffee, friend."

And in mountain style, "Glad you be above ground, Fitz!"

Diah and I embrace each other by both shoulders.

"Come sit by my fire," he says. It's his way to sit off by himself and spend most of his time there. But I notice two sets of rolled up blankets by the fire.

"Who's sharing your fire?" I ask.

With a big smile Diah says, "My brothers Peter and Austin. They want a taste of mountain life."

I know he's been eager to give his brothers a start in life, one way or another. "I bet you like having them along."

He fills two cups with coffee and hands me one. "Really glad," he says.

————

Time to launch in.

"What you want to know," I say, "is my partners and I, do we want to be supplied for rendezvous? The answer is, sure we do! We got a couple of hundred men to re-supply and a big bunch of Indians to trade with."

Uh-oh. I wait a little. Yes, I know they intend to sell their goods in Santa Fe. Maybe there's nothing left for rendezvous. It's my fault for being late.

I tell Jedediah why I'm behind the time. Four of the partners of our new Rocky Mountain Fur Company went back to Blackfeet lands, including me. The other two went to Shoshone country. And we four got no word from the other two about sending the express to St. Louis to order supplies.

"After too damn long," I go on, "my partners decided to go ahead and send this crazy Irishman with the express."

The problem is that "too damn long" means the express is two months late. I know that. The message that was due in April has arrived in June, and now the rendezvous to be supplied starts in less than two months.

"I'll go talk to Davey and Bill," Diah says. "You're tired. Spread your blankets here."

Just then two young fellows walk up.

"Austin," Diah says, "Peter, come meet my friend Tom Fitzpatrick."

They walk around the fire and I offer my hand.

"My brothers," Diah says unnecessarily.

I shake their hands and say, "Welcome to the life, wild and free."

Though he has a dubious look, Jedediah takes my elbow. "Throw your blankets here," he says, "next to mine."

———

Davey, Bill, and Diah want to help us partners of Rocky Mountain Fur. But they're on a different mission. So they chew it back and forth a bit and come to me with a proposal.

Bill says, "Fitz, if you'll ride to Santa Fe with us, we'll supply you there."

Davey adds, "Me and Bill will get together two-thirds of your outfit, Diah the other third."

The problem is that they'll be giving me the supplies in early July, and I'll be a month late getting to rendezvous. Lots of trappers and Indians will be waiting very irritably. Or maybe they'll run out of patience before I get there with what they want—and leave.

I shrug. "Deal. It's me who got the late start."

———

Near Council Grove our train gets a surprise attack by Indians that even we mountain men can't identify. All we care about, though, is that our cannon drives them off. Still, the four of us have the same thought: Maybe the Santa Fe Trail isn't as trouble-free as we've heard.

Then I get an idea. I can add some life to our campfires.

The train has already been enjoying some entertainment in the evenings. Back in St. Louis, Davey hired an

Irishman by the name of Paddy O'Shea as his clerk. When he took O'Shea on, the Irishman signed his name just "Paddy."

"Is Paddy the only name you got?" inquired Davey.

"No," said the applicant, "it ain't. My name is Michael O'Shea. But since I have an Irish accent, the lads will call me Paddy anyway, and I'm giving in to it."

Davey listed Paddy as hired.

The pleasure of having Paddy along is the jubilation he adds to our nightly fires. He plays the fiddle in the Donegal style, which I'm pleased to hear after all these years. Everyone gets a kick out of his lively tunes, which set us to tapping our feet and clapping our hands.

When he finds a willing dancer, Paddy teaches the fellow some steps of the jig. I smile while watching Paddy—he knows how it's done. The trick is to catch on to a step called the rise and grind. Paddy demonstrates over and over— "Hop, hop back—hop, hop back" he calls. But there's a problem. When Paddy's busy demonstrating and his fiddle isn't singing out, only he can catch on to how the steps coordinate with the music.

So I pitch in—the Irish in me is rising. I will dance, so now our evening entertainment will be an Irish fiddler and an Irish dancer.

Each evening we sit until the meat has gotten done just right and our bellies are filled with warmth, and then we *dance!*

Sometimes I can get one of the other hands to get up and try the hop, hop back. Each one, though, gets his feet tangled and ends up in the dust. Whenever the other dancer falls down, I pretend to fall and bite the dust myself. Paddy accompanies each collapse with an ominous-sounding double stop on the fiddle.

One night I get a little drunk and go after Diah. "Get

out here and try it. Hop, hop back, hop, hop back, there's nothing to it."

He grins and waves the idea off.

Then a couple of men begin to clap and chant, "Captain Smith! Capitano Smith!"

Soon all are clapping and chanting his name.

He gets to his feet awkwardly, calls out, "No promises!," and stands ready.

Paddy launches into a jig. I jump in front of Diah and model the steps to Paddy's call— "Hop, hop back, hop, hop back."

Diah starts tentatively but then puts some energy into it. Now he gives it more energy, and I join in calling out, "Hop, hop back, hop, hop back." On our fourth cry of "hop back," Diah plops down hard on his butt.

A burst of laughter and applause.

———

I help him up with both hands, then support him with an arm around his back and say to the circle, "Guess what?" I point to his chest. "There's a live one in there somewhere, ain't there?"

Lots more laughter.

Since my steps are unsteady from drink, Diah takes me by an elbow and leads me a little back from the fire. "Let's sit here," he says. "We'll be at what fancy folks call the penumbra of the firelight."

I smile, and we sit down cross-legged. "Penumbra? You have awful big words in your head for a mountain man."

Then I get to it. I say, "I've gotta ask you this. You said you want to be in St. Louis to be in the embrace of a Christian church, yet you no more'n get there than you're on the trail again. It's about time you wake up to something."

"What's that?" he asks, tickled.

"Listen to that wily heart of yours. It's telling you you're in love with the wi-i-lds." I make that last word sing.

Now I take thought, twist my mouth in a funny way, and go on, slurring my words a little. "Now from my reading this here child knows his loyalties. Atalanta, the Greek goddess of adventure; Abeona, the Roman Goddess of Outward Journeys, and Adiona, the Goddess of Safe Return; Ekehau, Mayan God of travelers and merchants. I ride flying those flags."

I put a hand on my heart.

"But your guide book? The *New Testament*? That song don't sing, not in this country."

I step back, get my feet tangled, and plop down. I'm too drunk for this.

JUNE 1831

As our train moves up the Arkansas River, we endure the endless drizzles, mires, the irritable behavior of the mules, and trouble getting our twenty-two wagons across the swollen creeks.

Then nature turns over and lies on her other side. We come to the Cimarron Cutoff, a shortcut from the Arkansas River to the Cimarron River. The Cimarron is what Diah calls an Inconstant River, one of those streams that gives a water hole here, then a stretch of flowing underground, and a water hole there, followed by far too much running underground. The name Inconstant River comes from a "stream" he followed for a while out in the Mojave Desert, trying to get across the sands to the mountains. That stream ran mostly underground, made an occasional water hole, and ducked back underground. The Cimarron is like that.

We could go along the Arkansas to the Rockies, turn left, and go through Raton Pass to Santa Fe. But that route is longer and we're behind time already, especially with me getting later and later to rendezvous.

We take the Cutoff. It's a water scrape, forty or fifty waterless miles to a river that plays hide and seek. Dicey, but we're going for it. Life in the wild is always dicey.

————

For the first three days we come to no water at all. And the land is cut up by countless buffalo trails, which confuse the route. Our horses and mules are desperate with thirst. The men are half-delirious.

Jedediah tells me, "It's time for us to step up."

So the two of us push ahead looking for a water hole or a spring.

Nothing.

More nothing.

Somewhere ahead is the Cimarron River, but...

We come to a hole that should have water. It's dry.

"Fitz," he says, "I'm going to ride alone toward that hill." He points further to the south, where I can see a bare smudge on the horizon. It's not really a hill.

"I don't like it, Diah."

"Crossing the Mojave Desert those two times," he says, "I learned how to find water. This is our best shot."

I just look at him, uncertain.

"You stay here and dig," he says. "Get some water to come up. You'll see our mules, our whole outfit coming." He points north. "When they get here and have a drink, point out the direction I've gone."

I say, "I don't like it."

My friend answers, "Fitz, finding water is what I do."

————

One hour, two hours, maybe three. No Diah and no pack train.

Then a line of smudge on the desert to the north, made by the dust our horses and mules kick up. It emerges as our outfit, 85 mounted men and 23 mule-drawn wagons in a big cloud of dust.

Though I've dug and dug, I have no water to offer them.

We ride on in the direction Jedediah pointed—parched, worn out, and desperate.

I ride out in front, more desperate. Ten miles, fifteen, maybe more.

And miracle—a water hole.

No Jedediah, but water. I let my horse soak himself and drink his fill. I lie down in the water, soak it up, and drink a belly-full.

Amazingly refreshed, the horse and I go back and lead the whole train to this water.

We make camp here.

Twilight, no Diah.

Dark, no Diah.

Dawn, no Diah.

I talk the situation over with his brothers Peter and Austin. When the pack train moves on, following the dotted line of the water holes made by this irritating Inconstant river, Peter, Austin, and I ride the other direction, upstream. Maybe five miles, then ten, still no Diah.

Under my breath I'm cussing the buffalo who've trampled all this ground and made it impossible to follow whatever tracks Jedediah may have left.

I tell the two young men their brother may have followed the dotted line of water holes to the west, or the east, no telling.

I'm afraid the brothers hear the weariness and grief in my voice.

We turn around and ride west. The clop, clop, clop of our horses' hooves sound like hope, hope, hope to me. But my hope is getting trampled.

We ride up to our outfit where they've camped for the night at a good hole.

Still no Diah.

Then dawn and still no Diah.

I confer with Bill and Davey, Peter and Austin standing close and listening.

We agree: We don't know what happened to Diah, but we have no more hope. When a man rides into country like this, death rides at his side.

The next morning we move on to the west, following the string of water holes. Peter and Austin want to ride to the east, looking for Diah. But I tell them we did that yesterday, no luck. If he's alive, he's ahead of us in the other direction. I try to sound positive.

But I know in my bones. My friend is gone.

Gone.

Gone.

July 1, 1831

The next day a miracle comes to me. I'll always be grateful for the unlikely miracles offered by the strange and wondrous life on this earth.

As I'm riding out in front of the dust of all the animals and wagons, I spot movement in some brush. Rifle ready, I approach and—behold, the moving figure is a small boy, probably eight or nine years old. He's emaciated from hunger, too scared and too weak to run.

He looks askance at my rifle. Looks like he would run if he could.

I swing off my horse, get my possible sack off my back, and take out several pieces of beef jerky.

I stick one piece in my mouth, bite, and chew. Then I hold out a piece to him.

His face goes through a couple of changes. I model eating jerky again. He takes a piece from my hand and raises his eyebrows to me, inquiring.

I nod yes. Will he understand this gesture? I put another piece in my mouth, and chew once more.

He nods and eases a piece into his own mouth.

Maybe the child is starving. Tentatively, warily, he munches.

I sit, stuff yet another piece into my mouth and chew hard and fast, modelling again.

He smiles and starts chewing fast. Soon we're having a smiling competition to see who can chomp it down faster.

Now we're both grinning and laughing.

I give him a hug—surely he'll understand that—and lift him up behind my saddle.

I swing onto my horse and after a few moments we join my companions, riding in front of the pack train. That evening we sit by the main fire, where an antelope is being roasted on a spit. The boy stays very close to me, entirely away from everyone else. I cut a good piece of one haunch of the antelope, cut it up, put it on a plate, and hand it to him. From the way he takes it I think he hasn't seen a plate before, but he knows well what meat is. He gobbles it down.

What on earth happened to this child's family?

I spread a blanket out and we sleep.

The next morning, when he wakes up, I urge more jerky on him.

Then I consider. It seems the boy is my companion now. What he needs first of all is a name.

I have an idea. I ask Sublette, "What day is today?" He keeps his journal more accurately than I do. "It's Friday."

So, I point to the boy's chest and say "You're, Friday," then to my chest and say, "Me, Fitz."

He repeats, pointing to his own chest, "You, Friday." And then to my chest, "Me, Fitz."

I can't help laughing. I'll have to teach him better

English, especially "you" and "me." I reach out and pat his thin back.

It will work out. For the time being I have a son, just as I wanted.

———

Our pack train rides into Santa Fe on July 4th. Though the Mexicans don't understand what the fuss is about, the men of this American outfit celebrate Independence Day with far too much whiskey.

I give Friday coffee with sugar in it, but not a bit of whiskey. He loves the sugary brew.

The next morning Peter, Austin, Friday, and I have breakfast in front of a Mexican restaurant. We'd like to talk to Friday but still don't know what language he speaks. At first he doesn't understand that the tortillas and beans put on a plate in front of him are meant for eating. I take his fork, lift some beans, and touch the fork to his lips. He opens, chews, and swallows. Then smiles.

Just then two men come up to our table holding...

I recognize Jedediah's rifle and pistols and know right off what has happened.

They ask us if we want to buy the weapons.

After a moment Jedediah's brothers also recognize his guns.

"You want?" asks one of the Mexicans.

We would have a problem communicating, but a man from the next table volunteers to help with the Spanish.

"He's asking if you want to buy the guns."

Peter and Austin say "Yes" at the same time.

I tell the stranger, interrupting, "We'd like to know how they got them."

"Yes, yes," says the stranger, and says something in Spanish.

The story comes out quickly. Some Comanches rode into town yesterday, wanting to sell the firearms. These two Mexicans got the weapons and they got this story from the Comanches:

The Indians rode up to a water hole that they knew on the Cimarron River. Looking down, they were surprised to see a white man and his mount standing in the water.

They spread out and surrounded him.

When the white man saw them, he mounted, put on a big smile, and made signs for peace. They ignored the signs.

They shot the white man and took the horse and the guns.

Now they've traded the guns to the Mexicans but kept the horse, which was a good one. They left the body.

When the Mexicans finish their story Peter and Austin don't say a word.

Friday just looks from person to person, puzzled.

I barter for the weapons, pay, and give them to Diah's brothers.

————

All of us ride back to camp in silence, Friday behind me on my horse. The way he holds on and presses his face into my back feels like a hug. He's a lonesome boy.

Peter and Austin are silent, their heads hanging.

Sometimes there's nothing to say.

I can tell that they want to be alone. I respect that. I also want to be alone.

I dismount and lift Friday down. At the nearest fire I borrow a cup, pour some coffee from the speckled pot, sip the brew, and offer it to Friday without sugar. He sips, makes a face, and spits the stuff out.

Now I pour in some sugar and offer the brew to Friday.

He hesitates and decides to trust me. Then a big grin. He loves the sugary stuff.

I pat his head and take a few minutes alone to sit with my thoughts and feelings.

Naturally, Friday is silent. I'm a stranger. A kind one, but still a stranger, not a parent, not a relative, no one he knows.

I get out my journal and my pen and stare at the blank pages for a bit. Then I show Friday with gestures that I'm going to write something. After some thought I pen this eulogy for my good friend, Jedediah Smith. No one will see it but me:

Jedediah, your body lies alone in a wasteland, observed only by the sun that circles above you every day and the moon that lights you by night.

Mother Earth knows you made altars of her mountaintops. She remembers that you sipped the sweetness of her mountain creeks as the grace of God. She knows you made an understanding of her myriad ways into your sacraments.

You treasured her so much you took numberless steps on her surface, and saw more of her bounty than any other man of your time. She knows you loved her.

Now she welcomes you home.

————

I take a long look at Friday. He seems to be about eight or nine years old. He's bewildered to see me making marks on paper with a pencil.

I take the boy by the hand and lead him around camp. I introduce him to several men I know to be kind, pointing to the boy and saying his new name, Friday, then pointing to the man and saying that fellow's name. When Friday figures out that I'm telling him the name, I remind him to add "Sir."

Peter points at him and says, "I'm Peter. You are Friday."

The boy answers, "You are Peter, Sir."

Good enough for now.

I get only that response from Friday until I introduce him to a trapper named Lewis. After one look at the boy's clothes, Lewis addresses him in a strange language.

Very oddly, Friday speaks back in a similar language.

Quickly, they're having a conversation.

Soon Lewis tells me, "This boy's an Arapaho. I speak the language. He doesn't know how he got separated from his parents, but it happened. And he thinks you're very kind to feed him."

Big stuff.

I say to Lewis, "Tell him my name is Fitz and his name in my language is Friday."

Done in a moment.

"He gets it."

Friday says to me, "Fitz, Sir."

Now I ask, "Please tell him that every man is "Sir" except for me. For instance, you're 'Lewis, Sir,' but I'm just 'Fitz' without the 'Sir.' I'm his family."

Lewis speaks to the boy in Arapaho.

Grinning, Friday says to me, "Fitz, not Sir."

Good enough.

When I've spent a little more time with this child, I'm going to bear hug him.

Now I feel like a father for real.

————

Without trying, Friday helps me with my feelings about Diah, and I go on with life. I've suffered a big loss and then been granted an extraordinary gift.

After a palaver with Bill Sublette, Davey Jackson, and Peter and Austin, I buy rendezvous supplies from Jedediah's estate on the promise of paying six thousand dollars for them. These items aren't worth much here in Santa Fe but will be in demand in the mountains. Or, if I miss rendezvous entirely, which seems likely, I'll sell them on demand to trappers wherever I find them. I can find out where the brigades have gone, track them down, and trade the men whatever they want.

I have to make all this work. I buy an extra horse and saddle from Jackson and Sublette and quickly discover that Friday is used to riding. His parents must have put him on a horse early on. Then I agree to pay a dozen men of the Jackson-Sublette pack train to go with me to rendezvous, or wherever we end up.

Our little outfit rides up the Rio Grande and across to the South Platte, where I hear that my partner Fraeb is looking for me, and he's not far downriver.

When we get to Fraeb's camp, he says happily, "I'm looking for you."

"I'm looking for you," I exclaim.

He sees the pack train behind me. "You've come to rendezvous," he says.

"Yes, very late."

"We wasn't surprised you was late. We didn't send you off soon 'nuff."

"Rendezvous is over?"

"Yeah, the brigades have set out." He grin about lights up the sky. "The damnedest thing done happen. I guess I got a little Indian religion. Anyhow, I decided to ask a Crow medicine man to play oracle and figure out where you was. First the feller demands payment of two horses, which I think is a lot for a bunch of hocus-pocus. Then he gets some drummers to going and sets out to singing and dancing and screeching—all day and all night for two days until he passes out from exhaustion. When he wakes up, he says he's seen you a-coming but you're on the wrong road."

Fraeb shakes his head in disbelief. "So I talk it over with our partners and then come a-lookin'."

I explain that I was on the wrong road. I had to go to Santa Fe with the Smith-Jackson-Sublette pack train, but now I'm turning all the goods over to him. The deal is that our company, Rocky Mountain Fur, will pay off the note for six thousand dollars that I signed, getting the money back by selling to our own men. The first item to go will be the whiskey—the men will have a memorable blow-out, which may well leave them without strong drink for the next year. In the end everything we have will get sold.

Friday and I camp with Fraeb for a couple days. When I drink some coffee, Friday points and says a new word of English—"sugar."

"Sugar, please," I correct him.

He says, "Sugar, please."

I'm proud of him for learning. But instead of giving him a spoonful, I put it directly into the coffee. Then I take thought and put two more spoonfuls in the coffee and hand him the cup.

He sips, gives a big grin, sticks the cup out, and says, "Sugar, please."

I put in one more spoonful. He sips and grins. He sure likes coffee. With plenty of sugar.

———

It's time to turn our faces downriver toward St. Louis. I have two plans: One is to buy plenty of supplies there, put together a pack train, and make sure I get to next summer's rendezvous in plenty of time. That's my duty for our partnership. The other is to put Friday in school. I'm sure my boy will like learning to read and write. He's learning English fast. I think he's smart and I'm eager to see what a year in school will do for him.

I spend the winter in St. Louis and somehow raise enough credit to supply a new outfit for the mountains. This is the plan: Next spring I'll head for rendezvous 1832, leading a pack train. It will be in Pierre's Hole, a beautiful valley on the west side of the Tetons.

SEPTEMBER 1832

At last we get to St. Louis—the long ride has worn Friday pretty well out. The first thing we do, after finding a room, is go for a confab with Captain Clark.

Friday intrigues Clark. This man grew up as an Indian fighter, travelled from St. Louis to the Pacific Ocean and back and negotiated with Indians all along the way, and he is the agent for all the Indians of the Louisiana Purchase. Clark says he's come across no one like Friday until now.

I've come to ask favors of the captain, but he and the boy hit on their own agenda. Clark wants to hear Friday's impression of white people. Friday comes up with an answer: "Rifles!" he says, and he mimes taking a shot. Then he throws his hands up in amazement. "Knives!" Hands and eyebrows up for amazement again. "Coffee pots! Tin cups! Sugar!" His list is long, and his body language is as impressive as his words.

The captain smiles all the way through Friday's recitation. Then he looks at me and says, "This boy is something very special."

Then Clark has an idea: "Friday, do you know what ice cream is?"

My boy is stumped. "Ice cream, Captain, Sir."

Clark considers. "It's a treat for children, Like sugar, only sweeter."

"I love sugar, Sir," says Friday, his eyes lighting up. I don't think he knows the word "sweeter" yet.

In a jiffy we're walking to the confectioner's store. Clark orders a scoop of vanilla with chocolate sauce for Friday, one for himself, and looks questioningly at me.

"The same," I say.

The captain pays with a greenback and some coins.

After a few bites, he asks Friday, "You like ice cream with chocolate sauce as much as sugar?"

"More!" says my boy. I think "more" is a new word for him.

As we're walking back, I decide I'd better get to business.

"Captain, I'll be here all of this autumn and winter. Friday will board with me and go to school during the day. But in the spring I have to go back to rendezvous with the supply train, and from there I can't be sure.

"I have two questions: What school would you recommend for Friday while I'm here, and then what boarding school for the time I'm out west?"

"You know my secretary, Florence," says Clark, "and her boys. "She can introduce Friday to the school and its teacher."

———

When we get back to his office, I make introductions. "Friday, this is Mrs. Price. Florence, this is my adopted son, Friday."

Friday sticks out his hand and says, "Please to meet you, Mrs. Price, Sir."

Both Florence and I chuckle at his mistake. And together we teach him to call her "Mrs. Price, Ma'am."

She adds, "And you don't shake hands with a woman, only with a man."

I add, "This may be too much to remember, but men are called 'Sir' and women are called 'Ma'am.'"

"I bet Friday can remember," Florence says with a smile.

"Yes, Ma'am," says Friday with a big grin.

———

Florence walks us over to the day school where her boys attend and introduces us to Mrs. Talbot, the mistress.

Now Friday shows off. He keeps his hand to himself and says, "Pleased to meet you, Mrs. Talbot, Ma'am."

Florence and I grin at each other.

"Very impressive," says Mrs. Talbot. Then she explains to me that the fee for schooling will be two dollars a day. "Plus, two dollars a night for room and board for when you're out of town."

I tell her that's fine. I'd had no idea what the cost might be.

"Since I have no idea how much he knows and doesn't know," she goes on, "I suggest starting him in school on the first day of September with the other first-year students."

"Fine." I'm pleased. That's just eight days away.

"Right now would you like to put him in a classroom for the last hour of school, for today? Just so he can get used to it?"

"Sure!"

"You may pick him up at three o'clock, no charge."

———

Later, back at Clark's office, I ask Florence, "Will you watch Friday for just a few minutes while I talk with Captain Clark?"

"Sure. I'll show him how to make marks with a pencil."

Clark's office is thick with those smells of pipe smoke and the hides hung on his walls that have come to mean comfort to me.

"Captain, I'm concerned about Friday. Not for this autumn and winter, while I'm here with him, but for the times I'm out west. I'm afraid he'll be lonely, and... I'm just afraid for him."

"Fitz, he knows a person who can and will rise up to help him. Me." As he lights his pipe, the captain peers at me through the swirling puffs of smoke. "I emphasize to you what an impression this child has made on me." He takes a deep draw and puffs smoke out. "I wonder if you've considered this. As agent for the Indians of the plains, I have to consider it. Within a few years we're going to need a lot of help with the plains Indians. The traffic on the route along the Platte River to the mountains is going to get more and more crowded, because more outfits will be going to the mountains, most of them emigrants.

"Your friend Bill Sublette tells me that he's going to build a fort and trading post where the Laramie Fork comes into the Platte. And more forts like that will spring up along the way.

"All the traffic on that river route will mean more hunting pressure across the plains. That pressure will mean fewer buffalo for the tribes, which means they'll be angry. They'll also be angry about permanent establishments like that fort getting built along the road.

"Fitz, we're walking into a crisis, not this year, maybe not in five years, but it's coming.

"So, give thought to this. I already have. How valuable will a young man like Friday be in ten years? He already speaks Arapaho, and his English is coming along fast. After a few years of schooling, he'll read and write well enough to set down what's said at big conferences.

"And we will have big conferences. We'll need to get the Indians to give us permission to travel on the Platte route, and let us hunt along the way. Note that every buffalo we take along the route means less food for the Indians. We need to persuade them not to attack supply trains or attack the forts. And while we're at it, if we're humane, we'd best persuade them to stop attacking each other. And I intend to be humane.

"Now imagine a big treaty conference at a fort along the river, maybe even this fort where the Platte meets the Laramie. How valuable can Friday be at a conference like that? We'll want the principal tribes of the northern plains at such a gathering. With the knack Friday has for eager learning, I think he'll be able to help with translation and far beyond even that."

He takes the short-stemmed pipe out of his mouth and clanks its ashes into a big ashtray.

"I hope you're going to ask me to keep a grandfather-like eye on Friday while he's in St. Louis, during the times you're here and the times you're not. As the representative of the government of the United States of America, that will be my duty."

He gives me a smile of satisfaction.

He's offered everything I was going to ask for, and more. A hopeful future.

On the way back to the boarding house I feel like I'm dancing on air.

———

Reading is big on my mind. When I was about five years older than Friday, I was already reading Magellan's account of his circumnavigation of the globe. I wonder whether my absence from St. Louis will affect his performance.

A new thought breaks loose in my head. Friday's been away from his people for only a couple of months. He must miss them. His parents. He probably has brothers and sisters. But only an orphan would be left wandering in the wilderness, I imagine.

Or is everything new and so exciting to him that...? Actually, I don't even know how long he's been alone.

I'll figure a way to ask him.

APRIL 27, 1832

I set out today with Bill Sublette, my old friend from our days with Jedediah and was a partner in Smith, Jackson, and Sublette before selling out to us partners of Rocky Mountain Fur. Bill is carrying the supplies to the rendezvous of 1832. I had planned on doing that myself, but have no money and can get no credit. Bill helped me with money to get through the winter and hire four men to go along on this journey. However, he'll be making the profit on supplying the men of the mountains this year, leaving out our Rocky Mountain Fur Co. That doesn't sit well with me, but business is a tough world.

We head out with 65 horses and mules and slosh all the way across Missouri in relentless rains. At Independence a group of men led by Nathaniel West falls in with us—more trappers to compete with us in the mountains, but also more men to buy supplies at rendezvous. Now we're a gang of 85 men, and we're driving 300 cows and sheep. At least the animals will provide meat until we get into buffalo country.

So up the Platte River we go. the route that will later

be called the Oregon Trail, and at the Laramie Fork we run into another outfit of trappers, a Gant and Blackwell outfit—yet another competitor in the mountains. I buy their 120 beaver skins, cache them, and make a decision: I'm going to ride ahead, go forward alone to the rendezvous in Pierre's Hole, and give all the men the good news that the supply caravan is on its way and will be in plenty of time this year.

———

Diary, I'm embarrassed by my behavior. I haven't kept a daily record of what I do and what I think, not even close to daily. It seems that instead I'm remembering my bigger experiences as a mountain man and recording the growth of the fur trade in the Rocky Mountains during my years as a trapper. Though that includes a lot of my experiences, it's not entirely personal. Still, it seems to me that mixing what is very personal, such as my relationship with Friday, with the larger picture of what's happening around me makes sense. This larger picture includes some of the business side of things. As a partner in the Rocky Mountain Fur Company, I know the business.

There are probably rules about how to keep a diary. Surely, I'm violating them—forgive me.

LATE JUNE 1832

The rendezvous of 1832 is in Pierre's Hole, the pristine valley on the west side of the Tetons. We trappers arrive early, as usual. Why not? The spring season has ended and we're eager for the big party that will start when the supply train arrives from St. Louis. Maybe the supplies will come in June—for instance right now.

I wonder where Bill Sublette and the pack train are. I started out with them but rode ahead. Maybe Bill will show up in July, or August. Maybe, if our luck is really bad, as it was last summer, supplies won't get here at all. Mountain life is unpredictable.

What's unpleasant is that June is wet, cold, and miserable. The friendly Indians, like Crows and Shoshones, are not here yet, so the usual sports like horse racing, foot-racing, wrestling, and contests of shooting and knife-throwing aren't as much fun. Worse, there's no whiskey to get crazy on. There's no foofuraw to tempt the women, and so no dallying. Instead, we're just a huge gang of dissatisfied, lusty, thirsty men.

———

While the men I speak of are waiting impatiently in Pierre's Hole, I'm actually far to the east at the Laramie Fork of the Platte and about to leave the Sublette supply caravan—I'm going to ahead to tell everyone at the rendezvous that supplies are on the way. There will be no repetition of last summer.

So I take two fast horses fellow never knows when he'll have to outrun Indians. But I'm eager for this adventure.

I ride up and over South Pass, remembering when Diah and I found it and became the first white men to cross it, and the first to put in on a map. Diah made a sketch showing where it is. Quite an accomplishment, and a good day that was.

As I ride down the pass on the western side, I run into a gang of Blackfeet. Bug's Boys—and realize I'd better ride like hell now.

I go hard toward the mountain on the north side. When one of my horses has trouble with its footing and slows me down, I leave it behind for the Indians.

I whip my remaining horse up a steep, rugged path on the mountain. When this horse starts to falter, I look back and see the Blackfeet have dismounted and are advancing on foot. I press my horse hard, but it's soon giving out.

I jump off and run. Now I can hear the Blackfeet whooping as they capture my second horse.

I spot a hiding place in the rocks and dive into it. Quickly, I block the hole with sticks and leaves. Before long I can hear the Indians creeping by, going higher.

I wait with sagging spirits. And wait some more. And wait longer, anxiety crawling up and down my limbs.

———

When it's fully dark and completely silent, I'm sure they've abandoned the chase for the night. I creep out, look around, and head in a likely direction.

Only to find myself on the edge of their camp.

Stealthily, I creep back to my hidey hole.

The next morning I can see Blackfeet walking all over the mountain, looking for me.

When the day seems silent, I slip out of the hole. But down the slope I can see them running races with my two horses. I go back behind my sticks and leaves and wait for darkness.

All night long I follow a creek down the mountain. When the sun comes up, I hide in some brush and wait for another night.

In the darkness I walk on downhill, angling north toward Pierre's Hole. At daylight, thinking I'm far enough away from the Blackfeet, I keep going. Famished, I rummage for some roots and berries and eat. I see an antelope but don't dare risk the noise of a shot.

When I come to a swift stream I have to cross, I build a crude raft and risk it. But the raft bangs into a rock and breaks. To swim to the other shore, I have to drop my rifle and my shot pouch. Then I sit on the far bank, my buckskins soaked and my body shivering, and look at my pitiful situation. I have no weapon left but a butcher knife.

I must get on to the north toward Pierre's Hole and the help of friends.

I come to a swamp and kneel to dig some roots for food.

Right off a pack of wolves circles around me.

I climb a tree, intending to outwait them.

It works. Impatient, they file off.

And accidentally do me a service. Walking on, I find the carcass of a buffalo they've killed and mostly eaten. I scrape the rest of the meat off the bones, dig a hole, make a fire by rubbing sticks together, feed my hungry belly, and sleep.

The next morning I feel stronger.

But the following days are worse. I find almost no roots or berries. As I get weaker and weaker from hunger, my steps turn into staggers.

At last I fall down and give up. Acceptance: I will die here, and death will be a grace.

————

Hands shake me I look at the owners of the hands. Two white men—trappers by their dress. They help me sit up. Give me water. Feed me jerked meat.

I sit, eat, and drink. After a while I can stand up with their support. After another while I can stand on my own.

"Yes," I tell them, "I'm ready to walk."

"It's quite a hike to rendezvous," the short one says. I don't recognize either of them and so can't call them by name.

"I'll speak up when I need to rest."

"Let's move our tails," says the tall one.

"You know I'm Tom Fitzpatrick," I tell them.

The tall guy says, "This coon is Ricky, and my partner is Alan."

I shake their hands and say, "You're saving my arse."

Ricky says, "That's the idea."

They decide that saving my ass will be done best if I

ride first one of their horses, then the other. I don't think I'd make it otherwise.

Along the way we're lucky—we shoot an elk and feed greedily on it.

———

The walk to rendezvous takes two days, and the meat we have barely lasts.

In turns out that Bill Sublette has already brought the supply train in to the gathering at Pierre's Hole. I can hardly believe my troubles with the Blackfeet took so long that his train passed me. But that's my good luck because he sent Ricky and Alan to look for me.

Later, in Pierre's Hole, friends tell me that when they brought me into camp I looked like a skeleton, my eyes sunken, my face emaciated, my hair stark white.

But here there's meat aplenty, and in a couple of days I feel almost normal.

Now I'm afraid I'll have the name White Hair instead of Broken Hand.

THE FIRST WEEK OF JULY 1832

This rendezvous is even more of a carnival than the previous ones. The trappers are indulging in their usual recreations, all of them exaggerated by two factors—Sublette has brought plenty of goods plus plenty of whiskey, and a lot of the trappers have had good catches of beaver and are eager to trade.

In the middle of all this chaos I get a big treat. My partner Bill Sublette has carried two letters to me from St. Louis—one written by Friday and one by Mrs. Talbot, the mistress of his boarding school.

April 21, 1832
Dear Fitz—After nearly a year of schooling I know how to write English well enough to set down a few sentences to you in pencil. Mrs. Talbot is helping me do this. I hope that you like my hand in cursive writing.

Although you have been gone for only a month, I miss you. I would enjoy being with you. I like to ride behind you on your horse and hold on. I also like to sit by the fire with you and drink coffee with a lot of sugar.

I also say that boarding with Mrs. Talbot is good. The bed is warm and I like the food, though she won't give me coffee, as you do. I am glad to go to school. I am happy here, and I want to keep learning.

Captain Clark has picked me up twice in this last month and taken me out for ice cream with chocolate sauce. He has also asked Mrs. Talbot about my progress several times. He is a kind man, and I'm glad to know he's watching out for me.

I hope to see you soon. School is good, but I miss being with you.

Your son by adoption,
Friday the Arapaho

Mrs. Talbot includes her own letter about the progress of my boy. She says he takes to reading enthusiastically. For instance, he likes Mother Goose and chants one song with great enthusiasm:

> *There was a man lived in the moon, lived in the*
> *moon, lived in the moon,*
> *There was a man lived in the moon,*
> *And his name was Aiken Drum.*
> **Chorus**
> *And he played upon a ladle, a ladle, a ladle*
> *And he played upon a ladle, and his name was*
> *Aiken Drum.*
> *And his hat was made of good cream cheese, of*
> *good cream cheese, of good cream cheese,*
> *And his hat was made of good cream cheese,*
> *And his name was Aiken Drum.*

And his coat was made of good roast beef, of good
roast beef, of good roast beef,
And his coat was made of good roast beef,
And his name was Aiken Drum.

Mrs. Talbot says she has not yet begun to teach Friday to add and subtract. She's waiting until the second year of schooling to teach him arithmetic, and yet another year before introducing multiplication, she says, and after yet another year, division.

I can hardly believe my boy will learn so much. My father educated me at his knees without advancing into arithmetic. Yet he truly did teach me to love books. These stories inspired me to have own adventures.

At the end of her letter Mrs. Talbot asks me to send back to St. Louis with Sublette sufficient payment for another year in boarding school for Friday. Unnecessarily, she adds that she can't afford to board, feed, and teach children without compensation.

I'm glad to do that. I'm grateful to her. With the payment I'll include a note promising to send another payment with the returning supply train each summer I'm away. Since his boarding costs over fifty dollars a month, and his schooling the same amount, I hope that my share of profit in Rocky Mountain Fur will be substantial.

I'm thrilled with Friday's progress.

———

However, trouble is heating up here in the mountains. The American Fur Company is competing hotly with our Rocky Mountain Fur outfit. They follow our brigades through the mountains, learning from us where the best trapping grounds are. Right now we can trap the creeks almost clean of beaver before they arrive, but soon they'll have stolen our expertise for themselves and will go ahead of us. They're even poaching some men from our brigades into theirs, offering good wages. We don't pay wages—just pay for the hides the trappers bring to us. I'm afraid that the deep pockets of John Jacob Astor will eventually give AFC the upper hand in the mountains.

And worse: Other outfits are showing up to compete for beaver. There's one led by Nathaniel Wyeth, another by Captain Bonneville, a company of Gant and Blackwell men, and other small groups. Seems like everyone wants to cash in on the mountain trade. I'm afraid there's not enough beaver to go around. For sure my partnership in Rocky Mountain Fur doesn't look as good as it did. When Jedediah left the mountains, he went back to a big bank account and bought a fancy house in St. Louis. I don't see a fancy house in my future.

———

When the business of rendezvous winds down in Pierre's Hole, the first trappers setting out on the fall hunt are a party led by two of my partners, Milton Sublette and Henry Fraeb as booshways, another brigade of trappers, and some tag-alongs. They head southeast toward the Snake River. When they wake up on the first morning, not yet out of Pierre's Hole, they see a long line of horsemen filing into their valley, plumed and painted for war. The booshways recognize them as Gros Ventres, one division of our long-standing enemies the Blackfeet.

Though the braves are whooping and waving feathers and blankets like they want to fight, a chief rides out in front, unarmed and holding up a pipe—a sign asking for peace.

Sublette and Fraeb send Antoine Godin and a Flathead out to confer. These men don't like Blackfeet and don't trust them. Godin's father was killed by Blackfeet, and the Flathead people have had a long history of hostility to the Blackfeet.

When the chief holds out his hand in friendship, Godin instructs the Flathead to fire. He kills the chief right off. Godin grabs the chief's blanket, and he and the Flathead ride hard back to the camp in a rain of bullets.

The fire of battle is lit in Pierre's Hole, with plenty of old scores to be settled—another round of mountain men against Blackfeet.

———

The Indians take cover in a dense thicket of willows, and their women throw up a breastwork of logs. After sending a messenger to the main camp for reinforcements, our trappers crawl into a ravine or hide behind the baggage and fire at long range.

When those of us in camp get the word, Bill Sublette, Robert Campbell, and I lead a lot of trappers and friendly Indians out toward the fight. There are about 200 lodges of Nez Percés and Flatheads in camp, and not one of us, white or red, cottons to the Blackfeet.

We ride up and immediately lead the way closer to the foe. Amazed at the number of their enemies, the Blackfeet send their women and children into the mountains and the warriors bunch behind breastworks.

We trappers have conflicting ideas about a plan.

"I want to charge them," says Bill.

"Too much risk," I say.

"I'll go with you," says my Irish friend Robert Campbell to Bill.

Daringly, the two crawl forward through the underbrush. I can hear each of them telling the other his will, in case of the worst.

I'm puzzled that they go on their own instead of working together with the lot of us. Before long, Bill gets shot in the shoulder and Campbell drags him back.

Another man, drunk from rendezvous revelry, goes on hands and knees across the no man's land, right up to the breastworks. There he climbs the logs, peeps over the top, and takes two bullets in the head.

After a while, though, our fire from superior numbers quiets the rifles of the Blackfeet.

"Let's burn 'em out," says a trapper I don't know.

"Damn right!" several other men cry.

Almost half our men jump to their feet, ready to go.

I wish we had a clear chain of command here. I want coordination, not impulse.

So I'm glad that our Flatheads and Nez Percés say, "No, no, no." They want their trophies—rifles, blankets, and whatever else the Blackfeet may abandon in their flight.

So the battle meanders on, a stalemate without much action.

Then, suddenly, comes a big outcry from the Blackfeet. I call one of Fraeb's men who speaks the Bug's Boys language to tell me what they're saying. According to him the shouts are a king-sized boast, a declaration of their virtues and a dare to us. But several of the other men say it's a triumphant statement that the Blackfeet have sneaked off in big numbers and attacked our main camp.

Right quick most of our men are on their horses,

galloping back to the unguarded camp. And before long, in the twilight, they're back with us, with word that the camp is safe.

But now it's too dark for an attack on the Blackfeet.

In the morning the hostiles have disappeared. They've abandoned ten bodies, the carcasses of about three dozen horses, and some live animals.

We're the victors, but we haven't gotten much loot, and two good men have been killed.

Still, the rendezvous has been a good one. Sublette has come in with his supplies. He's had a fine sale and will go back with money in his pocket, which means the pocket of my partnership, Rocky Mountain Fur. For whatever reason, American Fur Company's supply train didn't appear. However, we're sure their outfits will follow our brigades through the mountains in the coming hunts, profiting from our experience and the knowledge of our booshways.

———

Later we find out that American Fur has held an alternate rendezvous on Green River at the mouth of Horse Creek. Last year Bonneville, head of another outfit competing with us, built a fort there, which the men called Fort Nonsense because a lot of materials were wasted in the construction. That's where the AFC supply train went.

Good riddance, as far as we partners of the Rocky Mountain Fur Company are concerned.

June 1833

This year's rendezvous on Green River is chaos in the mountains. The two biggest companies are here. My company, Rocky Mountain Fur, and Astor's American Fur are competing by bringing supply trains to serve all the trappers. Smaller outfits led by Drips and Fontenelle have come in. A band led by a Captain Ferry has gotten discouraged and gone home. Our annual supply train, led by Robert Campbell, has brought even more people— William Drummond Stewart, a Scots sportsman who has come to shoot big game, and a St. Louis businessman, Edmund Christy—I wonder what he wants in the mountains.

I'm not sure what the devil is happening here in the mountains, but I know they're too damn crowded. The trappers are about to outnumber the beaver, and never mind the other travelers.

In all this disarray there's one great blessing: Campbell and the supply train have also brought along Friday. He's shot up what seems like half a foot and he's gotten a lot more schooling.

It's twilight when the pack train comes in, and Friday jumps off his horse and runs to me. I knew I would be glad to see him, but I'm more than glad. He's happy too. Maybe ten years old now, he's enthusiastically affectionate: When he gets off his horse after the long ride out from St. Louis, he runs to me.

"Mr. Fitz, Sir," he cries.

I grin, hug him, and remind him gently, "Just call me Fitz. No 'Mister,' no 'Sir.'

I hesitate and then add, "Mr. or Mrs. aren't used within the family, and I'm your father."

He wiggles to the ground, gives me a big smile, and corrects me. "White-man father," he says.

"Right. White-man father. And right now, your only father. You better keep me!"

Again the big smile. "You keep *me*."

I tousle his hair and speak with emphasis. "I *promise*."

Then I lead him around camp and re-introduce him to the trappers he's met before. Every man acts excited to see him.

As am I.

———

In the evening I roast a buffalo tongue for the two of us, slice it, and give him most of it. I know he likes tongue—who doesn't?—and he doesn't like what I'm completing my dinner with, *boudins*. They're an acquired taste, particular to us fur trappers.

After we eat, I fix a pot of coffee and give him a cup with sugar, as I know he likes it.

He takes a sip and then holds out the cup.

"More sugar, please."

Yes, he says "Please." Mrs. Talbot has been teaching him manners.

I put another spoonful in.

He says, "I mean a *lot* more."

I suppress a smile, put in another spoonful, and ask, "Who's been giving you coffee made like this?"

"The booshway, on the way out here."

In this way Friday is like most Indian folks, who think coffee a mostly an excuse for a big load of sugar.

Fortunately, I just traded for sugar, and it's easy to trade for more.

"Was the food on the way out here good?"

"Very good. We had buffalo most nights."

So the supply outfit had good hunters along, and the Platte River road saw some herds.

"Do you like Mrs. Talbot's food?"

"It's good. We have bacon and eggs every morning for breakfast. I love bacon."

"What else did you like?"

"Corn on the cob. And she makes mashed potatoes and *gravy*."

He's dressed like a white kid, and I hope this all works out for him.

"And cornbread," he adds. "Cornbread is great."

He gives a big yawn.

"Time for bed?"

He hesitates. "You haven't told me any of your stories."

"We'll have all day every day. Get out your bedroll."

He unrolls it—just one blanket. But this mountain country is a little high for that. I'll give him my buffalo robe and roll him up in it. I can get by with his blanket and my one blanket.

I kiss him goodnight on top of his head.

He closes his eyes and seems to be asleep immediately. Long ride today, for a boy his age.

Then I pour myself another cup from the speckled pot. I drink it black.

Now I start considering. First, Mrs. Talbot has written a letter to me about Friday's progress in education. I read it with some difficulty by the flickering fire:

Dear Mr. Fitzpatrick,

I understand that you will keep Friday in the mountains for all of the coming year, returning him to St. Louis and to my boarding school in the summer of 1834. Those twelve months wipe away the time I would have used to continue to develop his skills in reading and writing and would have introduced him to addition and subtraction.

In view of this protracted absence, I am sending along a copy of Mr. Hanover's Introduction to Arithmetic with the request that you instruct Friday in the basics. (When you send him back to school, please return this volume). I remember that you yourself have basic skills in arithmetic. I hope Friday will be proficient in adding and subtracting by the time of his return, so that we can proceed to multiplication and division. I have no doubt about his ability to master these skills—his intelligence is high.

Socially, Friday does well. At first the other children were wary of an Indian, but Friday's playful spirit soon proved infectious, and now they are delighted with him. His good looks help, too.

You have requested a copy of History of the Expeditions of Captains Lewis and Clark, 1804-05-06, published in 1814, and I am sending it along with Friday. I understand that you plan to read to Friday from the Lewis and Clark account, with the intention of teaching him the pleasure of

*reading books of exploration and adventure. Please let him
also read some passages on his own. And please send $36.00
for me with the returning supply train, reimbursement for
the cost of both the book on arithmetic and the Lewis and
Clark volume.*

*Finally, when you return him to school, if you do not
bring him to St. Louis yourself, please send along the cost of
the next year's tuition, $2.00 per day for schooling, five days
a week, and $60.00 per month for boarding, plus two dollars
extra for months that have 31 days and $4.00 less for
February.*

*If you have other desires or suggestions for Friday's
continued education, please write them down and send them
to me.*

*Yours kindly,
Alma Talbot*

When I'm finished with Mrs. Talbot's letter, I answer
her briefly:

*July 6, 1833
Dear Mrs. Talbot—*

*I have welcomed Friday and received your good letter.
Please be assured that I am fully committed to his education.
He will be back to school at the end of next summer. Meanwhile I will have instructed him well in addition and subtraction, as you ask. Also, I hope to establish in him a love of
reading books, especially those of adventure and exploration.
And I will have started on his education as a mountain man.
I consider it essential that he become proficient in the skills
needed to live here in the West and earn a living here. He was
born in this country and belongs here.*

I am sending the $36.00 you requested along with this letter. When Friday returns to school, I will send the cost of his tuition, room, and board for the next school year. Friday and I are grateful for what you contribute to his well-being.

Thank you,
Thomas Fitzpatrick

Now I find myself in a comical situation. A month ago, on the Platte River, I wrote to Robert Campbell, expecting to send it to him via the supply train that will come to rendezvous this year. But, to my surprise, Robert has led the supply train to rendezvous himself. So, I hand him what I wrote:

June 4, 1833,
Dear Robert,

Immediately after our separation last summer I repaired to the Salmon River and there made a deposit of all our goods &c from thence to the Blackfoot country and further north in it than a party of whites has ever been before in search of beaver. But found beaver much scarcer than I had any idea of. Our party in that section consisted of about 60 men. We made a very extensive tour and caught only about 20 packs of beaver. Mr. Vanderburgh overtook us with a party of 112 men on Dearborn River, which was a great disadvantage to us, altho in all they caught about 5 packs of fur while we got 20. They remained camped with us until we arrived at the Three Forks of the Missouri, where we separated—we up the Madison and they the Gallatin. And soon after we each had a fight with the Blackfeet. Mr. Vanderburgh was killed a few days after we parted. In our fight Bridger was shot in two

places. We lost one horse, one squaw & the gun which you
sold Bridger, besides one man who was killed out trapping.

Your partner and friend,
Thomas Fitzpatrick

I don't reread or in any way correct either letter, and I'm sure that Mrs. Talbot would want to correct me.

The next morning Friday and I have coffee (his with plenty of sugar) and jerky, and then we practice adding. I hold up my left index finger and say, "One finger." Then my right index finger and say, "Also one finger. Now," I go on, "One finger"—holding up the left one again — "plus one finger"—holding up the right next to the other —"makes two"—and I show him the right and left up at once, flush beside each other.

Then I demonstrate more rapidly—"One plus one makes two," arriving at the two together with a triumphant smile.

He repeats all of that, using his hands and fingers just right.

Then I explain that it's all right to say either "one plus one makes two" or "one *and* one makes two"—it means the same. You can also say "two plus three add up to five." We white people have tricky ways of saying stuff.

Friday and I spend the entire morning working with all ten fingers until we come up with every combination of 1-2-3-4-5 plus this and that I can think of, and until I can't stand the repetition any longer.

Several times trappers wander over, watch for a short time, and drift off shaking their heads.

I wonder how many of them know arithmetic. I hope

the traders here don't short-change them when they trade, say, two plews for any given amount of tobacco.

But I'm not teaching anyone other than Friday.

Late in the afternoon he and I wander around camp saying "howdy-do" to the various men Friday has met in the past and introducing him to some new ones. I say, "Be friendly, say 'I'm glad to meet you.' And don't worry about forgetting some of the names—there are too many to remember."

Then, as the light fades, we sit back down at our fire. I get the flames going again, put the coffee pot on, and open the book with Lewis and Clark's map of the West. It's very incomplete as a map of the West. The two captains went up the Missouri River all its way, crossed the mountains to the headwaters of the Columbia River with the help of their translator and his wife Sacajawea, and followed that river on to the Pacific Ocean. They didn't see the Platte River Road, the Rocky Mountains, South Pass, Salt Lake, the deserts on the west side of the mountains, California...

The West as I know it fills out a lot more of the map than what Lewis and Clark saw. Jedediah and I found South Pass together, the best route across the Rockies—that was a great day. But I wasn't along when he explored even more of the West, and mapped it. He crossed the desert from Salt Lake to California, marched north to Oregon, and rode back to the Rockies. What a circuit of the far West! He left his maps with a young fellow in St. Louis to be copied. I wonder if they'll ever get published.

As I'm building the fire to fry pemmican for our supper, Friday asks me about my crippled hand.

I tell him about the big mistake I made with my pistol (although I don't know exactly what I did wrong) and having it explode in my hand and ruin it. Actually, I try to use this episode to tell him how to load the pistol correctly, so that it doesn't blow up. I don't want him to go through what I've been through.

Then he asks, "Have you ever shot an Indian?"

I hesitate, and hesitate, and then say, "I shoot at Indians if they shoot at me."

He gets it.

"But I promise never, never to shoot at you."

He grins.

"Then I won't shoot at you," he says.

And we both chuckle.

The twilight in the west is beautiful, dinner is good, the coffee is great, the buffalo robe and blankets are warm, and he drops off immediately.

I ponder. Teaching him to add and subtract, using fingers—that's good. And I'm not worried about him falling behind in his studies. I brought him out here for a year because I want to teach him things that I think are just as important as book-learning—what a mountain man knows about travelling in the West and hunting, especially hunting buffalo. Learning how to handle, load, and take care of firearms. Learning to shoot buffler at a gallop, which is one hell of a skill. Learning how to trap beaver—how to place a trap, bait it with castor, and what way the stick floats (downstream!). Learning to pack hides on a horse so that they stay put and the animal doesn't suffer. Learning how to get along with Indians.

Does he need to be taught how to get on with Indians? Sure. The tribes out here are enemies as much to each other as to white men, and as quick to shoot at each other, or quicker. And since Friday speaks only Arapaho, he needs to learn the sign language, which some one of us trappers will be able to teach him.

So, you see, Mrs. Talbot, by spending a year out here with me, Friday will be getting *ahead* in his studies, the ones he really needs.

And, yes, I still want him to learn to read and write and add and subtract.

But live in the settlements? Not hardly. Work in a store and spend life talking to people across a counter? Farm and spend every day persuading a few acres of crops to grow? No, no, and *hell* no.

Life in the West is an adventure.

Risk? Risk is the spice of being *alive*.

July 20, 1833

This rendezvous of 1833 is tumultuous for business in the mountains. The American Fur Company is doing its bit to create confusion, as usual. And today our little Rocky Mountain Fur Company is changing its face. That St. Louis businessman, Edmund Christy, has pointed out to us that we could use someone to manage our affairs in St. Louis—get the best price for our furs when they arrive downriver, make deposits into our bank accounts, pay any debts we have, and other payments that may be due. So today we have an additional partner. Our firm is now Rocky Mountain Fur & Christy.

Praise be, I don't have to explain any of this to Friday... Instead I'll use today to lead him out away from camp and teach him to load and shoot a muzzle-loading rifle and pistol.

I thrust my crippled hand into his face for emphasis and say, "This is why it has to be done exactly, exactly right." From the way he stares at my poor hand I know I'm making an impression.

We go out onto the prairie. I have one log where I

keep my journal and another for the record I keep of income and expenditures. I tear a couple of sheets out of the journaling log and stick them onto bushes of sage.

Next I demonstrate how to shoot a hole in each piece of paper, one with the rifle and one with the pistol. Then I supervise his loading of the two weapons very carefully and tell him to fire.

WAIT! I wasn't thinking. He's too young to be strong enough to hold a rifle steady with two hands or a pistol steady in one hand.

I steady his hand while he takes a couple of shots. Beyond that, lessons will have to wait for a year or two.

As we walk back to camp, I'm thinking fast. He needs something to perk his spirits up.

Then I see Shoshone boys lining up for foot races. Friday and I watch for a bit. I say, "Want to have a go at it?"

"Yes!"

I learn why he's eager. My lad is fleet afoot. He wins one race handily and another narrowly. Then he takes on a boy who's probably thirteen, maybe fourteen, and loses by only a couple of strides.

As we walk toward our bedrolls, I say, "If I could, I'd buy you a vanilla ice cream with chocolate sauce."

He grins at me and smacks his lips.

"Who taught you that gesture?"

"I don't need teaching for everything," he says. "I'm smart, and I can see."

———

The next afternoon some hunters come back with buffalo meat, and I trade them out of some hump ribs as a treat for us, plus a haunch roast. Then I build a bigger fire than I normally would, put up a spit supported by two forks, and roast us ribs.

I take the roast I traded for, slice it, construct a low rack for the slices, and show Friday how we'll sun-dry it and make jerked meat. Then I tell him that jerky is a staple for us trappers because it doesn't go bad, and keeps almost forever.

The hump ribs make a damn good supper—Friday loves them. I can be a regular homebody when Friday needs one.

———

The next day I lead Friday all around rendezvous to let him see the various doings. He watches more foot races, horse races, and a lot of wrestling matches. When he sees card games being played, he wants to know how they work. I borrow a deck and show him the various cards, distinguishing carefully between the kings, queens, and jacks. He wants to play, but the men are preoccupied, and gambling is the last thing I want Friday to learn.

I borrow a deck and promise to bring the cards back the morning. I'm planning to teach Friday to play Go Fish tonight after supper. As a kid, I had a lot of fun playing that game with my brothers and sisters. I plan to let Friday win.

I notice a Shoshone woman peeling roots and give her a smear of vermillion in exchange for a double handful of roots to add to our supper.

Friday and I watch an attractive young woman scraping a hide in front of the next lodge. While we're standing there, a trapper approaches and dangles a string of Russian blue beads in front of her eyes. Indian women prize Russian blues. Understanding, the woman accepts them, stands, takes the man's hand, snuggles against him, and leads him into a grove of trees.

I'm not going to explain that one to Friday.

The great pleasure of rendezvous this year is showing Friday off. Trappers with Indian children aren't a rarity here, but Friday is a big surprise to everyone. An Indian who speaks English fluently? Who could imagine that? And whether they notice or not, Friday's English is a lot more proper than trapper talk. A schoolmarm would praise his speech. Matter of fact, his schoolmarm does praise it.

That night I spread the borrowed cards in one hand and realize something: Each card, one through ten, shows a numeral. Hey, we can use those numerals for learning to add, and even subtract. One plus two equals three, etc. That will be a lot easier than holding up fingers for him to count.

Then we play Go Fish. When he beats me, as he does two out of three hands, his eyes gleam. I love this boy's spirit.

I've thought about getting married again but have decided against it. No white woman would follow me around on my mountain adventures. And an Indian woman? I could take a Crow for a wife—the Crows are friendly to us trappers. But Friday would be better served by aunts, uncles, cousins, and grandparents who are Arapahos. And I can't give up my life of travelling and trapping to live in a Crow village.

So I need to be Friday's entire family, right now his only family.

That's good for each of us, I think.

———

Inevitably, rendezvous breaks up, and the different outfits scatter to the four winds. Friday and I go north with Campbell and my partner Milton Sublette to the Big Horn River.

For mountain men, hunting buffalo is important. Learn to recognize the tracks of a herd on the move. Learn to get close to it without being smelled or seen. Learn to put a shot in the one place that will bring the beast down, close behind the left front foreleg, where the heart is. Learn the skinning, which is more complicated than with smaller animals. Learn what meat to carry off and what to leave on the prairie.

After Friday has these skills, there's still more to hunting buffalo. Herds don't stand still and let themselves get shot at—they take off at a gallop at the first loud sound. Then the hunter has to ride after the herd to keep up—and ride at a gallop.

No hunting skill, I think, is harder to learn than shooting a buffalo from a galloping horse. Until he learns to move smoothly with his mount, the rider bounces around far too much. When Friday has mastered riding at a gallop, he'll still have to learn to rein the horse into good position alongside the target, recognize the one place where the lead will bring it down, and hit that spot.

Beyond all of these skills, a mountain man has to learn how to tell the print of a Shoshone moccasin from a Crow moccasin and from every other tribe's footprint. He needs to learn to tell how many horses were in a party that travelled through, and whether that party was a village or a war party.

The list goes on and on. Neither Friday nor any other beginner can learn the necessary skills in a single year.

But after another year in the mountains my son will be no novice.

———

This year our train will take almost a hundred packs of fur to St. Louis for sale. We did a good business at rendezvous.

Right where the Wind River changes its name to the Big Horn, we stop and build enough bullboats to float the furs down to St. Louis. The men of the supply outfit will go down the Yellowstone to the Missouri River and then on to the city.

After several days of hard work building the boats, it's time to say so long to the boaters.

The night before they leave, Friday and I have a reflective meal. We've talked over how he'll spend this year. He wants to stay here in the mountains with me as much as I want to have him.

After we agree on that, I squeeze his hands and say, "You're my son."

He squeezes back. "You're my father." Hesitation. "My write-man father." Embarrassed pause, followed by a grin. He looks down, embarrassed, and corrects himself —"I mean *white*-man father."

We've walked through these words before.

"Good night," I go on. "We'll see the pack train fellows off tomorrow and go out and find some adventure."

He squeezes out these words: "I *like* adventure."

I say, "Not *too* much adventure, I hope." I pat his head. "Don't want to get *this* shot."

"I like my head as it is," he says.

He slides into his buffalo robe, and I fold up in my blankets.

"Goodnight, Fitz."

"Goodnight, Friday."

September 7, 1833

Friday and I stand on the bank of the Yellowstone, waving goodbye to the men piling onto the bullboats. They'll have a long cruise down the Yellowstone, down that to the Missouri, and then to St. Louis.

Watching the boats, I remember how hard they are to steer and how easily they break on rocks. One cost me a lot of time and pain, diving in to get rifles and furs, the water was so cold even the arsehole froze.

Friday says he knows how to swim. Mr. and Mrs. Talbot have taken the students swimming in easy backwaters of the Mississippi, and he says he's good at it. Standing here, I tousle his hair and think how glad I am that this is one danger he won't face in the coming year. On the other hand, he will face hostile Indians. I haven't yet gone through the mountains without getting shot at by Indians. For his sake even more than mine, I take comfort in the wholeness of my flesh. As long as we're out here, he's vulnerable.

As the bullboats sail around the first curve in the Bighorn, we stand on the bank and wave and halloo. But

I can't tell whether any man on them can hear us. So long settlements for another year.

————

With all that taken care of, I ask Friday to pack our belongings onto our horses for the coming ride. He knows how to do this. Then I turn my attention to the outfit I'm about to lead on a hunt. I want to trap the Bighorn Mountains and then the Tongue and Powder Rivers.

We're taking a greenhorn along, Sir William Drummond Stewart, a Scot who is heir to a title back home but wants some good big-game hunting before he settles down on the family estate. Also, he's heard of the land of Absaroka, the home of the Crow people, and he wants to see that. If I were set up to live the stuffy life of a Scots baronet, I too would want a taste of the wild. A taste of real life.

I hope Stewart will make a good companion. However, I'll be damned if I'll call him Sir William, as the crew of the pack train did on the way out. That would stick in my Irish craw.

We've barely gotten started on the march down the Bighorn River before we see downstream a full village of friendly Crows—just what Stewart wants.

The chief comes out to visit and signs a suggestion that our party camp with his village. I take a quick look at Friday to make sure he and his mount are behind me, out of the way of any bullet meant for me.

Feeling a little wary, I say we'll pitch our camp on downstream a little way. Then I move the outfit down-river and get set up.

Now I ride back to the village. Leaving the outfit, I

say to Stewart, "You're in charge here while I'm gone. Don't let any Indians into camp."

"Right-o," says the nobleman.

"And will you keep a sharp eye on my boy Friday?"

"Right-o."

When I get to the village, I show my good will by visiting the chief in his lodge and have a friendly smoke of the pipe with him.

All seems well.

On the way back to camp, though, I encounter a band of young Crows. I see right off that they have all our horses and our beaver skins.

Damn, I think, *they've overawed Stewart.*

Their leader canters forward, and I go out to meet him. I look hard at the group of warriors to make sure they don't have Friday with them.

The leader stops and raises a hand.

I stop in front of him.

He calls out loudly in the Crow language, but I have no idea what he's saying. The other young men ride forward and make a motion to me—down, down, down.

I understand that I have to get off my horse. Reluctantly, I do.

In a couple of minutes they have my clothes, rifle, and pistol and I'm standing stark naked on the bank of the Yellowstone.

I hold up a hand to tell my men to stay back. They aren't moving forward anyway—they know better.

I can see now that our beaver skins, we had 43 hides, are still packed on our horses, which the young Crows are leading. Our traps are on those horses too. And our rifles and pistols are in the hands of the warriors. Our outfit has been stripped clean.

Damn Stewart.

I mount, ride with them into the village bare-assed, tie my horse to a tree, and scratch on the door of the chief's lodge. That's the Crow way of knocking on a door.

He bids me come in, and I do, boldly, naked as a jaybird in front of his wives.

I'm surprised and very pleased to see Jim Beckwourth sitting by the chief's fire. Beckwourth joined the party led by Jedediah and me in this same village nearly ten years ago. He taught us the custom of taking a Crow woman for a wife, if only for the winter.

It was Beckwourth, essentially, who created the friendship of trappers and Crows. Now my mulatto friend seems to be still living in this village, probably a respected senior.

I won't repeat here all the persuasions Jim and I use with the chief. We point out that my men and I spent an entire winter with his people not far upstream of this spot, just a few years ago. Some of our men are the husbands of women in this circle of lodges. Some of the children in these lodges are their offspring.

I don't deserve to have to stand naked in front of his wives. Nor do I deserve to be robbed. My men don't deserve to be treated like enemies.

Beckwourth vouches for our good will toward the Crow people.

First I get my clothes back. In the end we get all our horses. Most of our traps. My guns, most of the men's guns, and a few rounds of ammunition for each man. The young warriors are especially reluctant to surrender the weapons and ammunition.

I untie my horse and ride back to our camp. Jim rides along. As we go, I ask what the hell is going on.

"The American Fur Company," he says. He explains

that A.F.C. men have been here, denounced us, and bribed the Crows to rob us.

"I will damn well make the A.F.C. pay," I declare. Actually, I don't know how I can do that, but I will. "Also," I insist, "those 43 beaver hides will end up in the hands of the A. F. C, and I'm going to get them back."

But now we've arrived at our camp. Sir William Fancy Ass Stewart is coming up out to explain what the hell has happened.

Before he can speak, I brush by him with the words, "What's happened is that a high-falutin' Scots nobleman got handed his arse by a teen-aged Crow."

Then I dismount, walk over to Friday, and open my arms.

That night I have a good meal with Friday, tuck him under the buffalo robe, and write to General Ashley about this embarrassing affair. I sum up the Crow robbery, explaining that it was caused by the cursed American Fur Company, and then get to the point:

> In short, Genl., if there is not some alteration made in the system of business in this country, very soon it will become a nuisance and disgrace to the U.S. So many different companies a-going about from one tribe of Indians to another. Each is telling a different tale besides slandering each other to such a degree as to really disgust the Indians, and they will evidently all become hostile toward the Americans.
>
> I now appeal to you for redress as the only person whom I know would be likely to have Justice done us. I ask no more than the laws of the U.S. dictates in such cases. It is because they, the A.F.C, are more powerful than we are that they are allowed to be instrumental to such acts of violence on people who are licensed and authorized according to law…. If I was disposed to become an outlaw, I could very soon have satis-

*faction for the injury done me. But no, I shall await Justice
from the honorable members in Session. I would have much
more to say on this subject but the bearer of this is impatient
to be off.*

Thos. Fitzpatrick

Disgusted with the behavior of the Crows, I say to
hell with trapping the Tongue and Powder Rivers, which
are too close to the Indians who robbed and embarrassed
us. I take our outfit back up the Bighorn and across
South Pass into the Green River Valley.

Here we have some luck—we find a friendly band of
Shoshone people and combine with them to ride to
Ham's Fork of the Green, a rendezvous site we know and
like. There we find Captain Bonneville and his outfit and
discover that they have also gotten robbed back in Crow
country, to the east of South Pass.

This news truly provokes me. I sit down that night by
my fire with a full coffee pot and a dram of whiskey
(don't I wish it was Irish whiskey!) and write to my
partner Milton Sublette in St. Louis. First, I tell him what
I already wrote to General Ashley about our humiliating
and costly affair at the hands of the Crows, inspired by
the American Fur Company. Now other trappers are
suffering at the hands of Crows inspired by those great
meddlers the A.F.C.:

November 31, 1833
To my partner Milton Sublette—

*However, it is not quite so bad as you may suppose.
Bridger and myself have on hand about twenty-three packs of
Beaver furs. Fraeb is gone down the Seedskeedee (Green*

River) with Bill Williams for pilot and intends not to return before March 1st. I think they may do well. Jervey (their partner Jean Gervais) I have not heard from neither.

For next summer's rendezvous, study well the articles of profit. Liquor will be much wanted, and indeed all groceries. Come as soon as possible to the rendezvous and look out for the Crows on the way up. I believe that they will be hostile parties hereafter. They have good encouragement from the American Fur Company.

Perhaps they may not kill but will certainly rob all they are able and perhaps murder also. I intend to winter here and hereabout and will hunt nearly in the same section where I did last spring. Don't go so high up on Seedskiddee (Green River) as Horse Creek. Strike somewhere about the mouth of Sandy and remain until we come. Harrison is going after a small equipment. If you allow him to take up, make terms with him about it. He will be among us considerable.

Now I have given you a short sketch of the whole situation of our affairs and I expect you to act hereafter although according to your own dictations. Mr. Guthery was killed last fall by lightning and Biggs has since supplied his place.

Yours &c Thos F

June 20, 1834

I don't want to dwell on the rendezvous of 1834 on Ham's Fork. If the last rendezvous was chaos from a business point of view, this one is chaos times tumult. We of Rocky Mountain Fur have made an agreement with businessman Nathaniel Wyeth to buy the supplies he brings out. However, when the time comes, we have to pay off Bill Sublette. Bill arrives at rendezvous first and uses our debt to him to make us buy the supplies from him instead of Wyeth, who comes in several days later. Instead we're forced to pay a forfeit of $500 to Wyeth.

Then, on a single day, our Rocky Mountain Fur Company falls apart. Fraeb sells his interest in the company to Sublette, who takes on a fifth of our outfit's debt.

Then Jean Gervais sells his interest in our company to me, Jim Bridger, and Milton Sublette. By the end of rendezvous, I'm in a new outfit, Fontenelle, Fitzpatrick and Company. Rocky Mountain Fur exists no longer.

I don't know how, or even whether, I will explain all these crazy doings to Friday. The new arrangement changes the bank accounts back in St. Louis—whose dollars are in which account and who owns them—but they have little or no effect here on the daily routine of the fur trade. We'll still travel in brigades led by booshways to hunting grounds that seem promising to us. We'll read the sign for where beaver are, put traps in creeks and rivers, haul the beaver out, skin them, transport the hides back to St. Louis, and sell them. The routines of the trapper will not change.

But... But... But...

Tonight I have to have a talk with Friday.

————

"Build a low fire and put on some coffee," I say to him. "I'm going over there to get some meat." With a nod of the head, I indicate that "over there" is the big fire where roasting is being done on a spit.

I'm back in less than about five minutes. My son has a perfect fire going and the speckled pot is sitting on it, spouting the steam that promises good brew.

I hold out half of the meat to him on my knife. "Hump ribs," I say unnecessarily.

"Our favorite," says Friday.

"Yep."

We gnaw happily. From time to time each of us tosses a stripped rib onto the fire.

Finally, I get to it. "Tomorrow we leave with the pack train for St. Louis. "You feeling good about that?"

"I guess," he says. "Mostly."

We've agreed since the day we came back to the West that his stay this time would be a year. Now it's time for him to go back to school with Mrs. Talbot. I'll take him all the way there.

"Will you be glad to be back in school?"

"Yeah, I guess."

"Mrs. Talbot says you lead the class in reading and writing—you're a star pupil. You like that?"

"Yeah."

"Captain Clark will come to see you. And he'll take you out for vanilla ice cream with chocolate sauce. You like that?"

Now he smiles. "I sure do."

"You're a star pupil in the mountains too. I think you've learned a lot in a year. Trapping beaver, tracking game, shooting it, dressing it, cooking it. Hunting buffalo. Fording rivers. You've *really* learned a lot."

"That's true."

"I know, though, that you would have been learning the same things with your tribe, if you were there."

"… Right."

"Friday, you're going to end up with a rare, rare advantage. You can live as a white man or as an Indian, whichever you prefer. You speak both languages. You know both ways of life. You'll be fully equipped to go either way. You'll have a choice—the first and maybe only Indian to have that choice."

"I don't know," he says.

I'm puzzled. I hesitate and then ask, "What are you thinking?"

"As an Arapaho, I would be able marry a girl of my people. I would earn standing in the tribe by winning honors in hunting and in war. But I don't think I would be acceptable as a husband in the white world."

I'm stumped. I consider, and then say, "I think it would depend on whether you can support a family. You get along very well with people, and you have an excellent set of skills—reading, writing, and being able to add, subtract, multiply, and divide. You'd make a great catch as a husband."

"My color won't make any difference?"

I purse my lips, consider, and take a chance. "I don't think so. It may be an advantage. The parents will be persuaded by your achievements. With the girl, love will conquer all."

I hope I'm telling the truth.

Pause.

After a bit Friday says, "I'll miss you this coming year."

"You'll be in school, in the fall and the winter. I'll come in the spring, and we'll ride back to rendezvous together."

He doesn't say anything.

I slide over to him and say, "Friday, I'll miss you too. Every day."

I think of telling him I love him. That would be true —sure I do. But I don't think Arapahos use the word "love."

Long silence.

"Fitz," Friday says, "is life going to be okay for Indians? For the tribes on the plains and in the mountains?"

That's a stumper, so I take some time to think. "Yes," I say, "I hope so. I think it can work. What the Indian people need is to have their lands left alone, left for them to live on and hunt on. As long as they can follow the buffalo and eat by hunting, they'll be fine.

"There's talk that white people will migrate west and maybe take the Indian lands, but I don't think so. Neither the plains nor the mountains are any good for farming, only for hunting. Farming is good much farther to the west, in the lowlands of California and Oregon.

"So maybe a lot of white people will go across the plains and keep going. I think the tribes will be okay."

I wait but he doesn't speak.

"Regardless, I think this matters: I'll be here, and I'll care. I'll speak up for the Arapahos, the Sioux, the Crows —all the tribes. I feel strongly that they have a right to live as they've always lived, which is a beautiful way. I'll speak strongly for that.

"And I have the ear of Captain Clark, who's the agent for all these tribes. He agrees with me. I believe that he and I together can keep the peace between red and white."

A longer silence. Friday finally says, "I'll miss talking with you very much this fall and winter."

I hug him from the side. "You are fine company, Friday. Remember, I'll come for you in the spring. Then we'll ride back to the mountains."

Pause.

"Is there anything you want before we go to sleep?"

He grins and says, "Coffee with a *lot* of sugar."

I give him that, sure. He swills it down and rolls up in the buffalo robe.

I sit for a few minutes, looking at him.

Yes, we're father and son. A unique father and son, red and white.

Changes are coming to the West. I hope the tribes and the white folks can negotiate those changes and come out on the far side healthy.

I hope Friday and I can manage the changes.

THE SECOND WEEK OF
AUGUST 1834

The rendezvous of 1834 on Ham's Fork has ended. We're heading for South Pass, the first landmark of the long ride back to St. Louis. I've joined the pack train, along with Friday and William Anderson, a sightseer who came out from St. Louis and is now going home. We're going to stop by Fort William, the new trading post built by Bill Sublette where the Laramie flows into the Platte. About fifty miles above the post Friday, Anderson, and I ride ahead with an express for the post. Along the way Anderson writes a description of my lad and shows it to me:

> *Mr. Fitzpatrick's little foundling Friday is becoming every day an object of greater and greater interest to me, his astonishing memory, his minute and amusing inquiries interest me exceedingly. He has been from his band & kindred three or four years, yet some scenes and incidents he describes with wonderful accuracy. He still remembers that he was called Warshunin, which he tells me means "Blackspot."*

I Balk at the word "foundling", but he is *some,* my boy.

SEPTEMBER 30, 1834

Friday and I got to St. Louis yesterday with the pack train. Today my partner Lucien Fontenelle will go about the business of selling our furs, and I will get Friday set up in school with Mrs. Talbot. Since I'll be spending the winter here, I'm getting adjacent rooms for me and Friday in a boarding house.

The first stop on our agenda, naturally, is the confectioner, for the usual dish of vanilla ice cream with chocolate sauce. The second step is a stop to see William Clark.

Florence ushers us into Clark's inner sanctum immediately, and Friday walks across to him with right hand extended. "Hello, Mr. Clark," he says properly and with a big smile.

Clark shakes his hand, and mine. He waves us into chairs in front of the desk, and says, "I'm very, very glad to see you. I take it that your English continues to improve."

"Definitely, Sir. And Fitz"—my son nods at me—"has taught me to add and subtract."

"Excellent."

I put in, "During the last year he's also learned some basic mountain-man skills, like shooting muzzle-loading weapons." At these words I look down at my crippled left hand uncomfortably and slip it under my leg. "Also, he can set a trap and skin a beaver. He can pack a horse. He has basic hunting skills. And he can tell a Crow moccasin from, say, a Sioux moccasin."

"My, my," says Clark, "I'm proud of you, Friday."

"And now, Sir," says Friday, "Fitz and I are in town for this fall and winter so that I can go to school and learn to multiply and divide."

I put in, "Lucien Fontenelle is in town with me for the winter. He's my new partner, with Jim Bridger and Milton Sublette. He's in charge of selling our furs and buying the outfit for next summer's rendezvous. Also"—here I pause for emphasis—"he and I will buy Fort William from Bill Sublette."

I wait, and Clark replies, "You and I have talked before about a fort where the Laramie comes into the Platte. It's a central location, an ideal spot."

"It's Fort William, Sir, named after Bill. But everyone already calls it the fort on the Laramie, so…"

Clark grins. "Very impressive," he says. Now he fishes out a pocket watch for a quick look. "What would you say to lunch?"

Friday grins and says enthusiastically, "I love to eat."

Clark gets up, leads us out of the office onto the boardwalk, and off to his usual lunch spot. He orders ham omelets with croissants for all three of us. I watch Friday carefully. He's never had such fine food. I think, *If he isn't already completely sold on the white way of living, meals like this might nail it down.*

When we've finished and he's paid the tab, Clark stands and says, "How about dessert... Ice cream with chocolate sauce?"

Before I can protest that we've already had that treat this morning, Friday jumps up and bursts out with *YES!*

Maybe Friday would be happy in St. Louis after all.

Then I think, *No, he'd have to take a job, show up every day, and work inside.* I do a quick comparison with the life of a mountain man, which brings something new every day. Nope, St. Louis and Friday—that is a no-go.

———

Mrs. Talbot makes time for me and Friday by turning her students out to play. They rush out the door. Whatever schoolwork they were doing, they'd rather play.

Then she leads us into her office, sits at the desk, and nods us into chairs facing her. "Friday, Friday, Friday," she begins, "I'm so glad to have you back in school."

"Glad to be back, Ma'am."

I'm proud of his manners, especially the way he remembers to say "Ma'am." In the mountains we don't have white women for him to "Ma'am."

She fusses with a couple of pencils on her desk, apparently getting words ready. "Mr. Fitzpatrick, you're putting the boy back in school for the year, but he'll be rooming with you, not with me."

"I'll be in town this fall and all winter, and next spring Friday and I will head back to a new fort, the fort on the Laramie."

She shakes her head regretfully. "Mr. Fitzpatrick, you're making his education a hit and miss affair. Which is a disservice to such an extraordinary student."

"He gets one kind of education when he's with you, Mrs. Talbot, and another kind when he's with me."

Now she gives me a severe look.

"What he will learn from you, I'm afraid, is vagabondage. He needs to learn how to fit into society, not how to be a roamer. He needs ties to work, family, society in general."

I look long at Friday and think even longer before I answer. Even then my response is lame.

"I do what I think is best for him."

"You yourself are a vagabond, without ties to society."

I huff a little breath out. I don't like the idea of *ties*.

Long pause before I speak. Then, "Friday, do you like being on the plains and in the mountains with me?"

His answer is prompt. "I love it."

But I go on. "And do you like school?"

"Definitely."

I'm proud of his choice of words.

"He can't be white and red at the same time, Mr. Fitz-patrick."

I give her a hard look and stand up. Friday stands with me.

"At any rate," she says, in recovery mode, "he'll be in school for the fall and winter."

Friday speaks up ahead of me. "Definitely," he says.

Now she stands up, dismissing us. "I'm sorry he won't stay in school longer," she says, "but I bow to your judgment."

"Friday, I expect you in class on Monday morning." She lifts a book out of a drawer. "Here's our textbook on the subjects of multiplication and division. Read the first lesson, make sure you understand it, and work the problems at the end of that chapter."

"Got it," says Friday.

She nods toward the door, signaling for us to leave.

Outside on the boardwalk, as we walk back to our rooms, Friday says, "Fitz, will you help me with the problems she's talking about?"

"My boy," I say, "I don't know any more about multiplication than you do. But I'll read the chapter and see if I can learn along with you."

Then I stop him, take him by the shoulders, squat a bit, peer into his eyes, and smile. At eleven, he's almost as tall as I am. Soon he'll be taller.

"Friday," I say, "you're going beyond me, into new territory. You'll know more than I do."

He looks down at me, smiles, shrugs, and says, "Good."

I say, grinning, "You devil, you."

———

When we get to our rooms, he sits on his bed and reads the textbook. I stretch out on my bed and think:

Yes, Mrs. Talbot, I'm a vagabond. No, I don't have ties to society. I've gone off and left my family behind. I don't have a wife. I have only one child, Friday. I don't have a job. I don't go to work every morning and reappear at home every afternoon. I ride here and there, upstream, downstream, across hill and dale, all around the town. I'm not tied down.

Am I teaching Friday to live like this?

Maybe so.

Friday the vagabond. Fine.

But white men in the settlements aren't like that, I tell myself. *It's out to the hotel or the hardware store at the same time each morning and home to wife and kids at the same time every afternoon.*

Indian men aren't like that either. They have strong ties all around the circle of lodges they live in, the expectations of their people, the welfare of the tribe.

Am I teaching Friday a crazy, inhuman way to live?

Deep breath. Another deep breath. *No, I think it's very human.*

And I love my freedom. I do have ties—I'm a good partner to the men I ride with, a good leader of my brigades, a good friend, a good businessman. And I'm still free.

After a while, suddenly, I realize I'm drifting off. I look across at Friday, sitting on the other bed, doing something with pencil and paper.

Even now he's advancing beyond me.

"Friday, let's get some supper."

We enjoy sandwiches in a tavern. Is that the best kind of meal for a father and son?

It's perfect for us.

———

As it turns out, the fall and winter in St. Louis are boring. I make regular visits to Clark, a man who commands my respect. And regular visits to Ashley, an influential fellow in Missouri. Fontenelle goes around to merchants buying the goods we need for selling at rendezvous. I go around to traders who have horses and out to ranches where horses are raised, buying stock. I trust my eye for horseflesh. Slowly, we put together what's needed for the pack train headed back west. Toward the end, I also buy hogs and sheep for us to take along. Meat on the hoof.

At the end of each week, I check in with Mrs. Talbot, and she assures me that Friday is giving multiplication and division their due. I've given up on studying along with him. Though I've always done the work of clerking in my years in the fur trade, we don't do multiplication or division in the logs we keep. I can add and subtract—that's enough. Plenty.

When trouble comes, it's at Friday's school.

February 12, 1835

Mrs. Talbot doesn't want to talk about it. She purses her lips and fills her eyes with anger. "It's about the dance on Saturday night," she says. "Valentine's day. Talk to Friday about it."

I wait until school is out and walk him to the confectioner's shop. He acts strange on the way over, especially considering that ice cream is forthcoming. His gait is uncertain and his eyes are averted.

I buy our usual treat, follow Friday to a table, and sit cattycorner to him. He's picked the place in the farthest corner, where two windows make a right angle. He looks like he's about to cry.

I slide his dish of ice cream to him, hold out his spoon, and ask, "What's wrong?"

"I love her," he says.

Uh-oh. A boyish crush.

He's eleven years old, so it's no surprise.

"Love who?"

"Angel." He spoons ice cream into his mouth and looks with glazed eyes out the window.

"Angel who?"

"Angel Lajeunesse."

I know the girl he's talking about by sight. She has hair of spun gold. She really does look like an angel. And the family is evidently French—Lajeunesse. How appropriate—*jeunesse* means "youth."

A private school in St. Louis, which is a city with a big, influential French population, and to some extent French heritage. Of course, Angel is enrolled in a private school.

"She's a beautiful girl," I say.

"Very beautiful," says Friday, his voice holding back a sob.

"And?"

"She loves me too. We always sit together during recess. She *says* she loves me too."

"And?"

"I asked her to the Saturday dance. She said yes—she wants to be my date. But her parents are pitching a fit."

"A fit?"

"A big fit. They came to school and insisted on meeting with me. They told me to stay away from their daughter."

Now his voice is a big sob. "The father said..."

But now Friday is up against something. It wants to explode inside him. He *wants* to explode. Finally, he comes out with it. "The father is called Leo. The son of a bitch said to me, "No dirty redskin is going to put his hands on my daughter! Even to dance with her."

Now Friday lets his head and face drop into his hands and his whole body begins to shake.

I stand, bend over, put my arms around him and still his quivering body. I've never heard my boy use the words "son of a bitch," though they're plenty common among mountain men. And I'm outraged at the label "dirty redskin."

"What do you want to do now?"

With tears giving music to his voice, Friday says, "A herd of fifty horses couldn't drag me to their goddamn dance."

Quite an afternoon for cussing.

"What do you want me to do?"

"Kill the son of a bitch. And scalp him."

I squeeze my lips together and think.

After a while I say, "Actually, Leo had better hope I don't get my hands on him. But maybe it's best if neither of us goes near that dance."

Friday pulls back, grins, and whaps me on the shoulder. I tap his shoulder in return. That's how we say *yes!*

We're both laughing.

I say, "Have you ever had an ice cream soda?"

His face screws up. "What's that?"

"You're about to find out."

April 1, 1835

I keep Friday away from the dance and use Saturday night to buy us a roast beef dinner at the fanciest restaurant in St. Louis.

Fortunately, we get out of town soon. On April Fool's Day we head back West, setting out well ahead of the rendezvous supply train, which Fontenelle will bring later. Right now we're just three—myself, Robert Campbell, and Friday, and for the first time Friday is carrying a loaded pistol and a horn full of powder, plus lead bullets in a sack around his neck.

(I take time one evening to teach him how to shoot again. I'll make sure he doesn't make the mistake I made.)

Three makes a safe travelling outfit on the plains if they're all armed, primed, and ready.

Robert and I have business to take care of at the fort —selling it to the American Fur Company. Friday is happy to get away from school, away from St. Louis, and away from everyone named Lajeunesse.

Of course, he hasn't forgotten about Angel—he still

moans about loving her. And he's bitterly angry at her father and mother. This misadventure is going to be with him for a long time.

I'm hoping our life in the mountains will be soothing.

At first it will be life at the fort on the Laramie. Excellent meals three times a day, sweetened coffee and buttered corn for breakfast, game meat for lunch, and buffalo for supper.

I'll run the fort until we get paid and it's sold, and Friday will stay there with me. We'll have some very good books to read: I've brought copies of *The Travels of Marco Polo, Robinson Crusoe,* and *Gulliver's Travels,* celebrated stories of adventure which will be as new to me as Friday.

I hope he and I will take turns reading them to each other before bed. We're going to be in the mountains together for a year. I've told Mrs. Talbot I'll bring Friday back to St. Louis next summer. Then I'll pay for nine months of boarding and schooling with her.

For now? We I hope we find some adventure.

———

Yes, life here at the fort is good. Robert stays with us for a couple of weeks, then the American Fur fellows arrive and write a check to us for a lot of money. Robert goes back downstream with that big check and a promise to deposit half in my bank account.

I'll be rich, sort of.

THE FIRST DAY OF MAY 1835

April showers bring May flowers?

No, April showers bring May thunderstorms.

That's what May, 1835, is like for us.

I'm chewing on fried pemmican in the trading room. It's the central hub of the fort, a big, a spread-out room.

The main feature is the trading counter, where visitors, both white and red, come to buy or trade for whatever they want. The main objects for white travelers are coffee, sugar, jerky, and other groceries. Plus rope, and other gear for travelling.

For the Indians who come in it's the same plus powder, ammunition, weapons, knives, blankets, kitchen utensils, and colored cloth for their women to sew into blouses.

I hate to see Indians trading for weapons, gun powder, and lead for bullets. I know white people will get shot with these. But if the Indians can't trade for them here, they'll go to another trading post and get them.

The cook fries up pemmican for me, Friday, and the kitchen workers every day. I like sitting here, eating, chatting with Friday, and looking at the painted buffalo robes that adorn the walls and fill the room with a rich scent.

———

Just as Friday and I finish our meal, a tall, distinguished-looking Indian man, probably in his middle 40's, walks up to us, followed by two Indian women.

Instantly, Friday jumps to his feet and they go into an enthusiastic, mass embrace.

They're grinning happily and talking to each other in a language I don't know but assume to be Arapaho.

All right, this must be Friday's birth family. Or not so damned all right.

After a lot of chatter and a lot of embracing, Friday turns to me and introduces his parents.

"Fitz, these are my father and my mothers." He holds out a hand, indicating them one at a time.

"Gray Bear, Old Chokecherry Tree, and Singing Bird."

He turns back to them and speaks in Arapaho.

Still grinning happily, he turns to me and says, "I told them you saved my life and are my white-man father."

"Greetings," the man says with his fingers. His face is grave.

Dark clouds start gathering in my mind, low and threatening.

"Friendly greetings," I finger-flash the three of them. Still sitting at a trestle table, I motion for them to be seated opposite.

They sit, and Friday sits next to them.

I sign to them, "My name is Fitz," pointing to my own chest and saying aloud, "Fitz." Then I stand and reach across the table with a hand to shake. When Gray

Bear just looks at it blankly, I realize he's not acquainted this white-man custom. I withdraw my hand.

I sign, "Would you like to eat?"

Gray Bear signs, "Yes."

I ask Andrew in English to bring some food from the kitchen, whatever is ready to serve, along with black coffee and enough sugar for all of us.

Next comes a violent crack of lightning and thunder.

My life is breaking wide open.

————

After we finish eating and are drinking coffee—they like lots of sugar in it—I give Andrew a wave and he comes over. "Let's take them to the counter," I say, "and show them the kinds of things we trade to Indians and white people. Anything that doesn't have to do with firearms."

"As you're showing it, watch the women to see what pleases them the most. When they've seen a fair amount, let's make them presents of several items. Cloth, I'd say, and tin cups and a knife. Whatever the women show that they like."

But I can see that Andrew is puzzled. I get up, sign Gray Bear that I'll come back, and walk a couple of tables away, leading Andrew by an elbow.

Now that I'm here I wonder why I've walked away. Gray Bear and his wives wouldn't have understood what I'm about to say in English anyway.

I explain to Andrew in hushed tones that this is Friday's birth family, father and mothers, maybe with brothers and sisters back in their camp. I'm not sure what they want, but…

Andrew can read the shock and dread in my face.

He just nods. He understands.

———

This evening the trading room, which is also our dining room, is bustling. The entire staff of the fort is here, complete with the Indian wives and the children a few men have. The roasted deer makes first-class eating.

Friday, Gray Bear, Old Chokecherry Tree, Singing Bird, and I sit down, Friday between his father and mothers.

Now the head cook, James, comes to our table carrying a tray full of food. He puts the food in front of Gray and serves each of us one at time, Friday's mothers, and me last.

The entrees are slices of deer meat with brown gravy and mashed prairie turnips with more brown gravy.

Prairie turnips are a staple for the Indians of the Plains, like potatoes.

"What's the story, James?" I ask him. I haven't seen him make anything special before.

He makes another trip to the kitchen and comes back with a pot of black coffee and a full sugar bowl.

Then, almost comically, he comes back with five cups on a tray.

My cup is full of whiskey.

It's not Irish whiskey, but I'm delighted.

"Thank you, James," I call after him.

I'm not going to share the whiskey for one reason. Indians think whiskey is just to get drunk on. If you don't get dance-till-you-fall-down-crazy, they think, "What's the point?"

———

Since we can't sign while our hands are busy, conversation is stifled. I notice, though, a lot of eye-language going back and forth between Friday and his parents.

Supper is spoiled for me. I'm wondering whether this is the last meal I'll ever have with Friday. I'm even fretting as the kitchen staff clears away the dishes.

Now Gray Bear says something to Friday in Arapaho. His wives nod their heads in the universal language of nods.

I'm scared.

Friday shakes his head no and adds something in Arapaho.

Gray Bear grimaces. He and his wives stand up.

He flashes me the signs for "Thank you."

Gray Bear and Friday's mothers troop to the door and go out.

I look at Friday, waiting.

"They asked me to come back to their lodge this evening," he says. "But I told them I'll spend the night with you and see them at breakfast tomorrow morning. My brothers and sisters are here. I know where they're camped... I know our lodge."

So, I'm safe for tonight.

"Brothers and sisters?"

"Three brothers, two sisters."

Oh.

I wonder what tomorrow will bring. And tomorrow and tomorrow.

Maybe I'd better have another drink.

MAY 2, 1835

The next morning, I eat in the trading room with Friday, but his family doesn't come this time. The breakfast of fried pemmican is good. Then he and I set out for the Arapaho camp.

Friday leads the way to one circle of lodges and to one lodge in particular. He recognizes it by how it's painted.

His father, mothers, brothers, and sisters are squatting outside, finishing their breakfast with black coffee and probably a lot of sugar.

I recognize the pot and cups we gave them yesterday. We also gave them a full sack of sugar.

To my surprise, the display of affection is restrained. Friday stays on his feet, says a single word to his father, to each of his mothers, two brothers, and three sisters in that order, seemingly in order of age. I wonder whether they would be hugging and exclaiming if I weren't here.

Uncomfortable, I pick the pot up and find it empty. After a moment of hesitation, I walk it to the river, fill it with water, and carry it back. I show them that I'm pouring in grounds from a bag I've brought, then set the

big pot on their fire. Last, I pour in sugar from an enve-
lope I've brought—sweet coffee for all.

Gray Bear signs "Thank you" to me.

Then, one by one, he introduces me to the three
brothers and two sisters. Friday's oldest brother is
Golden Eagle, the other two are Young Raven and Old
Sun. His sisters are She Bear and Little Sun.

Friday sits next to Golden Eagle. They jostle, bump
shoulders, and smile at each other.

My sense is that I owe these people something, but I
don't know what. Whatever it is, I also owe them time to
themselves, so they can feel free to celebrate their
reunion. But not yet.

I launch in clumsily. "Friday, I think I'll tell them how
we met and what we've done in the years since. Will you
translate what I'm saying in signs?"

"Maybe I have a better idea," says Friday. "What if I
tell them all that and sign what I'm saying to you as
I go?"

His smile tells me that this will be a good approach,
so I smile at him and nod yes.

Now, speaking in Arapaho and signing to me with his
fingers. "Fitz found me along the Cimarron River, there
where it's not a river but just a series of water holes. I
was starving. I'd gotten lost from you three days before
and had eaten nothing ever since. And except for the
water holes I would have died of thirst."

Pause.

"Fitz saw me, rode over to me, and got off his horse. I
made signs to my mouth, and he understood that I was
hungry.

"He fished in a pants pocket"—here Friday plucked
one of my pockets—"and pulled out several sticks of
jerky and gave them to me.

"What a relief. *What a relief.* I could hardly believe the kindness of this white man.

"After I ate a couple of slices, he lifted me up behind his saddle, mounted, reached back, and drew my arms around his waist. I held on.

"He walked his horse to the camp of his pack train. They were taking goods to Santa Fe to sell. I ate the last stick of jerky. That night he gave me lots of fried pemmican for supper and supplied a buffalo robe for me to sleep under."

"I'd been a little chilly on the earlier nights. I was amazed at his kindness—I'd always heard that white men were cruel.

"With me holding to him on his horse, we rode with the train of mules and other animals to Santa Fe. And I discovered that, actually, all the white men along on this trip were kind to me. I was a very lucky boy.

"In Santa Fe we ate well—I like Mexican food. And then we rode to rendezvous. That was fun.

"After about seven sleeps we rode all the way to St. Louis, a *lot* of sleeps. There he bought more supplies for the white men and Indian people in the mountains, supplies to trade the next summer.

"All this time, as you would guess, I was learning to speak English by listening and speaking.

"When we got to St. Louis, he found a teacher to show me how to read the books white people make.

"Fitz, I've told a lot of this story. May I hold the rest until we all eat together—maybe tonight?"

"Of course," I said. I was surprised at how much of the story he had told himself.

The Next Day—Still At The Fort On The Laramie

At dinner the family came to the dining room, and we sat across from each other so that Friday's parents, brothers, and sister could read the signs he made.

James brought a full pot of black coffee, a sugar bowl with a spoon, and cups. I passed five cups around and poured for Friday and myself. Then I passed the coffee pot and the sugar to papa Gray Bear, who poured for himself, spooned a lot of sugar into his own coffee, and passed the pot and sugar bowl along.

———

Today Friday spends the day with his family, but walks to my room in the fort and we both fall asleep.

The next day we take all three meals with his family. Again, Friday spends the night in my room in the other bed.

The everyday crew is still serving breakfast, and it's good. Buttered corn and sugared coffee.

Another matter: During supper in the fort dining

room with Friday and his family, I notice that everyone in the family calls Friday "Vash." So, I ask him, "Do you want me to call you Vash?" He answers, "To you I'm Friday. Vash to the members of my tribe."

I must look puzzled because he adds, "I like being your adopted son Friday."

Then he busies himself showing them that they can use a fork to hold a pair of ribs down and slice them apart with a knife.

Watching while they eat and talk, I learn a bit. Friday's oldest brother, Golden Eagle, observes Friday carefully to see how Friday uses the fork and knife. But the two younger brothers are strictly experimental, fumbling to find out what works.

Also, of these younger ones, Young Raven is the scalawag of the family. He makes wisecracks about how clumsily the others eat. The youngest boy, paradoxically named Old Sun, is the family clown, pretending to drop a rib and then catch it with the other hand. He also spouts cracks that make the others laugh. Then he puts a rib in his mouth and sticks it out like an ugly tongue.

I imagine that Friday has his own role in this pecking order, but I don't yet know what it is. If he and I are with them enough, I'll probably see it.

Gray Bear is almost ceremonious in the way he eats and thanks me several times for the good food, especially his favorite, the buttered corn. Singing Bird, the younger of the two sisters, watches her sister for cues to behavior like putting the butter on the corn. I've already seen that the senior wife, Old Chokecherry Tree, watches me for how to do that.

Why is she called Old Chokecherry Tree? She looks close to forty, and her bearing is majestic.

I wonder which of them is Friday's biological mother. When I ask him, he says, "Makes no difference."

Maybe he doesn't know.

What the devil, with all the different characters, they may as well be an Irish family. Big differences? Their love for coffee instead of tea, and the amount of sugar they add. Otherwise, the families are alike. They gobble up food, and they like to tease. And there is usually just one mother, but really? Older sisters often play the part of another mother in Irish families.

When we've taken the dishes back to the kitchen, all of us stand around for a moment. Then Gray Bear says to Friday, "Why don't you come back and sleep in our lodge tonight?"

Not knowing what his father has said, I look at Friday.

He tells me in English.

Then he answers Gray Bear, "I'll sleep in my own bed tonight."

His own bed. I like that.

I consider asking him what's on his mind about going back to his first family. Yes? No? Maybe?

But I decide to leave that question alone.

———

We serve Friday's family breakfast again the next morning. The cooks give us the usual, fried pemmican, and this time offer a treat. I've asked them to bring a pitcher of milk to add to our coffee, and everyone likes that, as long as they get sugar too.

Then the senior wife, Old Chokecherry Tree, stands up and says, "Vash, I have a gift for you."

Friday flashes her words to me with his fingers. He's

told me the two wives are equally mothers to him, but when I watch the body language between him and Old Chokecherry Tree, I think she's his birth mother, and their bond is the tight one. When a woman gives suck to a child, something special is created. And whether or not you acknowledge that openly, you know it in your bones.

His mother isn't quite ready to show us her present. "This is the Moon of the Serviceberry," she says, with Friday relaying her words to me. "You were born in this moon, in the year when the white soldiers first made their appearance."

Now she shows off the present, a beautifully painted shirt.

As an aside, Friday tells me that was, in the way white people count the years, 1823, the year I arrived in St. Louis and boated up the Missouri with General Ashley's two boats full of trappers. When Ashley made the mistake of trading the Arikaras for too much powder and lead, leading to the Arikaras kicking our asses with a dawn attack.

Mike Fink saved me with a rowboat.

Roll of the dice.

Back to breakfast in the fort: Friday dashes around the table, takes the shirt, holds it up to his chest to model it, flips it around to show the other side, and gives her a big hug.

The painting is really fine. It's all red against the buckskin color, and the stylized hunter and deer are handsome.

Old Chokecherry Tree looks at me with a friendly smile, and Gray Bear signs, "We always have a couple of deerskins around for making clothes."

We mountain men wear cloth shirts in the summer and leggings of deer hide year 'round. Most of time cloth does well, but it gets torn in brushy country.

I can see that Friday is thrilled with his shirt. And in a just a moment he's more thrilled.

Golden Eagle, the oldest brother, says, "Friday, have you shot a bow and arrow?"

"No," Friday says eagerly.

"Today you will. Young Raven and I will teach you. We'll shoot tree trunks instead of deer. That's the way we learned too."

Hunting with bow and arrow. I've taught him to hunt with a gun, but not with a bow. His brothers hunt that way. If Friday was with his people, he would have started learning it by now.

Well, bow-hunting has one advantage over using a gun. The bow can't blow up in your hand and make it into a cripple, like mine.

———

Supper is even better than breakfast. A couple of our hunters have found the tag end of a buffalo herd, brought down two cows, and hauled the meat to our kitchen. The cooks are serving it.

Everyone in the family (am I now including myself in Friday's family, instead of him in mine?) knows well how to eat hump ribs and buffalo roast, a delicious food. I'll bet our cooks kept the tongue for themselves. It wouldn't stretch far in this crowd anyway.

Friday is seated among his brothers this time, and is excited by having hit the target tree trunk numerous times after several misses.

I tease him: "Would you be able to put an arrow into the right spot on a buffalo cow riding at full speed?"

"*Hell* no," he says to me with a smile, finger-flashing

the others. "I could do it with a rifle. You taught me well, but not with a bow." Now his smile is a grin.

The buffalo is supplemented by stewed slices of apple and more ears of corn. All of it pleases the visitors greatly, especially the sweetened apples.

We eat, linger a little over coffee, and separate to head for bed. As we sit down on the beds in our room, Friday exclaims, "Now I need to learn to make a bow and straight arrows!"

I can see he loved getting time with brothers Golden Eagle and Young Raven.

"What's their own news?" I ask.

"Well," says Friday, "Golden Eagle is eager to count his first coup. He's been on a couple of pony raids against the Pawnees and thinks he did his job well."

"First coup is a big event."

"Yes," says Friday. "Coups are how a young man gets standing among our people. Golden Eagle is ready. He has his eye on a girl his age, and he thinks she has eyes for him. Soon he'll be able to stake some horses in front of her family's lodge and…"

I know. That's the way to ask for her hand in marriage.

I ask Friday, "Is your mind still on Angel?"

His tone is muted now. "A little bit."

Pause, a long pause.

He says in a voice inflected with hurt, "She rejected me because I'm an *Indian*."

I breathe in, breathe out. There's nothing I can say to that.

Without another word we turn in for the night.

———

After breakfast Friday heads out for another day of learning to shoot a bow.

We don't speak much at supper.

Friday sits between his two mothers and seems happy.

I can't read the signs.

He walks with me back to our room. As soon as we're inside, he says, "I want to talk."

Dreaded words.

"Tomorrow morning I'll leave with my family."

Nothing to say.

"Go back to my people."

I'm silent.

"Fitz," he goes on, "I'm very fond of you. I'm grateful for all you've done for me, especially my education in the ways of books and in the trappers' skills in the mountains.

"But I'm an Arapaho. I belong with my people."

No words.

He asks, "Don't you have anything to say?"

I consider, fumble inside myself, and eke words out. "I think you want to marry, and that will be easier within your tribe."

He takes a breath and says, "It will be *possible* within my tribe."

I finally sit back on my bed.

He sits on his.

Silence.

I look at him, full of questions.

"I've thought it over," he says, "and you and I can make this work. This fort can be the point of connection for us. Here at this fort on the North Platte River, you're the boss. My band lives along the South Platte River, seven sleeps away. My people will travel to this fort to trade each spring. If not all of us come, some will. We will always need powder and lead. And I will come with the band—to see you."

I squeeze out words: "I may not always be here." Still fumbling, I add, "I may not be the factor at the fort." Meaning the guy who runs things.

"I know that," Friday says. "Still, we can connect. If you're not here, I'll leave you a letter about what I'm doing. And if not you're here that spring, I hope you will leave a letter for me.

"We *can* stay in touch," he says.

I'm silent for quite a while. Finally I say, "This is a lot to..."

"There's still some business," says Friday. "Reading is important to me, and I'm determined to keep it up. I'll leave *Gulliver's Travels* with you to return to Mrs. Talbot, but I'd like to finish reading *Robinson Crusoe* and Marco Polo's *Travels*. May I keep them until next spring?

"Eventually I'll return all the books to you, and maybe ask to borrow others. I want to keep on reading."

Now we're stuck for words.

I break the silence. "I want to sleep now."

He stretches out his arm and we clasp hands. We look at each other. We know each other's minds and hearts.

"Sleep now." I say again.

He says, "Me too."

I slide under my buffalo robe.

He blows out the lamp.

In the darkness, silently, I shed tears.

MAY 5, 1835

Friday is leaving this morning.

Painful words.

I'm going to stay in our room during breakfast. I'll grab a bite while the Arapahos are breaking camp.

When I can see that his band is making ready, I walk to their camp and into the midst of the family packing up. I watch the lodge covers coming down, being folded, and being laced onto the travois to drag behind the horses. Watch the parfleches—boxes made of hide—being tied on. Watch everything. I'd help out, but they have the routine down and are efficient.

No one says a word to me.

At last all is ready.

Friday comes to me. We stand at arms' length, holding each other by the shoulders.

We've said it all.

The band lines up to move out.

Gray Bear approaches me, erect, waiting.

I look into his grave face.

"Thank you for everything," he says with his fingers.

He waits, but I'm frozen stiff. I nod.

Now Gray Bear walks, mounts, and leads his family into the middle of the line, Friday directly behind him.

They ride.

Friday turns, looks across the expanding distance to me, and lifts an arm.

I lift my arm and wave my hand.

I watch, standing in an ocean of sorrow, barely able to breathe.

May 6, 1835

Friday is gone.

I wonder how many days I'll start writing this log with those two words—Friday's gone. My son is gone.

I hope the words aren't as big in my heart and mind as they seem in my log.

What is big for me is the thought of what future he may face.

I'm sitting here in the fort's trading room, which is also the room for dining. It's empty now—everyone but me has eaten and headed out.

I get up and stand here idly, wondering what I'm doing. I carry the empty coffee pot back to the kitchen and get a full pot. I sit back at my empty table. What the hell am I doing?

Fretting. Fretting about what future Friday faces. He has a choice: He can be white, or he can be Indian. He's one of very few who have that choice.

Some pros and some cons:

White people have a religion that sticks them with a

contradiction. At the same time they're the chosen people of God and they're wretched sinners.

When I was offered this religion as a youngster, I said no, no, and no.

I can't tell for sure whether Indian people even have a religion. I know they salute Father Sun, Mother Earth, and the powers of the four directions in their ceremonies. However, those are real—not imaginary, like Jehovah and Satan.

I'm sure, though, that it's better not to think you're born a sinner.

I do see that life is going to get difficult for Indian people, both on the plains and in the mountains. With the coming migration of white people to the West, the Mexicans won't be able to hold onto California, where farmers can actually grow at least two crops in a single year. Oregon is fertile too.

That's going to mean floods of wagons coming across these plains and mountains. Which will mean lots of hunting of buffalo, deer, and antelope along the way. Which in turn will mean less food for the Indians. And that will create conflict between red and white.

What's the best place for Friday in this scenario? There's no stemming the tide.

White people are arrogant about the superiority of their civilization, which they think makes them better than everyone else. Yet the white men who come out to the mountains don't have the survival skills of any Indian people. If we mountain men didn't teach them, they would die.

More important, I don't see superiority in people who enslave Negroes. Indians sometimes take slaves, but then adopt them into the tribe and treat them as family members. When did that ever happen between white slave owners and black slaves?

Do Indians have big faults? Yes. The tribes are perpetually at war with each other. They honor men who are warriors and make them leaders whether or not they're wise. This condemns them to never-ending conflict, blood, and death.

Another issue for the whites: Oddly, they don't yet see that slavery is a big bump in the road ahead for them. Eventually, it's going to tear this country up.

But the big deal is, what's the best way for Friday through all of this?

How can I help him?

Also, what's the best route for me? When the big migration of white folks to the West gets started, I'll be sympathetic to the plight of the Indians. But what will be my role then?

Maybe I can help. My friend William Clark is officially agent for all the Indians. Maybe I can talk to him and somehow affect the policies of the U.S. government. Or maybe not.

I finish the dregs of the coffee and take the pot back. Better to catch up with the fort's ledgers than to stare into darkness.

I don't know how to help Friday. And his other father doesn't see the whole situation and so can't help.

Being human is hard.

August 12, 1835

I've missed Friday every day since his band pulled out. Since then, I've endured too many days of being chief guy of the fort—keeping the books up to date, straightening out small problems in the kitchen, telling several fellows they're not welcome to room and board unless they do some work, and the like. This job isn't my cup of coffee with sugar.

When our partner Lucien Fontenelle comes in with the pack train bound for rendezvous, visions of a good time start dancing in my head. Over dinner Lucien and I agree that he'll stay and take charge of the fort while I lead the pack outfit on to the big gathering on the Green River. I'm eager to get to rendezvous. When I ride in with all the barrels of whiskey, it will turn into a king-sized party. Maybe I won't think about Friday for a few days.

I've decided to be back at the fort each year in May, when his band is likely to come in. Otherwise, I want to shake loose of that place. I like new vistas every day. Or faces I haven't seen for a year, as at rendezvous—"Hiya, Pard. Glad to see you still got your hair!"

On the way to this rendezvous, I've brought two missionaries headed for Oregon, Samuel Parker and Dr. Marcus Whitman. We've just arrived today.

Shortly after pulling in with his men, Jim Bridger begs the doctor for help. "I done had this arrowhead in my back for three year," he complains. "Damn Blackfeet planted it thar."

Whitman takes a professional look at the wound and says, "I can help."

He lets me watch. He makes an incision and uses a tool like a pair of pliers to lift the arrowhead out, ugly with blood.

"No wonder it hurt, Jim," he says. "The thing is as long as one of my fingers."

Just watching has made my stomach queasy. Jim didn't make a sound, but he squirmed a bit.

Now Jim will be okay.

———

I'll remember this rendezvous well because of a bully Frenchman, Chouinard, who's with an outfit of French-Canadians of the American Fur Company.

One more reason to hate the A.F.C.

Chouinard parades around like king of the camp and beats men up at will. The outfits have been here for a week or two, and he seems to have acted belligerent with half of the men and have beaten up the others. He's big—about a head taller than me and probably fifty pounds heavier—and he's very strong. In fact, he looks even more muscular than my pal Mike Fink, king of the boatmen.

Early this afternoon I have lunch with a man who's new to me, Kit Carson, out of Taos, New Mexico. He's a likeable fellow, and more likeable for inviting me to share some slices of buffalo tongue and a cup of coffee with him. If he's come to a rendezvous before, I haven't crossed paths with him.

After lunch Kit and I wander around, chatting. We stop to watch a game of cards with men gathered in front of a lodge. Chouinard is in the circle, and I'm curious to see how he gets on with others.

It's simple: He acts like he's going to win every hand. And if he doesn't trump you, he'll tromp you.

Now he does win another hand, rakes some money toward himself, and hoots, "Fellers, if one of you dare'n rise up and take money from me, I'll take all of you on, one at a time, and beat you like rugs. Unless'n you is Americans. In that case I'll cut a switch and switch you until you cry like babies."

Kit has been here all week, and now Chouinard has gone one step too far.

"Monsieur Bully," he says, "I'm the smallest American in camp." True. Kit's even shorter than me. "There's a lot of Americans who could thrash you, and would like to, but can't be bothered. But if you mouth off any more, I'll rip your guts out."

Chouinard gives a grin big and shiny as the sun. Then, without a word, he walks off. In seconds, it seems like, he's back, mounted and carrying his rifle, standing at the ready two horse lengths from our group.

Kit dashes off and gallops back on his own horse, draws up face to face with Chouinard, and says at large, "Gentlemen, I have no weapon. May I borrow one?"

Quickly, I prime my pistol, step over to Kit, hand it to him, and say softly, "It's ready."

Kit gives me a lopsided grin.

Now he fixes his eyes on Chouinard and demands, "Am I the one you intend to switch?"

Their horses are so close they could rub necks.

In the same instant Chouinard says "No!", raises his rifle, and shoots.

Kit lifts the pistol and both fire at once. Every one of us at the card game hears just one shot.

Kit shoots the bully in the arm.

Chouinard's ball whisks past Kit's head. It cuts his hair and the powder from the muzzle burns his eye.

They glare at each other, their weapons empty, the Frenchman clutching at his bloody arm.

He turns his horse and walks it away very, very slowly.

Chouinard has met his match. He will cause no more trouble in this camp. Or probably at any other rendezvous.

————

At the end of this rendezvous I haul the beaver skins we've traded for back to the fort on the Laramie, taking Dr. Whitman along. Instead of going on to Oregon and preaching the gospel, he wants to go back to gather up more missionaries to help with the job. I'm glad to take one missionary back to the States—one less voice to tell the Indians what wretched sinners they are. Still, the doctor is a good man for pulling that arrowhead out of Jim Bridger's back. Doctors yes, preachers no.

I left Fontenelle in charge of our fort back when I went to rendezvous. Now he wants to make the trip on St. Louis, taking 120 packs of beaver and 80 bundles of buffalo hides. He'll be Dr. Whitman's escort.

At the fort I spend my time trading with the Sioux. About fifty lodges of them are here, and others are still coming in. I find them amiable and intelligent Indians and like trading with them. And I see that our fort on the Laramie has become a gathering place for red and white people alike, every tribe east of the Rockies and every train of emigrants. Makes sense—who doesn't need groceries? And tobacco? And shirts? And cloth? And powder and lead? And more?

It's such a good center for trade that Gary, my assistant in running the counter, leads two strangers into my office.

THE DAY BEFORE CHRISTMAS
1835

"Arthur," says one stranger, his hand extended. I shake it while the other one says "Delbert." I'd list their last names, but I honestly can't remember them.

"Representing the American Fur Company," says Delbert.

I grimace and hope they don't notice.

Arthur goes on. "The A.F.C. admires what you've done in building this fort in such a good location, serving so many tribes and all the emigrants on the Platte River route. We like it so much we want to buy it."

Delbert has nothing to say. Maybe his job is just to look smart.

Buy the fort? Part of me wants to sell it right now, ride away, and go hunt some buffalo or trap some beaver.

Slow down, I tell myself, *and think things through. Our little company of Fitzpatrick and Fontenelle has debts back in St. Louis. We still owe Bill Sublette money, and we had to borrow more money to buy the supplies we took to rendezvous. I don't know how much we got for the beaver and buffalo hides*

Fontenelle just took back to St. Louis, and don't know whether we're still in debt.

Stall, I tell myself. I pull out a drawer, take out my pipe, fill the bowl with tobacco, find a lucifer in the drawer, light up, and watch the smoke circle toward the ceiling.

I don't have the temperament to work inside every day.

On the other hand, this fort makes a good profit. It's the only general store on the main route to the West.

After a few moments I fumble some words out. "Do you have an offer?"

"Yes."

"Which is?"

Arthur shrugs and states a figure, as though casually.

I answer with words I decided on before I asked the question: "Well, I'll take the proposition to my partner Lucien Fontenelle. He's in St. Louis right now, doing company business." Pause. "For myself, I don't think that's enough money. We do have the only general store on the Plains."

Arthur and Delbert look at each other like they're exchanging nods. My answer is what they expected.

The damned A.F.C. again. But Fontenelle and I have already agreed that in the end the A.F.C. is going to rule in the mountains—we aren't strong enough to stop them. Bill Sublette says the same.

So, I tell these men I'll write my partner in St. Louis. My recommendation will be to sell the fort when the offer gets high enough.

Arthur stands up, and Delbert follows suit. Arthur extends his hand again for a shake. "We'll get back to you," he says, very business-like. "How should we get in touch?"

"Write to General Ashley," I tell him, "St. Louis,

Missouri. He will forward your letter to us by the first pack train heading west. We'll get back to you promptly."

He and Delbert nod at each other. They know who Ashley is.

I think, *Time to be cordial now.* "Please," I say, "come back for dinner at sunset. Let me show you how hospitable the fort can be."

"Well, thank you," says Arthur.

They bow and smile their way out of the office.

January 3, 1836

By the first of January I'm out of patience with handling the daily management of the fort. Leaving that job in Gary's able hands, I leave for St. Louis on January 3rd, entirely alone for the mid-winter journey across the plains. I do take two horses, just in case.

I'll get the new bid from the American Fur Company from Ashley. If the dollar increase is significant, I'll write the A.F.C. back, accepting their offer.

The trip is as nasty as expected. When I get to St. Louis on February 27, I have frostbitten fingers and toes.

The next morning my first stop is to see Captain Clark. I go just before lunch time, and as I'd hoped, he takes us out to his favorite place for omelets and croissants.

When we get to our table, he begins heartily, "Well, Fitzpatrick!"

"Fine to see you, Captain."

We sip our coffee. This French restaurant serves excellent brew.

"What a career you've had in the mountains, Fitz.

Clerk, trapper, brigade leader, and now owner of the fort on the Laramie."

"You've talked to Fontenelle, then."

"I have. The fur men who come to St. Louis stop by to see me and I pump them for news."

"Well, Sir, I have even newer news. What will you think of this?" I tell him about the visit from Arthur and Delbert and the offer from the American Fur Company.

"I'm not a bit surprised," Clark says. "In fact, I think this is inevitable. You and I agreed long ago that the Laramie Fork is the ideal spot for a trading post, central to all the Plains Indians and all the travelers on the route along the Platte. We've even said that one day it may become the place for important talks between the government and the Indians."

"Yes. But I'm asking a high offer for our fort."

"And since Mr. Astor is determined to dominate the fur trade in the West, he'll increase his offer for certain."

"Yes."

"Do you intend to sell?"

I tell him about the issues. First, Fontenelle and I owe money here in St. Louis, to Bill Sublette and others.

"Let me ease your mind about that," he says. "Your partner came in with plenty of furs to pay that debt." He grins broadly at me. "I told you all the fur men who come to town tell me what's happening. When you hear Fontenelle's figures, you'll find that you're well in the black, not the red."

Clark chuckles and says, "I'd say you and your partner are in the clover. Most entrepreneurs have not done so well. When will you talk to your partner again?"

"Whenever I can find him."

He considers. Then says, "Come to my office at 5:00. I may have news."

———

Actually, his news is Fontenelle in person.

"Lucien!" I exclaim, delighted. He likes for his name to be pronounced in the American way, not the French way.

"Fitz!" he says softly, offering his hand for a shake. He smells like a brewery, but I shake his hand heartily.

"Go right ahead," Clark tells Fontenelle, motioning us into chairs in front of his desk. "Tell him."

"We got the furs down here, no problems," Lucien says, "and sold them for eleven thousand dollars above what we owed. Fitzpatrick and Fontenelle Company has that money in the bank, and half of that is yours."

I say "Hooray," raise my fists, and shake them.

"What's more," Lucien goes on, "the A.F.C. has already written me with a better offer…"

He hesitates before naming the figure. "Wait. Do you really want to sell the fort? It's profitable. When traffic on that trail picks up—and it will—it's going to be even more profitable. Want to keep it?"

Now he's slurring his words—"shell the fort," he says.

I almost the blurt out my answer out: "No, let's sell."

He looks at me with raised eyebrows.

"When I was a young man in Ireland," I explain, "I walked away from inheriting the family farm and spent every dime I could scrape up to come to the United States and find *adventure*. I still love adventure. I'd rather fight Blackfeet than spend my days behind a counter or in an office counting dollars and cents." Pause. "I'd rather dodge bullets than stare at numbers."

Maybe I've overstated my case, but I don't care.

Lucien chuckles. "Captain," he says to Clark, "it

seems that our good friend was not born to be rich." *Rich* comes out as "rish." *Yes, Lucien has had one too many.*

He goes on, "The A.F.C. has increased its offer by plenty. I've told their representatives that we'll have to get that much plus the value of our inventory at the fort, whatever that is on the day the sale is final and the full price paid."

He's being clear, and the deal is very good.

Lucien hesitates. "Do we know what we have in inventory? Are the books up to date?"

"Up to date as of the day I left the fort to come here," I answer. I may not have liked the work, but I damn well did it right.

"All right, then," he says. "I'll tell the A. F. C. man to send his representatives to the fort at a set time, let's say when our pack train will get there, in the first week of May."

He's still slurring his words, but it doesn't matter.

I smile big and speak with care. "Good. We'll re-supply the fort at that time and charge the A.F.C. for all those supplies, then take the pack train on to rendezvous in June."

Hey, Friday may come to the fort in May, and I'll get to see him.

When Lucien stands up and sticks out his hand, we shake and give each other big smiles.

"Very good, 'gents," says Captain Clark. "*Very* good. You've done well."

"As well as others?" asks Lucien.

"Better than the others," says Clark, "except for General Ashley and John Jacob Astor. They're still the big players."

Clark adds, "Congratulations!"

———

From Captain Clark's office I walk to Mrs. Talbot's new address. She and her husband have bought a roomier place—she must be doing well. On the first floor are the school rooms and her office. On the second are the rooms for boarding students, the kitchen, and the dining room. On the third are the couple's living quarters.

She holds the door to her office open. Then she sits at her desk and nods me into a chair in front of it. Her husband stands at the side of the desk, eyes hard on me. I feel like a pupil facing an examination.

"Where's Friday?" she asks right off.

Her husband disappears. He avoids everything to do with the school or the boarders.

I tell her my sad story, that Friday is now living with his Arapaho family. Though I plan to say it objectively and present matters in a good light, emotion seeps into my voice.

Finished for now, I pause. Then she says, "You've done a world for that boy."

I appreciate her sympathetic tone.

"But it's all going to be wasted," she goes on. "This was unnecessary. Had he been here, in school, in contact with white society, it would have been avoided."

Not so sympathetic.

I don't mention that here in school Friday would have had to face Angel Lajeunesse, the cause of his misery, every day.

"In one way it's a blessing that he's gone. Mr. and Mrs. Lajeunesse don't want Angel near him. And they won't send their other two children to school here, a girl and a boy, unless I promise not to take any more Indians as pupils. They don't want their children associating with…"

She stops short of saying it.

"But back to Friday," she says. "What a student! I'm impressed that he's kept those two volumes for reading. That boy likes to read, and he'll need all the books he can get."

"I think he'll ask for more," I put in. "He's promised to return the books he had to me, probably next May. I'll either bring them downriver to you or send them with the pack train that brings the furs down."

Pause. Then she says, "Will you be kind enough to pick out a volume or two to send back to him?"

She goes on, "Whenever you and Friday return books to me, I'll send more."

Good woman.

"But," she goes on, "he's missing out on a lot of his education. He can add and subtract when the numbers are low, but that's all. He can't multiply or divide at all."

I feel her blame and don't like it.

"He has no idea of the history of this country, which is noble. No idea of world history. No idea of religion, and no awareness of God."

The mention of God pisses me off. Doesn't belong in school.

"His present environment will make him back into a savage."

I swallow hard at the application of the word *savage* to Friday. Or to Indian people generally. It's not right. She's ignorant and doesn't know it.

"*If* he keeps his word and comes to see you at the fort," she goes on. "*If* his family lets him keep that promise."

"The fort may well get sold," I confess. "But I intend

to be there each May, regardless. If Friday comes, we'll get to see each other. If not, I really think he'll send a letter for me. I'll write one and send it to him. And ask for him to return whatever books of yours he has to the fort. If he hasn't returned them after two years, I'll pay you for them. He'll probably re-read them anyway."

"*Thank you*, Mr. Fitzpatrick."

I take a deep breath, realizing how forlorn I sound.

Quickly, I go on. "His education has been a great thing."

"And could have been better," she says. She won't ease off about that.

I struggle on. "After five years among white people, he speaks English fluently. He reads and writes very well. In fact, he's more educated than the average farm boy in this country."

When I hear a sort of snort from her, I add in a hurry, "That's thanks to you."

She stands up. "At any rate," she says, "what's done is done, and there's no undoing it."

I stand too, and say sincerely: "Thank you for taking my son in and educating him."

She's momentarily lost for words. Then she says, "I've been glad to have him as a student. He's been a pleasure."

I stand, make a small bow with my head, turn, and walk out. I'm thinking, *A pleasure until he and a white girl...*

————

I see Lucien Fontenelle in his cups all too often over the next couple of months. Out of patience, I set up another meeting with Captain Clark, make a new arrangement, and ask him to repeat it to the men of the American Fur Company.

Captain Clark makes a note of my words: I'll go to the fort on the Laramie in the spring and transfer ownership of the fort to the A.F.C. whenever its representatives arrive. John Jacob Rich Man Astor will pay the price agreed on plus the value of the inventory at the fort at the time. I expect that the money will have been given to Fontenelle in Clark's presence, and the Captain will see that half goes into my bank account.

I think Lucien has ruined himself in the fur trade. Now that he'll have some dollars in his own bank, he doesn't seem to give a damn.

April Fool's Day 1836

Milton Sublette and I are off with the pack train in good time to be at the fort by May 1st, in due time to meet the A.F.C.'s representatives. We'll transfer ownership of the fort on the Laramie to them and get a good sum in return.

I don't think it will be called the fort on the Laramie for long. Fort Laramie is too convenient a name.

It will feel strange and wonderful, both, to have that much money in the bank in St. Louis.

On this trip west we're escorting more missionaries to Oregon. This time it's Dr. Whitman and his wife Narcissa, the Reverend and Mrs. H. H. Spalding, and W. H. Gray. Some Indian boys are travelling with them.

These missionaries make me chafe a bit. They treat the Indian kids like black slaves. They act as though the titles of *Dr.* and *Reverend* grant them the right of deference. They don't realize that in the mountains they're just greenhorns who don't know what way the stick floats.

But no man gets automatic deference out here—

respect has to be earned. The missionaries think the best part of the buffalo for eating, the tongue, is odd, and they disdain it. They don't like the crisp, crunchy roots of Jerusalem artichokes either.

Whenever they talk about Indian people—especially when the two wives do—the word *savages* gets tossed around. But those "savages" have thrived while living on these plains and mountains for centuries, and these greenhorns would get lost, starve, or be killed right off if I didn't take care of them.

They have no automatic respect, really, for anyone who lives out here, red or white. When they learn respect, they'll get it in return.

I do appreciate, though, the writing ability of Mrs. Whitman. She shows me a letter she's written to a friend she calls E., and it has a good picture of our outfit on the move up the river:

> *The fur company is large this year. We are really a moving village, nearly four hundred animals with ours, mostly mules and seventy men. The fur company has seven wagons and one cart, drawn by six mules each, heavily loaded; the cart drawn by two mules carries a lame man, one of the proprietors of the company. [She means our partner Milton Sublette, who has an artificial leg made of cork.] We have two wagons in our company. Mr. and Mrs. Spalding and Husband and myself ride in one, Mr. Gray and the baggage.*

> *Your friend, Narcissa Whitman*

Tonight we had a gathering that was a bit silly. Who can imagine a tea party here in the mountains? No doubt, though, Mrs. Whitman thought she was bringing a touch of class to the wilds.

Pretty funny.

———

Gladly, I invite fancy Sir William Drummond Stewart to join me at my evening fire. On the coals the coffee pot is staying hot. I have a jug of whiskey at our feet and will keep our cups full.

Stewart begins with a surprising question: "Do the missionaries and their outfit pay you to escort them west?"

"Sure. They're like you. They pay for someone who knows the way and can get along with the Indians. Basically, the guests are paying for what they eat and for the service of having their asses kept safe."

"You're selling the fort on the Laramie to the American Fur Company."

"Right. I'm getting out of that business. Though I love trapping, I think it's done. Styles have changed, silk has replaced beaver as what men's hats are made of, and the value of fur is far, far down."

"Have you thought that you could make a good living as a guide? Take missionaries, adventurers like me, and even government outfits where they want to go in the West for a fee? That would be a great service."

"That's what I'm already doing."

"Excellent. This is the fourth straight year I've gone to rendezvous, and I love coming out here. I spend the winters in New Orleans and come West every spring for the hunting—buffalo, bear, elk, deer, antelope—love it, all of it. It would be better for me, though, to make the trip solely as a hunting expedition, not ride along on someone else's affairs, whether their business is beaver or Bible."

"I can see that."

"I would compensate you handsomely. I can afford it."

A baronet afford it? I guess so! When he becomes the baron, he can afford anything he wants.

So, I agree. "I think I can do that well. Can locate buffalo. Put you in position for a good shot. Are you good at long shots lying on the ground?"

"On the ground," says Stewart, "I'm very good. Here's what I can't do, or not yet. Can't run the buffalo and shoot them at a gallop like you mountain men do. At that gait I'm bouncing around far too much."

"Every man new to the West has the same trouble," I say. "Took me several years to get to moving with my horse smoothly enough to make that shot."

I go on. "Do you want trophies? Heads of buffalo? Elk with a lot of points? Antelope heads? Deer heads? Tanned buffalo hides? Elk hides? Deer hides? *Painted* buffalo hides?"

"All of the above," says Stewart. "I want to make a good display in my castle back in Murthly. I already have some trophies from hunting trips in North Africa, and fully intend to add the United States."

"That's your home, Murthly Castle."

"Our ancestral home. It's a bit more than a mile outside the village of Murthly in Scotland. Our chapel was built in the 16th and 17th centuries. It has a barrel-vaulted, timber-boarded ceiling with arabesque motifs and a beautiful font for holy water. Plus a series of hatch-ments with the heraldic components of our family coat of arms. Also a sandstone mural monument to Sir Thomas Stewart."

This recitation has lasted longer than I can hold a breath. Does he think the water in the font of his family chapel is holier than the water in a cathedral here? Or than the water of a clear, cold mountain stream?

I take that thought back. I'm sure a baronet is proud of his heritage, and he has a right to be. On the other hand, they can keep their baby barons-in-waiting out of Ireland.

I refill our cups with coffee and a lot of whiskey.

He sips from the cup. I watch his face but can't read it. I'll bet he'd rather have Scotch.

"What do you think?" he asks. "Would you guide me, just me, and make it an expedition to shoot big game and get trophies? Again, you would be well compensated."

I consider and admit, "I don't think so. It's not safe, two men riding across these plains and through these mountains alone. Too many Indian attacks."

I can see from the way he's pursing his lips that this isn't the answer he wanted, but it won't change. It's *not* safe.

I explain. "Think of this. There are war parties out and about from the various tribes, looking to raid the horses of other tribes, or anyone, and run them off. Those parties consist of young warriors on the make. They aim to count coup on enemies, steal horses, do war-like deeds of every kind. It's also to make their reputations within the tribe and gain appeal as prospective husbands for the young women.

"Suppose a war party like theirs comes on two men like us, a solitary pair who have horses to be stolen, guns to be grabbed, and scalps to be lifted. We'd be far too tempting a target."

I think these words but don't add them—"*especially since one of us is a greenhorn.*"

"I understand," says Stewart. "I know you travel in big caravans for safety in numbers."

"Damn straight. But I'll tell you what I can do, if you like. Take you along with the big caravans like this one, you and I being a separate unit, and give you particular attention. When we come to buffalo sign, I can lead you to the herd, approach in the best direction considering the wind, and crawl with you until we get a good shot. Help you skin the buffalo.

"And when we get to rendezvous, we'll hand the skin to an Indian woman who will do a first-class job tanning it. Even get a woman to paint the hide, if that's what you want."

I take thought and add, "William Clark has some tanned hides on the walls of his office, but not one painted hides."

That makes Stewart raise a smile.

Seems to me a little selling might be good now. "I can do more like that. Put you in a good spot to take deer, antelope, and elk. Skin them for you and show you how to do it. Get the hides and head ready to take back as trophies."

Now I have a pleasant thought, and speak it: "As a matter of fact I'd enjoy doing that."

He puts in, "And I'd be pleased to pay you for the service."

I smile, shake his hand, and say, "We'll do some good work together and have some shining times."

Then I take thought. "I can do one thing for you more if you like. When we're at rendezvous, I can help you find a nice-looking Indian woman to go into the woods with you for some pleasure. She'll charge something. Typically, two yards of red or blue cloth to make herself a blouse. Or maybe enough just enough vermilion to put a red streak in the part of her hair.

Stewart hesitates and tastes his whiskey with coffee. Then he says, "I don't do women."

Whoops! Am I understanding this correctly?

"You mean you go for men instead of women? You're a pansy?"

He takes a longer draft of the whiskey.

He gives me a wry smile. "I don't much care for that term," he says, "but it's a lot better than the term most common in Ireland, *poofter*. That word generally comes with a snicker."

Yeah, *poofte*r is derogatory—that's the way I remember it.

Stewart smiles easily. "Yes, I prefer men. Particularly big, rangy, strong-looking men."

Breathe in long, out long. Now I know. Actually, I guess I guessed earlier, but…

But it sure doesn't bother me. Even the Indian tribes have some men like that. They call it being born under a different moon, or two spirit, or the like.

Each to his own, I tell myself.

I refill his cup with whiskey, and mine, and lift mine in a toast.

"To good company," I say.

"Good company," he echoes, and we clink cups.

He stands up and says, "Time to head for my blankets, while I can still walk."

I stick out my hand, and he shakes it.

"To good adventures," I say.

"To adventure!"

———

The next morning I start by checking on Mrs. Whitman. She's a good sort, if somewhat out of place. White women are out of place in the West, period.

I'm not pleased with myself for conducting these missionaries and their wives to Indian country, bringing the bad news that every human being is a sinner bound straight for hell. Except, of course, for white people who are baptized. They *know* they're superior to Indians. And to us trappers.

What rubbish.

Dr. Whitman is a good fellow. I watched him do that surgery on Jim Bridger and save Jim from more years of pain. That doc took care. I'm glad to have him along.

I'm also glad to have Stewart with us, and am already thinking how to give him the most enjoyment as his guide. He will be thrilled. And since beaver trapping is a fading business, I'll still have a way to make a living. Thomas Fitzpatrick, guide of wild-hair adventurers, big-game hunters, missionaries, emigrants, and who knows what else?

————

Right now, I'm eager to get to the fort by the first day of the month, in case Friday and the family come in on time. On the other hand, Arapaho people count the months off by moons, and I don't know whether those moons square with the white-man's dates for May. Best just to get there as soon as I can.

MAY 7, 1836

As it turns out, neither the day nor week matters. When the Arapahos come in today, Friday's family doesn't come. But Friday has sent me a letter:

The moon named April
Dear Fitz—

Our family isn't coming to the fort this year. We need only a few things, and we've asked the family in the lodge next to ours to get those for us.

Don't worry, my family won't attack trappers or any other white people. They will only use the rifles, powder, and ammunition to hunt game. When we can get close to the buffalo, arrows do fine, but from a distance we need guns.

I'm very sorry not to get to see you this time. I miss you. I think my Arapaho father senses that and doesn't want us to be together. But I've made him promise that we'll make the trip next May.

Along with this letter I'm returning the copy of Robinson Crusoe. Please have it sent to St. Louis and Mrs. Talbot.

I'm keeping Marco Polo's Adventures until next year.
What grand stories! What terrific experiences! I'm going to
keep reading but intend to bring the book to the fort next
May, so that Mrs. Talbot gets it back.

With big thanks to my white-man father,
Friday

It's wonderful to have this letter, but I hope the same news doesn't repeat itself year after year.

What if I never get to see Friday again? Oh, that's silly. Friday and I will find each other. The West is big geographically but small socially.

On the other hand, *my* family and I...

Since coming to the States, I've written to my parents and brothers and sisters each year at Christmas, from 1823 forward. For the first several years I gave my letters to General Ashley to forward to County Cavan in faraway Ireland, paying him for the postage in advance.

Since he took Jedediah Smith as a partner and stopped coming to rendezvous himself, I've given my letter to the leader of each trade caravan to carry back to St. Louis to be given to William Clark forwarding.

The bundle of letters going from trappers back to their families with each rendezvous caravan is considerable. If we didn't pay the postage in advance, Clark or General Ashley would have quite a burden.

The letters carry a different sort of burden. They're full of merry exaggerations about how well we trappers are doing, how much money we're making, and how soon we'll be back with our loved ones.

We may have to leave the mountains soon, a lot of us, but with scarcely a dime.

I smile at all this because I have to write out a lot of

these letters for others. Most of us trappers can't read or write. I charge for this service—each letter earns me a cup of whiskey while I write it. I don't charge extra for improving the language of my fellows: I dress the letters up a bit. The phrase "This child he don't" becomes "I don't." The same for the phrase "this coon don't." Also, there are no statements like "After another year out hyar, I still got my hair," or "I'm still above ground."

Back in the States they speak more nicely than we do, and they're better off without knowing how raw we are.

Back to my own family. After all this time of writing faithfully each year, I have yet to get a word back from anyone—Father, Mother, brother, or sister. Yes, my feelings are hurt. Maybe Father is angry at his youngest son for leaving and has slammed the door on all communication with me.

Actually, when my partners and I sold the fort on the Laramie, I cut all the ties that keep me out here. Though I may end up with a career as a guide, I'm temporarily unemployed.

I thought of taking a year to sail back to Ireland, see how my family is doing, and find out how the old sod feels beneath my feet. But I'm too angry to make that trip now.

And probably too upset to write the family at this Christmas or any other. Here's a letter I wrote in my journal but won't send:

Dear Da, Ma, brothers and sisters,

> *I went looking for adventure and have found it in America, plenty plus plenty. I've explored a great part of the western half of this huge continent. I've fought Indians many times without getting shot. I'm fluent in the sign language*

and so am able to talk with Indians. I've been a leader of the fur brigades that march about the country hunting beaver. I've also become a partner in a fur company and have earned a lot of money. I've earned the respect of my companions and partners. I've gotten an adopted son from one of the tribes, and I'm proud of him.

When you have cause to be proud of your youngest son, why have you have forgotten me?

Your loving son, Tom

————

Joshua Pilcher has arrived with authorization from Pierre Chouteau to make all the arrangements for transfer of ownership of our fort to the A.F.C. Fine. I wanted to be done with it. We've conferred, we agree, and I'm free of the fort.

Now I'm impatient. I want to get on to the rendezvous of 1836, which will be at the mouth of Horse Creek on the Green River.

Off we go, a full complement of wagons, mules, William Drummond Stewart, and missionaries. At the fort we take our loads out of the wagons and off the mules and stack them on the shelves to become stock. Those goods belong to the A.F.C. now, and Big Bucks Astor will pay us by deposits into our accounts in St. Louis. That's good.

Our route beyond here is west along the Platte, straight on up the Sweetwater, over South Pass, and on south to Green River. Moving in the same fashion as before, we should get to South Pass about Independence Day, which Americans celebrate, and to rendezvous about three weeks later.

Now, as we labor up the Pass, it's in fact right on July 4th. My thoughts float back to the fine day Jedediah Smith and I found this route across the Rockies and became the first white men to ride over it. In our minds that was a great day. From here all waters flow to the Pacific Ocean, not the Atlantic. By the heavens we'd done it.

Today I'm tickled to see that the missionary women want to make a ceremony of this same passage. Mrs. Whitman, Mrs. Spalding, and Mrs. Gray dismount, kneel with an American flag in one hand and a Bible in the other, and Mrs. Whitman says quietly, "We're honored to claim this western part of the continent as home to American mothers and to the Church of Christ."

I think maybe our original crossing deserved some spiritual gesture too. However, I look at the reverends and their pious wives and wish the United States of America was not exporting the gospel of You-Are-Sinners to Indian people. It's cruel and unusual punishment.

Though I'm acquainted with a number of Indian tribes, I know of none with a hand-me-down of such guilt.

MID-AUGUST 1836

I don't know today's actual date and won't pretend I do.

This rendezvous is as raucous a party as any of our summer gatherings has been. Because our pack train has hauled even more barrels of whiskey than usual, maybe more raucous. Games of cards, foot races, knife-throwing competitions, shooting at targets, quarrels and fights, the escorting of Indian women to the woods for a few minutes of pleasure in trade goods—this rendezvous of 1836 is another grand extravaganza.

It also offers me the return of a good man I met last year, Kit Carson. Kit is out of Taos, down the river from Santa Fe. I don't know Taos at all, but a fair number of trappers make it their headquarters.

Kit came to rendezvous last year. Though among the smallest men there, he made a big impression on me, and on a lot of mountain men, by taking of the dare of a big French-Canadian bully.

Kit would be good for any outfit.

When I voice that thought to Stewart, he says, "Damn right."

I invite Kit to share hump ribs at my fire tonight and he accepts. He arrives with a jug of Taos brandy, what the Mexicans call *aguardiente*, and I discover right off that it's an improvement on the whiskey we bring out here in our barrels, though not as good as Irish whiskey.

We munch eagerly on the ribs, switch to black coffee, treat ourselves to more brandy, and switch back to stories. He doesn't have many. He came west only a couple of years ago with a caravan headed to Santa Fe. During the next year he worked as a cook for the family of a Taos fur trader, Ewing Young, and learned Spanish in that household. Next year Kit's planning to ride to California with Young on a southerly route.

I confess that makes me envious. When Jedediah led the first American expedition to California, I didn't get to go. I want to see the land of perpetual summer, but I still haven't had the chance.

I poke at the embers of my fire with a stick, pondering.

Kit's Taos stories intrigue me. From time to time, he says, the Utes ride into town with captives they've taken in raids on their perpetual enemies the Navajos. (Everlasting warfare between tribes is the curse of Indian peoples, including the Arapahos of my son Friday.) Some well-to-do Taos families buy those captives, who are usually children of

families whose parents the Utes have killed. The purchased kids become either slaves or adopted children in those households, depending on the good will of the families.

And, according to Kit, some of those adoptees learn Spanish and get sent to Santa Fe, where there's a boarding school.

Shades of what happened with Friday!

Kit hopes to become a full citizen of Taos, married to a woman of a local family, and part of the community with his own children. But there are difficulties. He'll have to become a Mexican and a Spanish-speaker. The language within his own family will have to be Spanish. Since his Spanish is good, that's fine. The bigger obstacle is that he will have to convert to Catholicism, and his children will be raised as Catholics. He doesn't like Catholicism any more than I do.

"And I want my children to get educated," he says. "I can't read or write, but I want my children to."

"*What?*" Though I shouldn't be surprised, somehow I am.

"No, you heard me. I can't read or write. I want my children to speak Spanish and English, and to read and write Spanish and English."

I take a moment to pour another whiskey for Kit and one for myself.

"If you can't read and write, how will you teach them?"

"We'll send the kids from Taos to boarding schools in Santa Fe."

Shades of Friday and Mrs. Talbot! The angel with a fee.

WINTER 1836-37

At the end of that rendezvous, I lead the caravan back to the fort on the Laramie.

My mind is not really on Kit, on reading and writing, on Friday, or schooling for Indian kids. It's on the prospects for the life of us trappers in these mountains. I had a talk with William Clark about this not long before heading west from St. Louis, and I'm going to record it here as a guide to my future:

Clark invites me to lunch at his favorite restaurant, and we're eating croissants and omelets, as usual. He's buying, also as usual. One of the benefits of being Secretary of Indian Affairs is the business lunch.

"How's the price of beaver?" he asks, his face bewhiskered by the steam rising from his coffee cup.

Though he surely knows, I answer, "Fallen and falling further."

"Fashion," he says, irony in his voice.

"Beaver has gone out of style in in the big cities," I agree. "For decades men wanted hats made of beaver fur.

Now silk is all the rage. As a result the pelts we trap aren't worth a tinker's damn."

"And yet," he says, shaking his head at the foolishness, "more and more beaver outfits are out there competing for the fur."

I agree: "John Jacob Astor is looking to expand until he runs the whole show. And soon the show will be worth nothing."

We're both shaking our heads at the madness. I sip my coffee and he crunches on a croissant. I'd never tasted croissants before coming to St. Louis, but now I think they're one of the best parts of living in so-called civilization.

"You've had a great run," he puts in.

"Thirteen years in the mountains, a fine time—I got the adventure I came to America to find."

"Fitz," he says, "you have the skills. You know how to travel out there safely, how to negotiate with Indians, how to fight when you have to, how to make peace when possible, how to hunt buffalo, and more. You've learned the rivers and mountains of the West as well as most men know the palms of their hands. You speak the sign language. You know everything."

"No. But a lot, anyway."

"Enough," he says, "that I pointed Reverend Whitman in your direction." He smiles broadly. "Sent you Captain Stewart too. Hope you charged him good price."

I did. The co-leader of the Lewis and Clark expedition wields a lot of influence. And Stewart has already been a repeat customer, paying me on each trip west.

I assure him that I got a decent fee from Stewart.

Clark sets his coffee cup down. "Beginners wanting to

go West generally come through my office," he says. "Mostly, I'll refer them to you."

"Thank you for the favor," I say sincerely.

At this moment our omelets arrive on heated plates.

"Have you thought about guiding as a career? You're top of the line—you could make a good living. And not just from missionaries and adventurers like William Drummond Stewart. From the many, many emigrants who will be coming."

Looking at me across his coffee cup, he sips and goes on. "For starters, I'd like you to take my sons along with the next caravan west. Their names are George Clark and Meriwether Lewis Clark. This boy is named after Meriwether Lewis, as you would guess. They want to get a taste of the West for themselves. Your trip up the Platte, stopping at the fort on the Laramie, and going on to rendezvous—that's a terrific introduction to the plains and mountains. I know you'll take care of my boys.

"*And*," he says after a pause, "I'll compensate you well. You deserve it, and I can well afford it."

"I'd be honored to do that."

He tucks a napkin into his shirt.

"Fitz, I see the near-term future of this country as westward expansion. People are hearing that Oregon is an agricultural paradise, and they're going to flood out there. Also, the government is going to encourage that emigration. Right now, Oregon is co-occupied by the United States and Great Britain. The U.S. is eager to make it ours alone, and American occupancy will accomplish that. Which means a lot of traffic on the route up the Platte, past the fort on the Laramie, and on to the Pacific. Wagons, wagons, and long lines of wagons. You can stay busy working as a guide. And I'll help."

I hold up my empty coffee cup, motion to our waitress, raise my eyebrows in a question mark, and say, "Please." She smiles, brings the coffee, and pours.

"Also," Clark plunges on, "after the rush to Oregon I anticipate a rush to California. When people hear about the land of four summers, where farmers can get several crops a year, they'll damn well go. My opinion is that our country will end up in a war with Mexico for California and all of the Southwest. Again, traffic will jam the Platte River road and on across the mountains and deserts."

The old soldier is thinking ahead and foreseeing.

I sip hot coffee again. I bet his foresight is spot on.

After a pause Clark continues. "All this emigration, by the way, is the real reason Big Bucks Astor has bought the fort on the Laramie from you. When these emigrants get going, that fort is going to be a gold mine. It will be the only trading post between the Missouri River and California."

"I didn't like running that fort," I tell him. "Staring at numbers, making calculations, more numbers, more calculations—figures without end. Book work, book work, book work. I didn't come to America to bury my head in numbers."

Clark says, "That would be my friend Tom Fitzpatrick." Then he downs the last bite of ham omelet. "You'll like numbers of people more than numbers on a page."

"Damn straight," I answer, although plenty of people will be exceptions.

"In that case," Clark says, pushing his empty plate away, "I make you a simple promise. When people ask, I'll tell them you're the best guide there is."

He's got a lot on his busy mind.

Clark proceeds, "In the end it may matter even more that I'll tell my superiors in the government that you'll be an excellent guide for military expeditions. Also for exploring expeditions. I expect the government to want more complete maps of Oregon, California, and all the regions in between. They can really use your knowledge."

I take a deep breath and let it out. *Mapping. Exploring. Going. It's my happiness.*

Clark says, "Add the occasional big-game hunter like the baronet and other adventurers, the emigrants, and the government expeditions—it all comes to a full-time occupation."

With that Clark smiles, pushes away from the table, and stands up. "You like all this?"

"I'm floored by it," I tell him honestly.

He says, "You're welcome, Fitz. You've earned it."

AT THE FORT ON THE LARAMIE—MAY 10, 1837

As we ride up to the fort today, we are for sure the craziest aggregation of people ever to get here. As guide I lead the carts, wagons, and livestock to the gates. Right behind me are William Drummond Stewart and the painter Alfred Jacob Miller. Stewart has brought this artist to the West. They intend to record his adventure in big game hunting in the wilds, plus the lives of trappers and Indians. Miller is making water color sketches that will become oil paintings for display in Murthly Castle.

Behind Stewart and Miller, ride two heirs to aristocracy in the West, the sons of William Clark, famed as the co-leader of the Lewis and Clark expedition, now the Superintendent of Indian Affairs.

Right behind them rides one last absurdity. The Reverend William Gray has come back to rendezvous this year. He spent half a year circling through small Eastern towns. He was looking for a white wife to bear him white children. His idea was to create a nugget of Christian virtue in the so-called morass of sin among trappers and Indians.

No luck, and what a joke.

They're shocked by our boozing and carousing. The Reverend said to me: "There's nothing but blasphemy out here."

No comment about this ugly judgment. But in my head, I say this: *That's the kind of white superiority that will corrupt red-white relations for generations to come.*

Though William Drummond Stewart doesn't lord his title over us, I'll be damned if I'll address anyone as "The Reverend," "Sir," or the like.

Of course, Mrs. Gray reminds me daily that I should.

This cast of characters is good comedy.

————

AT THE FORT

It's painful that for the second straight year Friday isn't here, and this time he hasn't sent a letter. Yes, my feelings are hurt. He promised to come to the fort or at least send a letter each May. Have I lost him for good?

There is no possible way for me to believe that.

Most lodges of Arapahos have come this time, though none from Friday's family. I'll write a letter and send it to him with someone in his band. And I've brought him a book as a present, which I'm sure he will like.

Now I'll go into the big dining room, get some lunch, and write the letter:

May 12, 1837
Dear Friday—

I miss you and am eager to see you. It has been two years since we saw each other, so you're two years taller and filled

*out stronger. I'm very proud of you and will be proud when I
get to see you. It's hard for me to picture now that you're
fourteen years old. You've probably learned to be a good
hunter and may have gone on a horse-raiding party and
perhaps counted coups. You're growing up fast.*

*As you can imagine, Mrs. Talbot criticized me for letting
your education to come an end. But it hasn't ended—you
kept Marco Polo's Travels and Robinson Crusoe to read.
Have you enjoyed those books?*

*Meanwhile, here's another book I think you'll like. I hope
you have fun reading it.*

Your white-man father,
Fitz

————

Now I have other young men to attend to, George and
Meriwether, twenty-one and nineteen respectively.
They've gotten a good dunking into experience of the
West on the way out here, and will get still more at
rendezvous. From there we'll go back to their father in
St. Louis. Clark is fifty-seven now. I envy him for the way
he's gotten to watch his boys grow up, and I'm glad he
has confidence in me to show his sons the West.

In the late afternoon the lads come in from hunting
along the banks of the Laramie River to the north.
Unfortunately, they've come back empty-handed. "Don't
be disappointed," I tell them. "The hunters hired by the
fort have probably hunted those banks until the deer and
antelope have fled farther north."

"What's for supper?" George says cheerfully. He's the
older brother.

I hope to have a chance soon to skin animals the boys

have shot. We'll cook the meat on a spit—they'll love it way. However, I've checked with the fort's cooks, and they'll provide us with hump ribs for our fire tonight. The crowd in the big dining room has plenty of meat for tonight's meal. That will serve all our visitors, the crew of our caravan, and more.

I'll eat the bread. We trappers rarely get it.

———

The boys spread their blankets out while I get the fire started and put a spit above it for the ribs.

The three of us sit quietly, watch the sun set in the mountains to the West, and keep an eye on the browning meat. I think the boys have grown accustomed to my being quiet when talk isn't needed. I don't know whether they're really comfortable with silence.

But we three have had a lot of meals together already. They've asked many questions, and I've volunteered plenty of information about the buffalo, the plains we're crossing, the Indians we encounter. Everything.

I look from one boy to the other, wondering: Do they want to live in St. Louis, where they've grown up, with its version of sophistication? Do they want to get some land and farm it? Do they want to travel *all* of the West and fill in the spaces on the maps of country that their father hasn't seen? Or perhaps work for the U.S. government, like their dad?

I don't know. Don't want to intrude by asking, nor hand them my own points of view. They must choose their own roads.

Now we gnaw the meat off the ribs greedily.

Just as they're finishing, the younger brother, Meriwether, lunges at George with a big grin on his face. "I'm going to stab you," he says, brandishing a rib like a dagger.

George seizes John's wrist and uses momentum to roll Meriwether over onto his back. "Back at you!" George shouts from on top. There's no risk here—the rib bones are blunt at the ends.

Now it's topsy-turvy, one above the another, rollicking everywhere in the dirt, shouting mock threats, with lots of laughing exclamations of "You son of a bitch!" and "You bastard!"

I let them have their fun until they knock the coffee pot over, and it seems like Meriwether is about to land in the fire on his back.

At that point, chuckling, I jump up and plant myself astride them. "Stay out of the coals, boys."

They ignore me.

"STOP IT!" I holler. George relents and pulls clear of Meriwether.

Now I stand between them.

"You want your father to get you back home, roasted?!"

They crawl apart on hands and knees in a tumult of laughs, curses, and grumbles.

It's not their first time for horseplay, that's for sure. but they can do it further from my fire.

"Take to your blankets," I say firmly. Heads hanging, they do.

———

Tomorrow after breakfast in the dining room I'll get our outfit started toward the rendezvous on the Green River. We'll empty the wagons to restock the fort's shelves with supplies needed by the visiting Indians and the passing visitors. Then the carts, missionaries, the Baronet William Drummond Stewart, his painter Alfred Jacob Miller, and French-Canadian trapper Etienne Provost—all these will come along to the rendezvous. We'll unload the carts there to re-outfit the trappers and whatever Indians come to rendezvous this year. That will earn rousing shouts of protest from the trappers about the high cost of whiskey, tobacco, coffee, powder, lead, and other necessities. But since the value of beaver has gone down, hauling the supplies from St. Louis out here is expensive.

———

My responsibility for the missionaries ends here at rendezvous (and I won't miss their company). I'll help them choose a reliable trapper to lead them on to join the other missionaries in Oregon.

Now some sleep.

George and Meriwether are taking turns bragging about who did what.

Young fellas!

July 1838

Osborne Russell, a veteran, recorded the arrival of our outfit at the Green River this year, and he's shown me what he wrote.

First, he celebrated the enthusiastic greetings of the trappers for the caravan and their eagerness for letters, news, and supplies. He recorded the high prices of what we've brought to sell, at least double the cost in St. Louis. Yet just $4 or $5 a pound is given for beaver, so that one blanket costs four beaver hides.

This madness surely can't continue—what we trappers can get for our furs falls and falls while the cost of living in the wilds sails higher and higher.

The biggest burden will be on the brigade leaders, and as one them, I sympathize. Back in the States people think tobacco and whiskey are just indulgences of crazy trappers, but they aren't.

Every brigade leader has led an outfit into the territories of lots of tribes. In each case we're obliged to make gifts of tobacco, whiskey, and other goods to the Indians, especially to the chiefs. These are in effect bribes for letting us travel in their territory and shoot their game. For us it's the cost of doing business.

———

When rendezvous disbands, I guide our outfit back across South Pass and down to the fort on the Laramie, guiding the aristocrat William Drummond Stewart, the painter Alfred Jacob Miller, the two sons of William Clark, and the carts and pack animals. Before leaving the fort, I'll buy supplies and leave what little we still have for the new owners to trade. That will settle our accounts with them.

So, I lead all of us down the Platte River, then down the Missouri to the boys' home, St. Louis. We're carrying the furs that the fort's new owners traded for at rendezvous. I'm not pleased about doing a service for the American Fur Company, once my rival. But they're paying for the job, and I'm now in the guiding business.

I wonder how long the custom of rendezvous can last. I wonder how long trapping can last.

———

Back in St. Louis I have lunch with William Clark right off, and he tells me that his sons can hardly stop raving about their marvelous trip to the West, guided by me. Clark expresses plenty of gratitude, and I'm pleased to have done a service for my good friend.

He also offers me a nice invitation. He's holding an open house at his big place for the display of the water-color sketches Alfred Jacob Miller made on our western excursion, and he invites me to come.

———

The sketches are marvelous. They capture the Indians and the trappers going about their daily lives, with good detail of what's worn out here, how Indian lodges are painted, how buffalo are hunted, and even how Indian brides are bartered. (Those sketches of bartered brides are going to upset some white folks. Is it really any different than the balls society folks put on so their daughters can find the best catch? I don't think so.) Better yet, here in St. Louis Miller has completed several oil paintings based on his sketches, and they too are impressive.

Right on the spot Stewart gets a bunch of good offers for the sketches and paintings. But he's holding tight to them for display back at Murthly Castle.

The American Fur Company then asks me to guide their caravan again next summer. I'm to lead an outfit of horses and mules, plus carts and wagons, full of supplies back to the fort on the Laramie and then on to rendezvous. This work alone will keep me and my bank account in good shape for the foreseeable future, and if William Clark is right again, the floodgates of traffic to Oregon will open over the next few years. Plus, he thinks, those government expeditions to map the West. He says I should be plenty busy.

———

Whoops! I'm laughing at myself. When I said I'll be plenty busy, I was figuring without what is called a "financial panic." Business is down everywhere, every kind of business. The fur trade was hurting already, and this crash in the economy will make it worse. As a result, the A.F.C. has let me know that now I won't be asked to lead their caravan to rendezvous next summer. They're sending their own man, Andrew Drips, to do the job.

In the end that's fine by me. Stewart wants me to lead him back to rendezvous, again with Alfred Jacob Miller, and I'll collect the same fee. He's intrepid, this Scot, and he loves Miller's sketches and paintings. Me, too. The sketches will become beautiful oil paintings to hang in that castle of his, castle alongside his other paintings. They deserve that.

I clearly can't depend on the A.F.C. to keep me employed each year. However, William Clark tells me that there will be parties of missionaries next year and probably in the years thereafter. And he emphasizes that a flood of emigrants on the Platte River road is inevitable. He's given that road a name, the Oregon Trail, he calls it, and he says he'll recommend me as a guide to all comers.

So my income looks secure in the long term.

Meanwhile, Mrs. Talbot has asked me to help out at what used to be the school my son Friday attended. She has more students than ever, and she wants me to help them along with reading, writing, and arithmetic. That will be a pleasure this winter.

It will also make me get suited to help out in the West. Several trappers are married to Indian women and have Indian children. Those children are able to do some reading, but usually not much. When I'm back out there, I'll volunteer to help those kids along with their reading, no charge, glad to do it.

That will bring Friday to back to my heart in a good way. As of now I haven't seen him in too long, and that's painful. I've gone to the fort each May since, but his family hasn't come, and he hasn't written.

Come to think of it, I've written to him only twice. Right now I'll get to writing him another letter:

January 21, 1839
Dear Friday—

I miss you. I remember well finding you when you got lost on the prairie. You were seven years old, starving, and half-dead of thirst.

I was glad to give you what food I had, and you swigged water greedily from my horn. Then you climbed up behind me on my horse, and we rode to join my outfit.

What a grand day that was.

We rode on to Santa Fe, and that was another grand time. And back to St. Louis for another one yet. All the way you were learning more English and even learning the body language of us white folks.

You're long since a master of speaking English, and thanks to Mrs. Talbot you read and write it just as well. You know how to add and subtract.

As you know, I'm immensely proud of you.

I've gone to the fort on the Laramie each May, hoping your family would come back to trade and I'd get to see you.

No luck.

Each year I gave one of the Arapaho families that did come a letter for you, and I once passed along two books I bought for you—did you get the books?

I'd speak of more that you remember between us, but it's not needed—we both treasure those memories.

I'm still going to this year's rendezvous. At this one I'll have a special pleasure. Several of the trappers now have Indian wives, and their kids are learning to read. So, in honor of you, I'll volunteer to use the time at rendezvous to continue the kids' reading lessons. I hope they will like that as much as I will.

Please send a letter to the fort with one of your tribe's families next May.

Friday, I hope you're happy and doing well.

Your white Father,
Fitz

I tuck the letter away to be carried to the fort on the Laramie with next year's fur trade caravan. Eventually Friday will get it. I hope.

THE RENDEZVOUS OF 1839

This year's caravan to rendezvous is a lot smaller than those of the past. The fur trade continues to shrink.

Black Harris, known among us trappers as the man to make mid-winter journeys back to St. Louis, is the A.F.C.'s choice to lead this caravan. I'm along as guide to another party of missionaries and to several independent travelers, including William Drummond Stewart again, and with him Alfred Jacob Miller for another trip to paint the West. Also with us is a German physician, Dr. Adolph Wislizenus. The good doctor is keeping a diary in German, which he translates into English for me from time to time. Here's a very small bit of what he has written, a brief description of the fort on the Laramie:

> *The whole garrison of the fort consists of only five men; four Frenchmen and a German. Some of them are married to Indian women.*
>
> *Sincerely, Your husband,*
> *Adolph*

At the fort I inquire again about whether the Arapahos have come in to trade and whether they have brought me a letter from Friday.

Yes, the Arapahos are here, but Friday's family is once again not among them. Again, there's no letter from my boy, and no return of the two volumes that belong to Mrs. Talbot. I'll replace those myself, a small price to pay for the good years he and I had.

Next, Dr. Wislizenus gives an account of our arrival at rendezvous on the Green River on July 5:

What first struck our eye was several long rows of Indian lodges, extending along the Green River for at least a mile. Indians and whites were mingled here in varied groups. Of the Indians there had come chiefly Snakes, Flatheads, and Nez Percés, peaceful tribes living beyond the Rocky Mountains. Of the whites the agents of the different trading companies and a quantity of trappers have found their way here, visiting this fair of the wilderness to buy and to sell, to renew old contracts and make new ones, to make arrangements for future meetings, to meet old friends, to tell of adventures they have been through, and to spend for once a jolly day....

At the yearly rendezvous the trappers are trying to make up for the sufferings and privations of a year in the wilderness. They use their hairy bank notes, beaver hides, to get all luxuries of the mountains, and live for a few days like lords.

Formerly single trappers at times like this have often wasted a thousand dollars. But the days of their glories seem to be past, for constant hunting has very much reduced the number of beavers. This diminution in the beaver catch made itself noticeable at this year's rendezvous in the quieter behavior of the trappers. There was little drinking of spirits and almost no gambling.

The doctor is mistaken about over-hunting being the

problem for the fur trade. It's the change in international fashion.

I told the doctor that his account was sharp-eyed and fair. He also penned a description of me which seems fair:

> *I have met the well-known Thomas Fitzpatrick, who passed through many an adventure in his life in the mountains. He has a spare, bony figure, a face full of expression, and white hair. His whole demeanor reveals strong passions.*

But instead of passionate, I feel forlorn. The life I've loved on the plains and in the mountains and among the trappers and Indians is lost, a pleasure of the past all of us trappers will miss greatly. If I were a poet, I would pen lines beginning "Farewell, ye days of glory…" and sing eloquently forth. But I'm no poet.

Regardless, it's no secret that the American Fur Company plans to send another caravan to just one rendezvous beyond this one. It's a money-loser. The rendezvous is dead.

April 30, 1840

Today the last fur trade caravan is pulling out from Westport for the last rendezvous. Andrew Drips is again in charge. I'm going along as guide to Protestant missionaries headed for Oregon, plus a Catholic priest, Father Pierre De Smet, and Joel Walker, the brother of my friend Joe Walker. Joel declares himself an Oregon settler, which will make him the first of what William Clark predicts will be a flood of settlers bound there. Probably brother Joe will head for Oregon as well. If William Clark is right about emigration to Oregon, I may end up wandering back and forth, back and forth, from here to there, guiding, safeguarding, guiding, safeguarding.

Father De Smet is the first Catholic priest to Oregon. Though I had hoped a Jesuit would be more understanding of Indian people, De Smet is as judgmental as the Protestants. He shows me his description of the Shoshones who greeted us at rendezvous:

Three hundred of their warriors came up in good order and at full gallop into the midst of our camp. They were hideously painted, armed with clubs, and covered all over with feathers, pearls, wolves' tails, teeth and claws of animals, outlandish adornments, with which each one had decked himself according to his fancy. Those who had wounds received in war, and those who had killed the enemies of their tribes, displayed their scars ostentatiously and waved the scalps they had taken on the ends of poles, after the manner of standards.

I concluded that this representative of God's church feels as superior to the people he has come to help as his Protestant predecessors do. And all these well-intentioned saints come carrying the message, "You are uncivilized wretches hopelessly lost in sin, repellent to the eyes of God."

I wonder why they expect to be received well.

Welcome to salvation.

———

This is the finale to the sequence of rendezvous started by General Ashley sixteen years ago. We trappers who remember that rendezvous and its grand successors are bewildered and bereaved.

I heard the veteran trapper Doc Newell put it well to Joe Meek, whose brother has gone ahead of us to Oregon as a settler:

"Come, we are done with this life in the mountains—done with wading in beaver dams and freezing or starving alternately— done with Indian trading and Indian fighting. The fur trade is dead in the Rocky Mountains, and it is no place for us now, if

ever it was. We are young yet and have life before us. We cannot waste it here; we cannot or will not return to the States. Let us go down to the Wallamet River in Oregon and take farms."

Farms? My heart rebels. Farms pin men down. Farms have pigs—and pigs stink. Farms till forty acres. But mountains reach forever in all directions.

Nevertheless, Doc is right. Our old life is done, done, and done. Let the funeral march sound forth.

But from the loss of this one kind of life, I'm determined to rescue a new life for myself. The would-be settlers need a knowledgeable man to guide them across the plains and mountains to Oregon or California. They think their destiny is manifest.

The Indians think, *Not hardly*.

So, these would-be emigrants need a man who can cope with the Indians along the way, Indians who will be angry at the white intrusion into lands historically tribal, angry at the emigrants for stealing their food—shooting the buffalo and other game the emigrants will kill along the way, angry at white people who think all Indians are savages—just plain angry.

I can do the guiding, and apparently, I will. It will be a living, and I'll still have a life of adventure on the plains and in the mountains.

————

The energies rampant among the American people have come together to create the Western Emigration Society. People have signed a pledge to meet at Sapling Grove, west of Westport, Missouri, on May 9, 1841. Some have been scared off by the report of one man who had a bad experience in the far West. But others are determined to make a go of it, and about sixty local men, women, and children have come together here for the great journey.

They talk things over and discover a major handicap. The maps some of them have brought are worthless, and no one knows the way.

Father Pierre Jean De Smet appears with a party of missionaries, led by a man well equipped to guide these innocents across a vast continent full of Indians—me.

The locals throw in with the missionary outfit eagerly. What they need most to learn is that my function will not be to show the way so much as to negotiate with the Indians for passage across their lands. Fortunately, the emigrants catch on.

When at great length, in fact, we get to California, one of them comes to me to show what he has written in his journal about the whole experience: He says they have been lucky to get me as their guide:

> *"For otherwise probably not one of us would ever have reached California, because of our inexperience. Afterwards when we came in contact with Indians, our people were so easily excited that if we had not had with us the old mountaineer, the result would have been disastrous."*

Exactly right.

———

It comes to be that May 10th, 1841, is an historic date. On that day the first emigrant wagon train sets out from the settlements for the Pacific Coast. We move out, combined with Father De Smet's missionary party. We have thirteen wagons drawn by mules, horses, and oxen. The missionaries, who are mounted, bring along five carts drawn by pairs of mules. In the next few days half a dozen other travelers catch up, bringing our whole outfit to about 80 people.

Procedure: I give the signal to get up and get going, indicate the rest stops, choose the place where we camp, set the guards through the night, and maintain discipline. When I pick a camping place, I make sure it's close enough to drinking water and to wood for cooking.

I set the arrangement of the carts and wagons in a big circle or square, according to the lay of the land. We keep our animals within that enclosure so Indians can't run them off.

One of the preachers disapproves of me thoroughly. When he thinks he's out of my hearing he tells the others that I'm "a wicked, worldly fellow."

That's fine, I don't like him either.

Near the Platte River we have our first Indian problem. One of our hunters, Nicholas Dawson, charges back into camp without his mount, rifle, and most of his clothes. He says he's been attacked by a horde of Indians, robbed, and in every way mistreated.

These claims get everyone excited and soon our wagon, carts, and all are banging-banging toward the river.

Fortunately, I get there first and direct everything into a hollow square with the

people and loose animals in the middle.

Soon about fifty Cheyennes come into sight and calmly pitch their lodges nearby. Since I know Cheyennes to be friendly to whites, I breathe a lot easier.

I make signs for peace and walk out to the lodges.

Chiefs come up and sit down to talk. They didn't mean to frighten the young guy, they sign, but he was so scared they thought he might shoot at them. They hand over his mule, his rifle, clothes, and pistol, no problem.

Our own man nearly caused a crisis. I wish I were surprised.

———

The going gets better as we ride up the Platte. Since we've gotten into buffalo country, we have plenty of meat.

One night "plenty" in fact turns into a threat. A nearby herd goes into a stampede and we're afraid our entire camp will be overrun by the sheer mass of beasts. But I take a dozen or so men out toward the herd, and we keep up such a constant fire that we turn the herd in another direction. Nevertheless, the thundering of hooves goes on all night. Had we not diverted them, the beasts would have trampled us—animals, wagons, and people—everything.

After we ford the South Platte and go up the North Platte, we come to the fort on the Laramie.

Disappointment. Once again Friday's family is not here. Worse, there's no letter from him, and no books left for return to Mrs. Talbot.

Discouraged, I write him another letter and leave it at the fort to be picked up whenever he and his family are here, or there's an Arapaho family willing to carry it to him. I don't actually know whether he's seeing my letters.

But no regrets. I promise myself, no energy wasted on regrets.

———

On up the river we come to where we have to cross the North Platte to get the Sweetwater and beyond that to South Pass and down to Green River. But the Platte looks nasty. Our missionaries are intimidated.

I get an idea: I approach one of our hunters, Gray. "Does it look safe to you?"

"Easy as getting a baby to suck," he says.

Though that sounds like an exaggeration, I keep going: "Will you and your family go across to show them that this is safe?"

"Sure."

Not only does he go into the river, his wife leads the way and he follows, leading a colt with their one-year-old daughter on its back.

Nervy, I think.

But now De Smet and his fellow missionaries are embarrassed into setting forth, and the rest of us follow.

The crossing is still not easy. One wagon tips over, another gets swept downstream for a way, and one mule drowns.

And on to rendezvous.

If only there was going to be a rendezvous.

At Soda Springs our party splits, half heading for California and the missionaries going on to Fort Hall. There they will join their friends the Flatheads and head for their home in Oregon.

In the spring of 1842, I ride back to the fort on the Laramie. I'm too late for the visit of Friday's family to the fort, and they didn't come this spring anyway. So he hasn't picked up my letter or left one for me. The plan of meeting here each May, or exchanging letters, just plain isn't working.

At the fort I meet an emigrant train bound for Oregon, the second one to take this trail. It has been organized by Elijah White, formerly a missionary but now appointed Indian sub-agent for Oregon. This outfit is huge—more than a hundred people, eighteen wagons, and big herds of cattle.

They've been quarreling among themselves and by now have split into two factions. When I tell them that hostile Indians are around, the factions come together under me and Dr. White. The Dr. writes in his journal a message of full-blown paranoia and prejudice:

> *I am now in Indian country with foes on every hand,*
> *subtle as the devil himself; but our party is large and strong,*
> *and I have been able to obtain the services of Mr. Fitzpatrick,*
> *one of the ablest and most suitable men in the country in*
> *conducting us to Fort Hall, beyond the point of danger from*
> *savages.*

When he shows me these words, I thank him for the compliment and say nothing of his mad paranoia or the prejudice in the term *savages*.

At Independence Rock, though, our troubles confirm him in his fears. When we move on, two of our members, L. J. Hastings and A. L. Lovejoy, stay behind to carve their names on the rock, as so many travelers have done in the past.

When I realize that the two have not caught up, I ride back and see that several hundred Sioux have come up, seized them, stripped them, and are acting like they're about to kill Lovejoy.

While our men are being held captive, I prepare the camp for battle. After two hours the Sioux start towards our camp.

I ride out to meet them, making signs for peace and asking them to stop what they're doing. They ignore my signs and ride on toward us.

Then, just as they get within our rifle range, they stop. I'm sure they can see that our wagons are in formation for a fight.

As I ride out to parley, Hastings and Lovejoy come running to our camp, tears flowing down their faces and words of joy spouting from them.

While we count our blessings, the Sioux just move on.

We take a couple of days to hunt buffalo. When we go forward, we come to the main village of the Indians we met earlier. Again, we see signs of hostility, so I stop the train and form for defense.

With three other men I ride out for a palaver. "Don't show the least sign of fear or uncertainty," I tell my companions. "They can see that there are a lot of us and we're well armed. But any indication of weakness can bring on an attack."

Chiefs come to meet us. I ride a few yards ahead and offer them some presents, and they seem satisfied.

That night the Sioux go away. Usually Sioux are friendly, but there's no telling what their most recent encounter with white folks was. It could have been all smiley or full of arrows and gunshots.

After I guide Frémont on his first expedition next year, he writes a savvy comment of this event in his published report:

Long residence and familiar acquaintance have given to Mr. Fitz-patrick great influence among them [the Indians], and a portion of them were disposed to let him pass quietly; but by far the

greater number were inclined to hostile measures; and the chiefs
spent the whole of one night, during which they kept the little
party in the midst of them, in council, debating the question of
attacking the next day; but the influence of "The Broken Hand,"
as they call Mr. Fitzpatrick (one of his hands having been shat-
tered by the burst of a gun), at length prevail and obtain for
them an unmolested passage; but the Sioux sternly assure Fitz-
patrick that his path is no longer open, and that any party of
whites which hereafter be found upon it will meet with certain
destruction. From all that I have been able to learn, I have no
doubt that the emigrants owe their lives to Mr. Fitzpatrick.

I was not officially the guide on this Frémont expedition—my friend Kit Carson was. But perhaps Kit spoke
to the Pathfinder about me, because he chose me as
guide for the next expedition. I call him "the Pathfinder"
with a sense of irony, because I was his guide on most of
his expeditions, and Carson on the others. We did the
work, but in the national mind he got the credit.

———

Meanwhile, back on the road to Oregon, we ride on to
Fort Hall safely. From here no Indian danger is expected
and as agreed my duties are terminated and my fee paid.

I ride back toward St. Louis with a man named Van
Dusen, carrying some letters and reports from Dr. White.
On the way down the Arkansas River, we run into a war
party of Pawnees. When I get to St. Louis, I write a
report of the encounter to the new Superintendent of
Indian Affairs there, D. D. Mitchell.

St. Louis, November 28, 1842

Sir:

*I take the liberty of laying before you a case of robbery
committed on me by the Pawnee Indians, on 28th ult., about
three hundred miles from Independence on the Arkansas
River. I left Fort Hall (Columbia River) August 20th) in
company with one man and thot I might more easily avoid
Sioux and Chiennes (who are now considered hostile). I left
the usual route and came by Mssrs Bent & St. Vrain's
trading post on the Arkansas. From there I anticipated little
or no danger to the settlements; however about half way
between that place and Independence I met with a war party
of the Pawnees coming from the South. They first appeared
friendly, but on our attempting to leave them and continue
our route, they showed symptoms of hostility and in a scuffle
which ensued they got possession of my gun. In the meantime, my travelling companion fled and I have not since heard
from him. I was therefore left at the mercy of the savages and
they made good use of the power they then possessed as they
rifled me of all my travelling equipage, save my horses which
they politely returned to me. They did not leave me where-
with to make a fire, which you know is very inconvenient and
one of the greatest privations. I will herein enclose a bill of
the articles they robbed me of, in order that I may obtain
redress according to the laws existing on the subject. The loss
I have sustained is very trifling, but the insult is very great to
have occurred as it were on the very borders of the
settlements.*

*I have appeared before a magistrate of the city, as you
will perceive, and have sworn to the correctness of the
enclosed bill; however, I will make some remarks on the
different articles for your satisfaction. They are all priced and
set down at what I believe they cost me except the spy glass,
which would be worth here about fifteen dollars, but in the*

Indian country I could at any time get a good horse or about forty dollars for it. There were many other articles amongst my losses which I could make no estimate of and therefore left out altogether, such as Indian curiosities, many curios, petrifactions, mineral specimens, etc.

MID-MAY 1843

In mid-May of 1843, the 2nd Frémont expedition
assembles on the site of what is becoming Kansas City,
with me as the guide. We are 39 Americans and Canadian Frenchmen. Our hand-held arms make us
formidable, and we're taking a twelve-pound brass
howitzer for a show of force. Our gear comes along in
twelve carts pulled by pairs of mules.

The nearby towns are thronged with emigrants
heading for Oregon. Streets and stores are crowded, and
the countryside is dotted with camps. Horsemen gallop
hither and yon, and the sun is half-blocked by clouds of
dust. The racket of hammering on blacksmith's anvils,
mules braying, and cattle bellowing interferes with all
hearing.

The whole conglomeration is quite a sight. What will
soon be called the Great Emigration is about to take its
first steps, a major shift of the population of the U. S. to
its western shores.

Our outfit heads out and pretty quick we're suffering.
The sun blisters us, the nights are frigid, and there's not

enough water. I push ahead to find some that's drinkable
but have no luck. After a couple of parched days, the men
don't care whether it's palatable or not. We camp at
some wallows where the buffalo drank, pissed, and shat,
and men are so thirsty they drink the fouled water.

On July 8th we strike the South Platte River and get
the huge relief of plenty to drink. Several days further up
the river we come on Indians acting like they want to
make friends, Blackfeet together with Arapahos.

And…

Hey, that's Friday!

My son and I jump off our horses, dash forward, and
crash into each other's arms. 'Round we swing, holding
onto each other. We thump on each other's backs.

When we let go, we're so dizzy we almost fall down.

At the same instant we cry, "I can't believe it!"

Still dizzy, we clump to the ground, grinning at each
other.

"Friday!"

"Fitz!"

"Friday!"

"Fitz!"

I turn and holler, "We'll camp here by the river!"

The men of my outfit are staring at the two of us—
they're stupefied. After a long moment they dismount to
make camp.

I bump my butt to the ground, reins in my hand, and
slap the earth with the other hand.

Friday sits just beyond my knees, facing me.

Behind me the men of the expedition, though disbe-
lieving, dismount, unsaddle their horses, and start
making camp.

Friday's companions start putting up their lodges.

———

Yackety-yack, yackety-yack, yackety-yack.

Friday and I are sitting by a low fire, across from each other. I've made coffee and poured us each a cup, his sweetened a lot, as he and other Arapahos like it, and mine black. Our conversation is animated and non-stop.

We haven't seen each other in seven years, and he's altogether a different man. Or I should say a young man instead of a teenager. He's a little taller and a lot filled out—husky, muscled, and moving gracefully as an athlete. *He moves a lot more gracefully than me.* As I've frequently learned, grace is not my heritage.

He's also full of reports about what's been happening. Along with other young men of the tribe, Friday has gone on raids to steal horses from other tribes each summer. On these he has stood out, doing his job, and counting several coups of his own. He hunts when the men of his tribe do and knows poor bull from fat cow. He can ride alongside buffalo at a gallop, put an arrow in exactly the right place, and send the beast crashing to its knees, a skill that takes a long time to learn. He's adept enough at hunting elk, deer, and antelope that he doesn't mention them.

Why did he abandon life in St. Louis, his education, and me to go back to his people?

The yearning of mind and body for union, for love, is understood the world over.

Hesitantly I ask, "Any flirtations?" and immediately curse myself for the clumsiness of my question.

He shakes his head *no*.

For a moment it seems like he's too embarrassed to answer.

Now he says, "One of the young women in a nearby lodge has my attention."

Pause.

"And I have hers."

Pause.

"I have a lot of horses and have counted more coups than any other man my age in our village."

Happy for him, I nod my head.

Pause.

"Later I will stake whatever horses I've stolen from the Pawnees this summer in front of her lodge."

The traditional way of proposing marriage.

"I think I know what her parents will say."

Pause.

Now he's waiting.

"I have a very good reputation."

Then probably my boy will…

I give him a big grin.

Now he turns our conversation to the really difficult subject: "I'm sorry we haven't seen each other in a long time."

We get it all ironed out.

After several days Friday rides on with his family.

See you again, son. I hope it's soon.

————

Instead of following the clear track of what is now the Oregon Trail, Frémont leads the expedition straight across the plains. Soon we're in trouble—we're high and dry here. By the first of July we're suffering acutely from the heat at midday and the cold at night. We're also suffering from thirst. On July 5th, I push ahead but find no drinkable water. The next day the men are not so squeamish. They drink again where the buffalo do, adding their own excrements to animals'. The sun has warmed the water holes for weeks, but the desperate men drink it anyway. What would a dainty connoisseur think of that?!

On July 8th, to our great relief, we strike the South Platte River. Four days later we come on three Indians who've been hovering near, and they finally come up to us. They're Blackfeet who live with the Arapahos, and one is a long-time friend of mine.

In the evening forty or fifty Arapaho warriors visit our camp and bring meat. They've just given a band of Pawnees a good beating. They have proof of that in the fresh scalps dangling from their belts.

Among these warriors I'm again thrilled to meet Friday. We embrace enthusiastically and we chat, but have no new news. When we reach the Arapaho village, whites and reds smoke the pipe of peace. Three days later Friday and I have to say goodbye. I march my part of the expedition on to Fort St. Vrain. Frémont has gone on ahead. After getting here first, he has gone toward Bent's Fort by way of the nondescript village of Pueblo.

I move my part of the expedition upstream to a new trading post, Fort Lancaster. On July 21st I get a delightful surprise: I come upon Carson, who has just arrived from Bent's Fort with nine mules and a good stock of food. That unknown youth I picked up at Taos and took into my company has now become famous. Frémont's published reports of the first westward expedition, full of references to Carson, have been printed and reprinted all over the United States. Yet there is nothing to show that his sudden leap into fame has affected my friend at all. Like his preceptor, he is a modest fellow, and he bears his honors modestly.

Carson goes back to his camp, and I move mine next to his. Two days later Frémont, and his half of the expedition, joins us. Since his own search for supplies and animals has failed, he's gratified to discover that I have carefully husbanded what we've acquired here. There's plenty of flour, rice, sugar, and coffee in camp. We're faring luxuriously.

During the week before Frémont's return, I've enjoyed a visit with Marcelline St. Vrain and his employees here. I know most of them well through my months and years in the West. I note that the trade is now almost entirely for buffalo robes. Fort Jackson and Fort Vasquez, a few miles up the river from here, are already deserted. Frémont has seen their crumbling walls on his way to and from the Arkansas River. The Bent and St. Vrain Company is dominating the trade in their regions through efficient management and good will. Lieutenant Lupton maintains his post by running livestock and doing agriculture.

Frémont is determined to force a way through the Colorado Rockies, and I can't talk him out of it. On July 25th he again splits up the expedition, damn it. He takes thirteen men, a Shoshone widow, and her two children—they want to get to Fort Bridger. They go up the Cache La Poudre, and we don't see them again for two months.

He takes along our camp cook, Courteau. I'm glad of that. I'm tired of his French cooking.

I take my part of the outfit up the usual trapper trail to Fort Laramie and get there on August 5th. On the following day we set out west along the Oregon Trail, a path made clear by the Great Emigration. The going is tough, with lots of discomforts, but the grim business of plodding along is lightened by some episodes that tickle our funny bones. (That's a great American expression, "tickle my funny bone." I wonder which bone it is.)

A good-for-nothing one of our members, Sam Neal, who gets into a lot of trouble, is riding a horse as useless as he is, and I've assigned him a pack mule again as useless. On a torrid day, as we're going through a stretch of hard-baked desert, Neal thinks he sees a clear stream a short distance off. Mounted on his so-called charger, "Old John," and leading his big-headed mule, "Jane," our adventurer turns aside. But on getting to the edge of the alleged stream, the three sink almost out of sight into the milky ooze of an alkali pool.

Shouting for help, Neal clambers to solid ground. His companions rush up with ropes to heave the animals out and make sure the three are safe. But they're thickly coated with a slime that in the open air quickly hardens into stony armor. Neal goes back to his place in the column amid jeers and laughter.

————

At Independence Rock, which we reach on August 15th, I tell them the story of the Indian scare here last summer. One of my men finds the inscriptions of Hastings and Lovejoy on the Rock.

On the Sweetwater we have an Indian scare ourselves. A band of forty or fifty mounted Sioux rush down on us shouting, "We are Oglalas! We are good friends of the whites!" I order them to halt and threaten to fire on them if they come further. So they stop, and I send a man who can speak Sioux to confer with them. He finds that they are Miniconjous, who have claimed to be Oglalas only because they suppose Oglalas to be in greater esteem with us whites. He calls them dogs and liars for their attempt at deceit, and then comes back to us. Nothing happens, and both outfits go on amicably.

Near the eastern entrance of South Pass we see a trail which we take to be Frémont's. Later we discover that it is indeed his. Baffled in his efforts to scale the Rockies, the Pathfinder turned north, reached the valley of the Sweetwater, where he found the emigrant trail, and followed it through South Pass and on to Soda Springs.

My outfit crosses South Pass on August 22nd and moves on south to Black's Fork. In earlier years the trail ran westerly from here, but now it has dipped down to Fort Bridger, the new trading post of Jim Bridger and Louis Vasquez. My men and I pass by the old fort on August 30th, but find the crude cabins, which are built of logs and plastered with mud, deserted and dismantled. Neither Frémont nor I go to the new Fort Bridger.

Soon after we get to Black's Fork, Vasquez gallops up with what he calls his "gallant party of mountaineers" and a band of Indians. Soon these are followed by fifteen or twenty lodges of Utes, and all of them camp together. Vasquez has just gotten back from a hunting trip, and Bridger recently started out with forty men to trap on Wind River. Evidently there is still some market for beaver in the mountains, so I missed a meeting with my old companion and partner.

Soon I learn that the Cheyennes have been on a rampage recently, and have raided the post and run off the horses of the trappers and also a band of Snakes camped in the valley. Some men rode hard after them—they overtook Indians and got the trappers' horses back. The trappers have kept up their spirits, even though they've suffered losses.

One man here at Black's Fort describes the scene like this: "They say it was a beautiful sight to see the

Cheyennes, formed in the shape of a crescent, driving the stolen horses at full speed before them. A party of skirmishers followed close behind,

zigzagging, or as it's called "making snake" along the line, which they endeavored to prevent the pursuers from breaking."

Though that outfit of trappers got most of their horses back, several men were killed. The Cheyennes escaped with just one fatality.

My men and I leave the fort the next day and ride toward Fort Hall. On September 8th, near Bear Lake, we meet a big lot of Shoshones. They're old friends and have a lot to say to me. Shoshones are generally in favor with us whites.

One veteran brigade leader, though, Peter Skene Ogden, hates them. He can't forget the thieving of those he came across in the 1820's. On the other hand, Theodore Talbot, one of the West's best explorers, told me that he joined most trappers in preferring Shoshone Indians and Shoshone horses to any other race of men or horses in the world.

————

We get to Fort Hall on September 13th. Before we arrive, I get a letter from Frémont saying he got this far on September 6th, then went to explore the Great Salt Lake, and is now returning. He writes, "I'm in great need of provisions."

The Pathfinder seems to have a gift for getting his men into spots where they're short of food or water. I lead a small escort out to meet him, carrying food to the men, and about a week later our entire expedition is reunited at Fort Hall.

This trading post, established by Nathaniel Wyeth, was sold to the Hudson's Bay Company in 1837 and Richard Grant is in charge. As a matter of fact, the entire Oregon country is now dominated by the Hudson's Bay Company. As a faithful employee of his company, Grant isn't sympathetic to American exploration or settlement. Still, he sells us several horses, which are poor ones, and five oxen, which are fat.

Frémont, though, favors establishment of a strong military post right here, one where emigrants can refit themselves for the rest of the journey. He says to me that it's deplorable for American travelers, tired out by the long haul from Independence, to have to depend on an unfriendly British outpost for aid.

For sure this Irishman agrees. I have no sympathy for the British anywhere, any time. To hell with the Hudson's Bay Company—let's kick the Brits out of Oregon.

––––––

Cold weather is coming on us now. Frémont gathers the men together, tells them that our journey is going to be a hard one from here forward, and offers to release anyone who wants out. Eleven elect to stay at this fort.

On September 23rd, in a chill drizzle, the rest of us set out for Fort Boise, another Hudson's Bay post on the route to Oregon.

The weather's turning cold. We get snow and ice. Frémont calls the men together, tells them what hardships lie ahead, and offers to release any who want to back out. Eleven more withdraw from the expedition.

On the same day our outfit sets out for the Hudson's Bay Company outpost of Fort Boise, which is on the way to Oregon. Just days later our captain divides the expedition yet again. As usual, I object, and as usual, he pays no attention to what I say. He goes forward, leaving me and the crew with the baggage carts. We have to follow a rough, volcanic terrain along the Snake River.

Damn, but I wish he would stop splitting us up and going his own way. Every time he gets his men into trouble from lack of food and water.

We force our way across the rugged terrain along the river. While eating dinner the next day we're approached by a little family of Diggers, an old man, a middle-aged, care-worn mother with an infant on her back, a handsome boy eight or ten years old, and a girl just coming into womanhood. They're very poor, ravenously hungry, and watch us eat intently.

The girl is strikingly beautiful, with a delicate, slender form, oval face, black eyes, a Grecian nose, and finely chiseled lips; but her brilliant eyes and flushed cheeks show a touch of famine.

We give them food and talk with them. I offer to take both the children along with us. Though the mother knows how desperate the struggle for life is, my pleas don't move her, no matter how often I repeat them.

"Paleface, I *love* my child," she answers, her eyes tearful as she draws her children closer to her bosom.

The next day our outfit moves on, never to see our guests again or learn what becomes of them.

————

A few days later a big hunting party of Nez Percés and Cayuses comes in from a good hunt on the upper Missouri. They're happy. They sing and dance and give intelligent answers to our questions about the country ahead. Moving on, we come to the Boise River and follow it to its mouth, where Fort Boise sits. Here we're told that Frémont has left with our people five days ago.

Damn him.

Following the emigrant trail, Frémont has gotten to Whitman's Mission and stopped there to get flour and corn meal. However, some Cayuse Indians burned the mill while Whitman was back East.

Frémont has then pushed forward and on November 5th reached the Methodist mission at the Dalles. From there he sends word back to us to abandon the carts at the Whitman Mission and come forward with the pack animals. Then, leaving his men in the charge of Kit Carson at the Dalles, he goes down the river to Fort Vancouver, where the big-hearted chief factor, Dr. John McLoughlin, sells him a liberal supply of flour, peas, and tallow.

Back at the Dalles, I come in with the rest of our men on November 21st. Frémont is here, preparing for our next adventure. He's finished what the government authorized him to do: He's made a reconnaissance all the way to the Columbia River.

However, he has no intention of going back to the States yet. He wants to see the Klamath Lakes, the region west of the Great Salt Lake, the fabled Buenaventura River, and he's dreaming of a visit to sunny California. I can't convince him that the Buenaventura is a myth. Jedediah Smith looked and looked for it, no luck.

Frémont has bought a small drove of beef cattle, and our number of pack animals has risen to 104. Not only the carts but the wagons have been abandoned, and our only equipment on wheels is now the howitzer. With twenty-five men, led by a Chinook guide, Frémont and I set out south on November 25th in nipping cold weather and amid flurries of snow. Foreboding about what's ahead prompts us to give thought to our mounts. On the second day of travel, in anticipation of coming hardships and to spare the horses, we walk.

———

We get to Lower Klamath Lake, which is the northern one, on December 10th, and we rest here for two days. The Indians have been reported hostile, but one shot from the howitzer convinces them of the virtues of peace. From here our party moves east and then south to Warner Lake, where we celebrate Christmas.

Then we move on, south and southeast, into what will become northwestern Nevada. The going is rough, the weather cold, and snowfall blocks our way. Our food supply is getting scanty, and only one cow is left to feed us. On January 10th, 1844, we come to a big lake full of salmon trout. From the high rock rising from its waters, Frémont names it Pyramid Lake. We go to the south and on January 18th arrive at the Carson River.

Since our last steer has been killed five days earlier, the men are hungry. Also, our equipment is in a sorry state. Fifteen of our pack animals have died or disappeared, and the remainder are footsore. The country to the south and east does not invite adventure. Frémont decides there's just one thing to do—scale the snowy Sierras and recoup at Fort Sutter. We have no business on the other side of the range, because a Mexican decree early in the previous year has closed the Santa Fe Trail and barred Americans altogether from entering California. This venture has turned into one of appalling danger.

Neither political nor physical obstacles, however,

discourage Frémont. From a point that is a day's march east of Virginia City, we start out on January 19th. Five days later we meet an Indian of the Washo tribe who volunteers to lead us to a good pass, but two days later he quits.

The way gets rougher and steeper. On January 27th and 28th we force our way forward to one of the first passes, and our party gets through, but we're forced to abandon our howitzer. Now we hire a young Washo as a guide, and on January 30th he leads us to the head of Antelope Valley. Getting cold and discouraged, though, he abandons us there.

Some other Indians we meet advise us not to go further lest all of us perish. We push on, though, and on January 31st see before us the towering peaks of the central chain of the Sierras.

There we stop for a day and a half to repair our clothing and get ready for the big climb. The temperature is zero, and the snow lies in places three and four feet deep. Food is scarce. Pea soup is the main ration, though one of the messes feasts on a fat dog. If any of the men have faltered and fallen down, it's not mentioned.

Frémont exhorts us to be resolute. He draws us pictures of the smiling plenty that awaits us in the valley of the Sacramento River only seventy miles away, as shown by his instrument. The men are silent while he's speaking, and there's no talk of retreat.

———

On February 2nd, led by a new Indian guide, we begin to break paths. Each man of a party of ten, mounted on one of the strongest horses, works forward until he's tired and someone else takes his place.

Over this trodden path the rest of the company makes its way. We make sixteen miles the first day, but less than half of that on the second, and on the third our progress is stopped. Two more Indians come up and harangue us whites about the dangers ahead. For the first time some of us begin to despair. The Chinook guide weeps, and on the morning of February 5th he deserts us.

The next day Frémont sets out on a reconnoitering party on snow shoes, and I go along. We march in single file, trampling the snow as heavily as we can. After crossing the open basin for about ten miles, we get to the top of a peak to the left of the one indicated by our guide. Far below, dimmed by the distance, is a big, snow-less valley, bordered on the western side at a distance of about a hundred miles by a low range of mountains.

Carson recognizes them with delight as the mountains bordering the coast.

Having seen the promised land, and greatly encouraged, we struggle back through the increasing cold to where our main party is waiting for us.

We make the turn towards our camp late in the day, and it gets cold in a hurry as night falls. One of the men gets tired and his feet start freezing. Building a fire in the trunk of a dry old cedar, I stay with him until his clothes are dry and he's able to go on. When we catch up, Frémont says to me, "You're a noble fellow."

I have nothing to say in response.

―――――

On February 9th we launch into our climactic effort. Our path has been filled with snow, but it's now beaten down. Struggling to follow it with the pack mules, though, I find that the packed snow will not support their weight. Some plunge around in the drifts and others sink beneath the surface. We now turn our entire force out with mauls and shovels to make a trail and strengthen it with pine boughs. Hungry, weak, and almost blinded by the glare of the snow, we keep to the task as we push forward day by day.

On February 20th, to our great joy, the whole company comes to the summit of the main pass, 9,338 feet above the sea. Fifty-seven animals have survived the ordeal, and though the howitzer has been sacrificed, all the baggage has been saved.

Now the weather clears, and under promising skies we head down. On February 24th another horse is killed for food.

Further on, Frémont, with a small escort, hurries ahead, reaching Fort Sutter on March 6th and then starting back with provisions for the rest of us. Our men in the rear section are a sorry sight. We're all on foot, every man weak and emaciated, leading a horse or mule as weak and emaciated as we are.

A few days later, well fed, reclothed, and re-equipped, we stroll in leisurely fashion around the fort. We laugh at the recollection of what we've suffered in crossing the snow-bound Sierra.

I had met Captain Sutter, now lord of an entire domain, when he accompanied the missionary party of 1838 to the Columbia. This adventurous Swiss, who landed in New York in 1834, has big dreams and boundless energy. From Oregon he sailed to the Hawaiian Islands and back to San Francisco Bay. In California he obtained a big land grant on the Sacramento River and in five years carved out an inland empire. His adobe fort is mounted with brass cannon from the Russian Fort Ross, which he purchased, and an ample guard makes the fortress safe from any likely attack. American overseers are already assisting him in managing his estate and dealing with the hundreds of Indians and Kanakas employed on his vast acres and in his varied industries.

Sutter is hospitable. He makes all the facilities of his establishment available to Frémont. He provides fresh horses and cattle. The mill furnishes flour, and the blacksmith shop is kept busy making shoes and bridle bits for our animals. The little company is soon transformed. With 130 horses and mules, plenty of equipment and supplies, and thirty head of cattle, including five milk cows, we're soon ready to get back to our journey.

———

We break camp on March 22nd, linger for two days a few miles further on, and then set out to the south. The valley is green, a carpet of grass and gold patches of waxen poppies. We ride along the San Joaquin River, with the snow-capped Sierras on our left, for about three hundred miles. Then we turn east and cross the range at Oak Creek Pass. Turning southeast again we wind through the northwestern border of the Mojave Desert.

On April 20th, after a difficult march of eighteen miles, an outcry among the men announces that we've found the object of our search—the Spanish Trail. This well-known route, carefully traced from one watering place to another, has been broken through from New Mexico, the land of sheep, to California, the land of horses and cattle. Opened in 1830-31, it has become a well-beaten path carrying traffic between Santa Fe and Los Angeles.

On April 24th, while the men are in camp, a Mexican

fellow and a boy, dazed and nearly exhausted, come running up, crying out their pitiful story. The man, Andreas Fuentes, and the eleven-year-old boy, Pablo Hernandez, are the only survivors of a party of six, including two women, who with thirty horses were travelling from Los Angeles when a band of Indians attacked them. The man and boy were somewhat apart from the others, guarding the horses. Starting the herd ahead, they rode at break-neck speed back along the trail where they met the Frémont party. Frémont adds the two to his outfit and rushes on to Resting Spring, where the attack took place. The women are gone, but the naked bodies of two men are there, pierced with arrows.

I'm surprised—in fact, dazzled—when two of our men, Kit Carson and Alexander Godey, come to Frémont with a proposition.

"We want to get the horses back," Kit tells the Pathfinder.

In disbelief, Frémont says, "What?!"

"We ain't gonna let them damn Injuns get away with killing all them people and making off with the horses. We're gonna take the horses back."

"All right," says Frémont, "the outfit and I will wait here."

All of us are staggered at this thought: Two trappers against an entire war party.

Carson and Godey follow the trail of the horses until late at night, when they lose it. At dawn they get up and soon see the Indians' camp. They creep close to check out the scene in detail. The whinny of frightened horses gives their presence away.

Caught, the two men look at each other. What should we do?

"What the hell?" one of them says. "All or nothing."

They charge the camp, whooping wildly as they go.

Two Indians fall to their fire.

The rest—miraculously—assume that the two men are the first of a big bunch. They run off in a panic.

Carson and Godey check out the bodies of the two Indians who are down and scalp them. Seeing that one is still living, though, they give him a fatal shot. Then they round up the horses and head back.

Cheers of amazement and congratulations ring through the air as they ride into camp. Frémont puts a lot of energy into slapping the men on their backs.

We ride to the scene of the crime. A dog comes charging up to the mother of the boy Pablo, and the two welcome the dog with hugs and tears. We find the bodies of two men the Indians captured and then mutilated. We don't find any of their women, who apparently are captives.

On May 3rd we get to Las Vegas, which at that time is just a creek and a meadow. But our horses, which are worn and half-starved, get well on the good grass.

Early the next morning we start onward. What faces us now is a *jornada* of fifty miles with no water. About midnight Frémont calls for a stop and a dry camp. But our mules, smelling water ahead, push forward frantically. Before long we come to the Muddy River and make camp.

Here in the Moapa Valley we rest for a day. However, we're continually threatened by Indians, and one of the best-liked of our men disappears, probably captured. Our men want to go after their friend, but Frémont rules that our animals are too worn down for a pursuit.

Forward we push and before long come to Mountain Meadows, a paradise in the desert. We approach the Wasatch range. Here Joe Walker, travelling with a caravan from Los Angeles, rides in with his outfit. Since he knows the route ahead very well and I don't know it all, I surrender the role of guide to him.

After resting for a day, we ride to Utah Lake and then cross the Wasatch Mountains. Then we ride to Fort Uinta and get re-supplied. Now we're in country both Carson and I know well, so we're sharing the guiding. We ride into Brown's Hole, a fertile, well-watered area we trappers love.

Fort Davy Crockett, on the east bank of the Green River, is now in ruins, a testament to what's happening to the beaver trade. We ride on to the North Platte, just a few days' journey from the Oregon Trail.

However, Frémont doesn't want that—he's choosing again to see what he hasn't yet seen. We turn south into a region of the Colorado Rockies. We trappers know it well, but it will be new to science, history, and Frémont's book about this expedition.

When we've traversed the park area, we push on south to the Arkansas River. We ride down that river and soon get to the village of Pueblo and then to Bent's Fort. At the fort, Carson and Walker leave the outfit. I continue guiding us down the river to Kansas Landing. There we board a steamboat to St. Louis and disband there on August the 7th.

1844

I spend the winter of 1844-45 in St. Louis. On May 18 I set out on another U.S. government job of guiding—this one under Colonel Kearny. Our task is clear: We're to determine whether it's better to establish a series of forts across to the Columbia River to facilitate emigration or to make a periodic show of military power to persuade the Indians to behave. I favor the forts. Frémont favors the forts. Kearny favors the shows of military might.

Soldiers always want to flex their damn muscles. They think fear works better than friendship.

Naturally, the government will heed the military, not the men who know Indians.

We set out with five companies of First Dragoons, 250 men altogether. We're well mounted and armed with sabers, carbines, pistols, and two howitzers. One of the lieutenants, a man in charge of the commissary, describes our outfit in his journal. He has shown me his description, and since it's accurate, I've copied it into my journal:

First the guide (that's me) is seen by himself, some quarter mile ahead of all: then the commanding officer, followed by his orderly and the chief bugler. Then the staff officers: then a division mounted on black horses, marching by twos: then another on grays—another on bays—another on sorrels and another on blacks again, with an interval of a hundred paces between each division to avoid each other's dust: then the howitzers, followed by a party of Dragoons to serve them under the charge of the sergeant major; then the train of wagons, with a detail to assist them in getting over bad places, under the immediate command of the quartermaster-sergeant, who receives his directions from the quartermaster; then the drove of cattle and sheep, under the command of a corporal; and lastly the main guard, under the command of an officer to bring up the rear. Each day the divisions alternate in taking the lead—as do the several wagons. Such is the usual order of march—though occasionally, where the ground allows it, the command advances in two columns abreast.

———

Moving north and then west, our expedition gets to the Oregon Trail. This year, 1845, the emigration will number almost 5,000 men, women, and children, with hundreds of wagons and thousands of horses, cattle, and mules. As our expedition of Dragoons keeps up its steady march, we pass party after party of emigrants. Kearny takes charge of counting the people we pass, and his figures total more than half of the year's emigration.

Our Dragoons ride on to the Platte River and along its south bank to the ford of the South Platte. So far, all this is territory I know very well—I first travelled this route to the Sweetwater more than twenty years ago. We ride along the south bank of the North Platte to familiar landmarks—Chimney Rock, Courthouse Rock, and Scotts' Bluffs. On June 14th, 27 days out, we get to Fort Laramie, now enriching the American Fur Company instead lining the pockets of me and my partners. As William Clark predicted, the great emigration is a windfall for whoever owns it.

This time the fort is swarmed with an incredible mix of men, women, and children, speaking a wild variety of languages—English, French, Spanish, and Indian. Many of the women and children are the families of the trappers, hunters, and traders.

Their Indian relatives are here in droves, and about 1,200 Sioux warriors are camped nearby with their families, along with some other tribes. This fort has turned into the principal trading center of all the plains. It has taken in two thousand pounds of beaver in trade so far this year, and nine thousand buffalo robes.

We haven't forgotten the main purpose of our expedition, which is to impress the Indians with our might. For that purpose, Kearny holds a big meeting with all the tribes between the fort and the Platte River.

At this meeting Kearny has three flags raised—two are the Stars and Stripes and the third is an Indian design —crossed bands to represent the winds, nine stars representing the nine tribes present, and clasped hands to indicate brotherhood.

We smoke the peace pipe, and Kearny addresses the crowd. He assures the Indians that their great white father in Washington loves them. He says that the emigrant road must stay open and the emigrants' travel must be unmolested, and he urges them not to trade for the liquor brought up from Taos.

At this point a principal chief, Bull Tail, gives a

friendly response to Kearny. Then presents are distributed—scarlet and blue cloth, red and blue blankets, knives, looking glasses, beads, and other gifts. As a final bit of show, a skyrocket is set off and three shots are fired from Howitzers. These are not only displays of power but threats—*you'd damn well better behave.*

Francis Parkman wrote about the discharge of the howitzers:

> *Many of the Arapahos fell prostrate on the ground, while others ran away screaming with amazement and terror. On the following day they withdrew to their mountains, confounded with awe at the appearance of the Dragoons, at their big gun, which went off twice at one shot, and the fiery messenger they had sent up to the Great Spirit.*

The best part of the whole affair is that Friday is there with the other Arapahos. He and I have long talks in the evenings, roll up in our blankets next to each other to sleep, and eat meals in the fort's dining room.

He apologizes for his people's behavior: Some of the depredations protested by Kearny, he admits, have been done by his people. I judge from this that he isn't yet a man of much influence in his tribe. Too young, probably.

I remind him that the white folks travelling the emigrant road aren't taking away his tribe's lands, just passing through. He says, "True, but they're shooting some of our buffalo." Which I can't deny.

I tell him I'm expecting that within a few years a big council of the U. S. government and all the tribes of the plains will be held at Fort Laramie, resulting in a major peace treaty. "William Clark has predicted that," I remind him. I say it's probable by that time that his people will choose him as one of the spokesmen for the

Arapahos, because his understanding of English and of white people is so good. And I say, "I'm pretty sure I'll be at that meeting to speak for the white folks." That pleases him. And neither of us has any idea how that meeting would turn out.

When the Arapahos leave to rejoin their tribe, I say to him for the first time ever, "Friday, I love you."

He gives me a hug and says, "Fitz, and I love you."

I watch him walk away. He turns, walks backwards for a bit, waves, and walks away.

"My son," I say quietly.

———

Now I lead our Dragoons on a march to South Pass, where we arrive in late June. Here, on the decision of the Pathfinder, we turn around and go back to the fort on the Laramie. Frémont is still planning to go across territory he hasn't seen for himself. At the fort, instead of taking the Oregon Trail, we follow a familiar trappers' trail south to Bent's Fort.

On the Chugwater branch of the Laramie River we come to another village of Cheyennes and other Indians, and here we hold another council. Though useful, it proves to be the last council we'll have on this expedition.

On the upper waters of Pole Creek, we encounter four Arapaho braves, and I'm excited again to see that one of them is Friday. We greet each other with exclamations of joy. Then our soldiers and the other three Arapahos insist on hearing the story of how we met, how I took him in and got him educated—the whole shebang. But after a couple of days we have to move on, and so do the Arapahos, in different directions.

After we come to the mouth of the Cache la Poudre, I lead us on past two abandoned trading posts. We ride to the Arkansas River, follow it downstream, and come to Bent's Fort. Frémont and I congratulate each other on having ridden about 1,700 miles in 72 days, with our horses subsisting entirely on grass.

At the fort we encounter Kearny and his Dragoons. There the Colonel is writing his report to the government with recommendations of what to do about the Indian "problem." He disagrees with Frémont and me about establishing posts along the Oregon Trail, saying they would be too expensive to maintain and that the trail is too roundabout. To his credit Kearny recommends me as the best guide for finding a better route. He writes in his report that "Mr. Fitzpatrick had as good if not a better knowledge of that country than any other man in existence." I'm grateful to him for that.

When Kearny and his Dragoons have gone on, Frémont lays out his plan to set out further west with this expedition, his third. He says he's sent down to Taos to bring Kit Carson up as guide. Ouch!

I wonder if he he's gotten tired of my complaining about his splitting the expedition up and leading his part of it into country starved for food and water.

The result is that I've been praised by one officer of the army and insulted by another.

Yes, I feel underappreciated. I've been more than a guide for Frémont. In practice I was the commander of the entire expedition most of the time, especially when Frémont went off one of his explorations and ended up shorting his men of food and water.

But now, without notice, I get another set of orders from the army. I am to guide Lieutenant Abert and 32 men on a scientific study of country to the west along the

Arkansas River. Abert thinks we don't have enough scientific equipment to do the job properly, and I agree with him. But the job is ours to do as best we can.

Old friends join us now—Alexander Godey and Basil Lajeunesse. I don't hold his last name against him, despite the way the Lajeunesse family in St. Louis mistreated Friday.

———

Luckily, Lieutenant Abert recognizes and appreciates my experience in the West more than Frémont did. He wrote in his report:

> *I was at once delighted with the carefulness of our guide. He directed one man to loosen a noose, which, passing around the mule's nose and neck, held them so closely together as to prevent its eating; another, never to tie his mules in the bushes, for they get alarmed at every rustle and are constantly looking wildly around, expecting some enemy. These things may appear trifling, but those who have been on the prairie know well how much depends on the care and attention bestowed on the animals.*

Now we set out through the upper part of Comanche country on full alert. Recently a band of Texans and a group of these Indians had a big fight— forty Comanches were killed. So, we expect the Comanches to be completely riled up and ready to go at it. Since Lieutenant Abert wants peace, he's bringing with us John Hatcher, a trader well known to the Comanches. At the trading post, Adobe Walls, Hatcher will later bring the Comanches and the Kiowas, who are just as difficult, into peaceful and productive council.

But that is then, and this is now. Now lieutenant Abert and I are taking every precaution.

The outfit rides south on a part of the Santa Fe Trail up the valley of the Purgatory River, which the Mexicans have poetically named Rio de las Animas Perdidas en Purgatorio, the River of Los Souls in Purgatory. Up that valley we ride toward the Spanish Peaks, which the Indians call *Wah-to-yah*, the breasts of the world. On the third day we meet an Apache village on the move, their dogs and horses dragging travois packed with camp equipment and baskets full of dark-eyed children.

The Apache warriors present themselves peacefully. In fact, they apologize for killing an ox from a passing wagon train. They were very hungry, they explain, and needed the food. We tell them white people will not be angry about such a theft if the Apaches acknowledge it in a forthright way and offer to pay for the beast.

We cross Raton Pass and go down to the headwaters of the Canadian River. After several days of travelling south, we see signal fires on high points around us. I explain to Lieutenant Abert that Indians are letting all their villages know that white people are in their country. Right away we tighten our precautions even more.

I order the building of a corral from the trunks of big trees, interlacing the trunks with small branches and strengthening the circle even further with wagons and tents.

We keep up these precautions all the way through Comanche country. When there isn't enough wood, we back our circle up against some natural obstruction, like a deep ravine, anything that will make a charge difficult for their warriors.

Where the Canadian River makes a sharp turn to the east, we find a trappers' trail that leads deeper into

Comanche territory. We follow that, occasionally passing
broken bits of wooden carts discarded by Mexican travelers. We find plenty of deer, antelope, and buffalo,
welcome additions to our menu. Some of the French
voyageurs among us eat a skunk, which offends the noses
of the rest of us.

————

We encounter a lot of Comanches, Kiowas, and even
Crows far from their mountain homes. These Indians
stay away from us, and since we don't give them a
chance to catch us off guard, there's no trouble. We keep
riding along the Canadian River for a long way, even
through the Texas Panhandle. Finally, we turn south to
explore the headwaters of the Washita. Then we cross
back to the Canadian and ride to Cross Timbers, a band
of woods full of fine trees and luxurious grass. Buffalo
graze all around us, and deer and turkeys are abundant. I
love being here.

We lay in a supply of buffalo meat and move on.
October brings us cold drizzles, which dampen and chill
our spirits and our bodies. On October 10th we come to
Fort Holmes, which has been abandoned. Pieces of
wagons are scattered all around, and the fireplace seems
to dream of when soldiers gathered around its flames. To
the east of the fort we march through a dense forest of
oaks and hickory trees, but before we can pull the
wagons along, we have to clear away the fallen trees and
fill in the deep gullies.

Shortly we come to some Creek Indian settlements.
These Indians are a model of dress and behavior that we
rough-looking soldiers could learn from. They dress
tastefully, work for a living, and keep the peace. This

time instead of the whites being alarmed at the approach of Indians, it's the other way around. We look wild, and they probably suspect us of going around the country robbing Santa Fe traders and shooting Indians. However, misunderstandings are soon behind us and all are friends.

———

Now our command crosses onto trails well worn by the wagons of emigrants coming into Texas. From here we come to Fort Gibson, then on across Arkansas and Missouri to St. Louis on November 12th.

Here the outfit disbands. Both Frémont and Lt. Abert now will proceed to give the information they've gathered to the government and to the public at large. That information, though not always accurate, will bring even more wagons to the emigrant trails next year and more emigrants to Oregon and California.

I believe a war with Mexico for possession of most of the Southwest and California is now unavoidable.

1846

All of the talk is an impending war with Mexico. Texas has already been annexed to the United States over Mexican objections. Thousands of Americans want to claim land in Mexico, regardless of a Mexican edict disbarring American entry.

There's no stopping the pressure to go. Mexico has already ordered an army of 6,000 men to the Rio Grande in anticipation of war. The new President of the United States, James Polk, has sent a small force to take a position some distance east of the Rio Grande. He's also sent out three small expeditions to be close to California, ready. Frémont has been put in command of one Of these. I'm assigned to the other two as a guide.

America is raring to go to war.

––––––

War is on. This month General Taylor advances from Corpus Christi to the Rio Grande, and it is there that a detachment of 63 men under the command of Captain S.

B. Thornton is ambushed, sustains severe losses, and is captured.

When President Polk gets the news, he appeals to Congress, saying that because of the acts of Mexico herself, we are in fact at war. Immediately the House and Senate authorize him to spend ten million dollars on prosecution of the war.

That news, flashed by the new telegraph to the western frontier, is greeted with national enthusiasm. American merchants involved in the trade with Mexico welcome the prospect of removal of the high import taxes at Santa Fe. Colonel Kearny is ordered to prepare to invade New Mexico, and the Governor of Missouri is asked to raise eight companies of mounted troops and two companies of light artillery.

Soon I get notice that an Indian agency is to be established on the upper Arkansas River and I am in charge of it. This notice comes after I'm en route to the action with Colonel Kearny. Hearing that one caravan of American traders to Santa Fe is carrying arms to be sold to the Mexicans, the Colonel appoints me as a guide to take two companies of Dragoons ahead. We meet a train coming into Santa Fe and from them get the news that hostile Indians are collecting on the Pawnee Fork. We push on, passing various trading caravans and telling them that they're ordered not to cross the Arkansas ahead of the army.

Unfortunately, orders don't reach us until we catch up with an outfit led by a man named Speyers, which we find waiting for us at Bent's Fort. Trading outfit after trading outfit is coming to the fort, and soon there are more than 400 wagons here, with over a million bucks worth of merchandise.

———

The fort is full. One of the women here painted a lively picture of the scene:

> The fort is crowded to overflowing. Colonel Kearny has arrived, and it seems the world is coming with him. There is the greatest possible noise in the patio. The shoeing of horses, neighing and braying of mules, the crying of children, the scolding and fighting of men, all are enough to turn my head.... The servants are all quarrelling and fighting among themselves, running to us to settle their difficulties; they are gambling off their clothes until some of them are next to nudity, and though each of them are in debt to my husband for advancement of their wages, they are coming to him to get out of their scrapes.

Here at Bent's Fort I get word that my appointment as Indian Agent will get made, but I will be permitted to continue with Kearney throughout the campaign. I write my friend Bill Sublette to give him the latest news:

> News which we have received from Santa Fe would indicate that we shall have no fight, and indeed it has always been my opinion that there would not be a blow struck at Santa Fe. Whatever the case may be elsewhere I know not, but from what I can learn, the campaign will not end in New Mexico.

On August 1st the Army of the West, as it's called, pulls out of the fort with me as guide and William Bent as an additional pilot. We follow the course of the Mountain Division of the Santa Fe Trail, but our long-legged infantry does more than keep pace.

Their cavalry moves on. The days are hot and the water scant. Three days later we send Bent and six other men ahead to scout the mountain passes. They meet a squad of five Mexicans and capture them. Their mission was to get knowledge of the American approach and detain whoever was trying to get out of New Mexico. These captives look wretched.

We march over Raton Pass and into the valley of Mora. In Las Vegas, Kearny, who has now been promoted to a brigadier general, climbs a ladder to a flat-roofed house, and in front of the *alcalde* and the citizenry reads a proclamation that they no longer own allegiance to the Mexican government. And they must not take up arms. They're now under the protection of the United States government.

He tells them that those who stay at home peaceably will be protected by me in their property, their persons, and their religion; not a pepper, nor an onion, will be disturbed or taken by my troops without pay, or by the consent of the owner.

"But—listen up! If you promise to be quiet and are then found to be in arms against me, I will hang you."

———

We mount up and move along. At the little town of San Miguel, southeast of Santa Fe, Kearny repeats this speech. However, the *alcalde* is hesitant to recognize his authority. This fellow wants to wait and see who will win the forthcoming battle.

The general replies, "All you need to know is that I have captured your town."

Those words are enough.

For a while we expect some stiff resistance. The swashbuckling governor of the province, General Manuel Armijo, has issued a proclamation defying Americans to enter Santa Fe, and assembled several thousand troops in Santa Fe Canyon. That's a good stronghold to defend, and excellent leadership might have beaten us invaders back. But in the meanwhile, James Magoffin, the U.S. trader-ambassador, has negotiated with the Mexican leaders skillfully. Most of them have lost patience with their governor, and as a result Armijo has lost heart. He decides it's useless to oppose us Americans and flees. His following disperses, and the way is wide open for us.

———

On August 17th we approach the old town of Pecos and its fat *alcalde* rides a small mule at full speed toward our troops. Over a roar of laughter, he shouts to General Kearny, "Armijo and his troops have gone to hell and the canyon is all clear."

We march into Santa Fe unopposed, and the Stars and Stripes are raised above the governor's palace. The next day General Kearny addresses the people, declaring himself governor, the inhabitants subject to his control, and Santa Fe entitled to the protection of the United States. Some officials retain their positions, and the oath of allegiance is administered to them.

I myself wrote an account of the events and the military situation:

> *Previous to our arrival great preparations were in progress to accomplish our defeat and Governor Armijo had collected a large force in order to "chastise the invaders and drive them from the sacred soil of Mexico." But on the near approach of our little army, the brave and magnanimous Mexicans with their general fled without striking a single blow, and now we are all here enjoying very peaceably the pleasure and luxuries of Santa Fe.*

We are not yet "reveling in the halls of the Montezumas," but in
those of Armijo, as the general has taken up his headquarters in
the palacio.

The army is entirely quartered in and about the city, with the exception of a small detachment sent off about twenty miles for the purpose of grazing and taking care of the stock, as there is little or no grain in the country for feed—indeed the keeping of horses in this place will be very difficult and is a much greater obstacle in the way of conquering the country than Mexican valor.

We have had no late intelligence from Colonel Price but expect him in about three weeks when General Kearny will again resume his march for California where he also intends to plant the Star-Spangled Banner.

The troops dislike the expectation in prospect for California as they apprehend much difficulty and suffering in getting there by land, and indeed my own opinion is that it would have been better to send the troops for that Country by sea, but the General has determined that your humble servant will accompany him. As I presume you are aware, I am the last person that would desert the cause whilst I can be useful to it.

A few days ago, General Kearny gave me permission to return to the United States and enter upon the duties of the office which is in contemplation for me, Indian Affairs Agent. However, the general has changed his mind on that subject and desires that I should go with him.

On September 3rd I again wrote from Santa Fe:

The inhabitants of this place who fled on the approach of
the army are now returning, and apparently are reconciled
with the new order of things. Indeed, one would think from

the present aspect that the conquest of Mexico is now
complete; however, much remains yet to be done, and General
Kearny is using all his exertions to prevent any occurrence
which might be prejudicial to the interests of the United
States in this quarter.

Ex-governor Armijo is yet in the province and is said to
be prowling about in the mountains with a band of two
hundred men. Strange to say, the inhabitants of that vicinity
where he is said to be are more in dread of him and his band
of guerillas than they are of the American army; and well
they may be, as they have nothing at all to fear from us
should they conform to the laws—on the contrary they have
a great deal to fear from a guerilla war, which Armijo is
disposed to wage, not only against us but against all the
inhabitants of New Mexico. His dastardly conduct and his
inglorious flight have left him not a single partisan, save
those with him, in all of New Mexico. This, together with his
already having been an outlaw in some of the lower prov-
inces, leaves the poor wretch hardly a hole by which to
escape. All this will have a tendency, no doubt, to make him
desperate.

Had Armijo acted as a brave and patriotic man should
have done in defense of his country and the government
which supported him, with the advantages that the nature of
the country afforded, together with the exhaustion of our
troops and horses after so long a march, he certainly could
have given us very hard work to perform, and he would now
have held a very different position in the opinion of mankind.
But he has fallen, never to rise…

…General Kearny will be absent about fifteen days.
After that we expect to depart for California. But much is yet
to be done before that is undertaken; and let it be conducted
as it may, its accomplishment will be attended with great
difficulty, and its performance, by an army, will be a feat

such has never been done before. But I will not dwell longer
on this subject, as those unacquainted with the nature of the
country would suspect me of seeking an excuse to back out
from so arduous an undertaking. Far from it. On the
contrary I am anxious for it, so far as my individual comforts
are concerned; moreover, I hold it a high honor to belong to
the advance guard of that American army which will have
the glory of planting the stars and stripes on the shores of the
Pacific.

The traders have all arrived here, together with the army,
making Santa Fe a crowded as well as a lively place. But very
few important sales have been made here this year… I think
many of them now wish they had stayed at home, for, with
the immense number of stock and men, with everything
double what it was before, their outlay is necessarily much
more than they can afford from the profits of any sales which
they are likely to make this trip.

Thomas Fitzpatrick

———

We have started building Fort Marcy on a height
overlooking Santa Fe. More of our troops have arrived,
and still more are on the way. The citizens seem to
welcome the new regime. Since all seems to be safe here,
Kearny is getting ready to march to California.

On September 25th Kearny starts for California,
taking 300 Dragoons. I go along as guide and Antoine
Robidoux is our interpreter.

We march down the Rio Grande to the vicinity of the
town of Socorro. Here we meet Kit Carson and his escort
of fifteen men, who are carrying dispatches from
Stockton and Frémont in Los Angeles. Carson, who had

heard nothing about the revolt that broke out when he left California, reports that everything is quiet there and American authority is supreme. Kearny then decides to retain all but 100 of his Dragoons and to send the others back to Santa Fe. Since Carson has just travelled the Gila River route, and I've never been on it, Kearny sends Carson west as guide with the expedition. Carson protests this order. He's been away from his Taos home for more than a year, and he's now within a few days' ride from home. The order means that he will be away from home for another year. But he sullenly resigns himself to going west with us.

First Carson turns the dispatches he's carrying over to me, and I'm to take them to Washington. I go to Santa Fe with 200 Dragoons. Here I report to Colonel Sterling Price. Price has arrived in Santa Fe with the Second Regiment of Missouri Mounted Infantry only three days after Kearny left, and he's now in command of the military district.

I start east from Santa Fe on October 14th and get to St. Louis in mid-November. Just a week later I go on to Washington with the dispatches and deliver them to the War Department. Next, I report to the Commissioner of Indian Affairs, get my commission as Indian Agent, and start my service as Indian Agent in December, 1846.

I'm happy about this appointment, even proud. It means I can do good service for my Indians friends *and* for my adopted country. I'm the agent for all the Indians of the upper Platte River and Arkansas River areas. I'm responsible for their care and for the safety of hundreds of emigrating Americans.

Yes, I belong here. However Irish my accent may be, after more than twenty years here, I feel like an American.

———

I establish the headquarters of my agency at Bent's Fort, but this location turns out to be impractical. The tribes welcome me as their agent. Some had complained earlier that their great white father must not care about them— otherwise he would have sent them an agent—other tribes had agents. So I came to them with a smile.

I can summarize my decade as the representative of the United States to the Indian peoples of the Great Plains briefly: Both sides, Indians and white, claim to respect my judgment and assert their intention to follow my counsel. I make my reports to the government regularly, in writing, and it pays attention now and then. I speak with the Indians continuously, and they listen as best their cultural slant allows. The army, on the other hand, never listens at all. Soldiers see no solution to anything but fighting.

———

The difficulty with communicating with the Indians is that cultural slant. I urge them to stop warring against each other. They can't make that idea fit into their minds. As they see it, war is the way a man shows himself to be a man, gains respect within the tribe, and especially proves himself to be worthy of the hand of the young woman he fancies as a wife. Life without honor? Unthinkable! Worse than death!

Much the same attitude applies to their relations with white people generally. Like other tribes, white people are enemies, and enemies are people you fight against and steal from. You protect your family. You protect your people. You protect yourself.

Your forefathers, grandfathers, fathers—all have known this.

This is the big issue we face from the start.

Here's a good example of why our ideas don't fit together: We grow corn and other grains and vegetables and eat them. Since the Indians are facing a shortage of food—there aren't enough buffalo left—we urge them to plant and harvest. Those who live next to rivers could do it. They could divert river water onto their fields.

But they're roamers. Hunters. They've always gotten food by roaming and shooting game. A sedentary life of staying in one place and cultivating crops—there's no slot for that in their thinking. I understand. I also like their way of thinking, in regard to their respect for the power of nature.

After ten years of striving in my work as Agent, I see little or no progress. Not yet.

Fort Laramie Peace
Treaty 1851

The Senate of the United States gives me hope. In its majesty, the Senate decides to send me and D. D. Mitchell, of the American Fur Company, to Fort Laramie to negotiate a peace treaty with principal tribes of the mountains and plains—the Sioux, Cheyenne, Crow, Arikara, Assiniboine, Mandan, and Gros Ventres.

I'm pleased. Mitchell also has a lot of experience with the tribes.

And I'm surprised and delighted when he says, over coffee when we first get to the fort, "Fitz, you be the point man, and I'll pitch in when I see fit. Your experience with Indian peoples is wider and deeper than any other man's."

"Good. And thanks."

In late August, 1851, all parties gather for a grand council. Hundreds upon hundreds of lodges are erected around the fort, bringing representatives of the Sioux, Cheyenne, Arapaho, Crow, Arikara, Assiniboine, Mandan, and Gros Ventres. I have my work cut out for me.

I ask our translator, Stanley, "Who's the leader of the Sioux delegation?"

He indicates a tall, stately fellow sitting at the right end of four chiefs. "That's Sitting Bull," says Stanley. "He's a force to be reckoned with."

Sitting Bull is sitting with his legs crossed, in the usual manner of Indians. I step over to him, squat down to his eye level, facing him, and say in the Lakota language, "*Háu, Kola,*" which means "Hello, friend."

I hold out my hand for a shake. He knows this white-man custom and gives me a handshake with his fingers only. And he's looking at his own legs, not at me. Well, here at the beginning of our talks it's too soon to expect to be called "friend."

I stand up and tell Stanley, "Now I want to greet my adopted Arapaho son, Friday."

I walk to Friday and, since he's also sitting, I squat to eye level. Then we grin and reach out with both hands for a vigorous clasp. I say in the Arapaho language, "*Héébe,*" which means "Hello." I'd hug him, but that would undermine his credibility as a man to do tough negotiating with me.

We all start ceremonially by smoking the sacred pipe, handling the bowl and stem with respect. As each chief is passed the pipe, he holds it high with both hands, then draws smoke into his mouth, looks skyward, and puffs the smoke up toward the home of the great powers of our planet—Mother Earth, Father Sky, the east, where the sun rises, the south, where we are always looking, the west, home of the thunderbirds, and the north, home of the cleansing winds.

When this prelude has been completed, Sitting Bull stands up, reaches out with his left hand, and recovers what is apparently his pipe.

Then he lifts the pipe up with both hands and prays. "Mother Earth, Father Sky, the winds of the four directions, we have come here to face each other, red man and white, with good hearts. As we talk, let us keep in mind that we are all related, that we must be considerate of each other, and let us then go to our homes in enduring peace. *Mitakuye oyasin*."

Those are final words in all Lakota prayers. They mean we are all related, a fine sentiment for mankind. What if you regarded every human being as your relative?

And with luck, probably over a lot of days, I think we'll reach an agreement. I'll present the terms being proposed by the government in English, and our translator will tell the chiefs in signs what I've said. Then back and forth, of course, then do a lot of painstaking negotiations to arrive at an acceptable agreement.

That night, as Mitchell, Stanley, and I are having a good supper of deer meat, corn, and *pommes blancs*, they get on my case:

D.D. challenges me: "What's this praying to the sky, earth, and the four directions? Do you believe that stuff?" He emphasizes "believe."

"Sure."

Now Stanley, our translator, jumps in. "Crazy Irishman."

"You weren't cursed with growing up in Catholic Ireland, being sent to the priest to get inculcated in the baloney that Father Donovan was handing out."

"Christianity?" asks D. D. "What's wrong with Christianity?"

"I read everything I could get hands on when I was a teenager," I say. "My father encouraged that, bless his soul. Didn't take me long to start seeing the stories about Jehovah and the Garden of Eden, Jesus Christ his long awaited son, come to save the Jews. In my opinion, these stories were myths invented to give emotional satisfaction to their readers. And I could see that the stories about Jehovah and his savior son were myths too. Myths may have poetic truth in them, but they're not to be taken literally.

"And I wasn't interested in those stories. I liked the stories of great explorers. I had a terrific yen for adventure. Before I was a full man, I was sailing to America to find adventure. Lewis and Clark had done a lot, but most of the West was unexplored, and I wanted to lead the way, or at least be part of it."

D. D. smiles at me across his steaming coffee cup. "Worked out pretty well, too, didn't it, Fitz?"

"Damn well."

"Still," says Stanley, "it doesn't make sense to me. How can you do it, worship heathen gods?"

I feel my neck and back get a little stiff, but keep my smile directed at Stanley.

"It's not worship. It's praying to natural forces because they're powerful, and they help us in our lives. The sun gives us heat and light, Mother Earth gives us living things, and the four winds do blow.

"When I thank Father Sun for the gifts of light and heat, when I ask Mother Earth to bless me or my friends, I'm praying to powers that are real. Jehovah—he isn't real, not to me."

Whoops! I sense that Stanley and I are headed for an argument, and I don't want that.

"D.D. and Stanley," I say, "what say I go see what's for dessert?"

D.D. says "Sure," and Stanley nods yes.

I come back with three small bowls of stewed apples.

Big smiles now.

"Just think," I say, "what a journey these apples have had to get into our bellies. The pack train has brought them all the way from St. Louis.

"And just think," I go on, "how these trading posts are changing the lives of native peoples. They have coffee, sugar, tin cups, knives, clothes made of cloth, coats sewn from blankets…"

I take the last sweet bite of apples and give my friends a quizzical smile.

All three of us stand up, ready to adjourn to our rooms. I'm sharing my room with Friday. Which is a big blessing.

———

The process of negotiations is amiable, with friendship on both sides. One episode in particular shows the good will of the process and the obstacles that remain:

On September 17 we come close to agreement and decide on a treaty with the representatives of the Arapaho, Cheyenne, Sioux, Crow, Assiniboine, Mandan, Hidatsa, nations. The agreement sets forth the traditional territorial claims of the tribes among themselves.

The United States acknowledges that all the land covered by the treaty is Indian territory and does not claim any part of it. The tribes guarantee safe passage for emigrants on the Oregon Trail and allows roads and forts to be built along that route. In return the government promises each tribe an annuity of fifty thousand dollars for fifty years. The treaty is intended "to make an effective and lasting peace" among the eight tribes, each of them often at odds with the others.

I remind my fellow commissioners regularly that our

job is not to lay down the law to the "savages." It's to listen to their grievances, to make clear the desires of the thousands of white people trekking across their lands and eating their game, and somehow arrive at solutions that satisfy both sides and allow all to live in peace. A tall order, but in the end, I like the terms we agree on.

I'm glad we assure these Indian people that the white man has not come here to take away the lands that are traditionally theirs, but have come only to cross this country and then disappear to the west. We will make remuneration for whatever we take of theirs and then pass on.

I point out to the other commissioners that these Indian lands, the plains and the mountains, are not the kind of country white folks want anyway. Very few of us could support ourselves in this high, dry country by farming, and that's how we feed ourselves. We want the fertile lands of Oregon and California, not the uninhabitable stretch in between.

———

One of the great pleasures of this Laramie conference is spending time with Friday. I'm glad to see that, even though he isn't yet a chief, his tribe has chosen him as one of their representatives. That's surely because of the good education in speaking, reading, and writing English, and I arranged and paid for that education.

We also travelled all over the West together, while I taught him skills needed to live on that land.

And we were each other's family. I love Friday and he loves his white-man father.

I also get to enjoy his company on the long journey to

Washington to confer with the Senate. We ride by horse-back to St. Louis and take trains all the way to Washington, sharing seats and meals all the way.

January 1854—In A Hotel In Washington, D.C

Now, in January of 1854, I am lying in a hotel room, confined to my bed. I have pneumonia in both lungs. Of the countless times I could have died, the irony that I will die in a large, noisy city does not allude me. I look forward eagerly to one great pleasure: Friday visits me every day.

The government will pay for his trip all the way back to his tribe's village in the foothills of the Rocky Mountains when the conference is over. On the way he'll stop in St. Louis and give these ledgers with my account of my adventures to my great friend William Clark, agent for all the Indian peoples of the plains and mountains. And Friday says he will ask Clark to find a publisher for my story.

More important, he will give Clark my will, specifying that whatever I have is given to my Arapaho wife Margaret and our two-year-old son Andrew. I'm comfortable with asking so fine a friend for this last service.

———

Right now, in this bed, in this hotel room, the critical word is that I'm *confined*.

I don't know exactly how many weeks I've been in bed, getting along on meals brought by room service. I do know that I can't get up and walk around. Even a circuit around the hotel would be impossible.

I'm only 55 years old. I have no regrets except leaving my wife, my son Andrew, and my son Friday.

For all these weeks I've been copying the words in the journals I kept for years. I want very much to finish the job.

So, it's scribble, scribble, scribble, get up and let in someone bringing a tray with a meal, scribble, scribble, scribble, get in and open the door to Friday happily. One of these days, I'll just peter out and drop the pen, unable to go on.

I will have given all I can.

I wish I had written letters of goodbye to my family in Ireland.

I'm grateful that during this time of the negotiation of the great treaty, I'm quartered in the same hotel as the Arapaho delegates.

It's a great blessing, this gift of time.

A knock on the door.

Did I order something from room service?

I struggle the few steps to the door, pull it open, and *It's Friday!*

I hold my arms out to him, and we hug each other. I fall against him, and he helps me into bed. I hand him a piece of paper with words for him to read. Breath comes hard. The world turns dim. And I hear Friday's beautiful voice, sending me home.

I give myself back to the abundant rivers, this lush earth, and to the stupendous sky, for I am their child. Air is the breath of this planet, and there, as everywhere, abide the spirits of all who live or have ever lived. With every breath, I am with those I love.

THE PEOPLE

THOMAS FITZPATRICK

Tom Fitzpatrick was born in County Cavan Ireland in 1799, and he died in Washington D.C. on February 7, 1854. He was well-educated, longed for adventure, left home, and headed for America at the age of 17. He became a sailor and went up the Mississippi River in the winter of 1822. That same year he went to work as a fur trader, having answered an ad placed by Andrew Henry and William Henry Ashley, stating that they were looking for "enterprising young men to ascend the river Missouri to its source, there to be employed," for their company, The Rocky Mountain Fur Company. And Tom's grand adventures began.

He survived an attack during the Arikara Way of 1823. With his friend Jedediah Smith, he led a small group of men to find an overland route through the Rocky Mountains. He rediscovered South Pass, one of the first white men to do so, for the route through the Rockies to the Pacific Ocean. He was part of the first

Rendezvous, an important gathering for trappers and Indians to trade and create relationships.

By 1830 he was senior partner, along with Jim Bridger and several others, in the Rocky Mountain Fur Company. (A terrifying experience, while being chased by a Gros Ventre tribe through wild country, made his hair go prematurely white.) In 1831 he found an Arapaho boy, named him Friday after the day he found him, adopted him, and educated him with schooling and also in the ways of mountain survival. That boy grew to become a respected Arapaho chief and interpreter.

Fitz went into business, out of business when offered a lucrative deal, and began adventuring once more. He had no fondness for ties to towns or society and was in love with the natural world.

After being named Indian Agent, he went to Washington DC to hammer out a peace treaty that would allow whites to travel over Indian land and hunt, for pay or trade, in the hopes that Indian culture would survive. Ironically, after years of dodging death, he caught pneumonia and died there in the city.

The list of people who passed through his life is a Who's Who of that era. The people he met, and befriended, included Jim Bridger, Jedediah Smith, Mike Fink, John C. Fremont, Jim Beckwourth, Charles Bent, William Bent, William Clark (and his two sons), Ben Bonneville, James Clyman, Edward Rose, and Kit Carson... and that's just a sampling.

When the floor fell through the fur trade, he became a guide and took the first two emigrant wagon trains to Oregon with the Whitman-Spalding Party. He was John Frémont's guide, and Colonel Stephen W. Kearney's guide, along trails to the far west. And he accompanied Kearney's men at the start of the Mexican American War.

As an Indian Agent he was well-resected by both Native Americans and white settlers. He negotiated with Arapaho, Cheyenne, and the Lakot Sioux. He was the negotiator for the Fort Laramie Treaty of 1851, at the largest council that was ever assembled of Plains Indians. At the time of his death, Fitz was a negotiator for the Treaty of Fort Atkinson with the Plains Apache, Kiowa, and Comanche.

MARGARET POISAL FITZPATRICK

Four years before his death, Fitpatrick married Margaret Poisal. She was the daughter of a French-Canadian trapper and an Arapaho, Snake Woman, as well as the niece of an Arapaho Chief. They had a son, Andrew, who was born in 1850. Margaret was pregnant with their daughter at the time of Tom's death.

She often worked beside him at the end of his life, and she became a well-known translator for her Arapaho people after his death, serving as the official interpreter during the Little Arkansas Treaty Council in 1865. He left her a considerable fortune. Upon remarrying, her new husband lost the money, and she divorced him. She was a force, and it's no surprise that she and Fitzpatrick were drawn to each other.

FRIDAY FITZPATRICK

Born ca 1822-1881, Friday was found, at around the age of 7, by Tom Fitzpatrick. The boy had been separated from his tribe, and was wandering alone, near starvation and without water. His Arapaho name, Warshinun, means Black Spot. Fitzpatrick named the child for the day of the week he found him, Friday. He was schooled in St. Louis and went on trapping expeditions with his adopted father, Tom Fitzpatrick. When he was an adolescent, he was recognized by his mother during a chance encounter and went back with his tribe.

Members of his tribe dubbed him the Arapaho American. He grew up to be a translator, interpreter, and peacemaker who was central to negotiating treaties and clearing up misunderstandings. He translated for John Frémont, "the Pathfinder" and one of California's first two senators. He assisted in surveying expeditions and became a leader of a band in the Cache la Poudre River area, near modern Ft. Collins, Colorado. After the loss of traditional hunting grounds, he moved his people to the Wind River reservation.

He and Tom Fitzpatrick remained close throughout Fitzpatrick's entire life.

A Look At Rendezvous: Volume One

DISCOVER THE UNTAMED BEAUTY OF THE
AMERICAN WEST WITH THE AWARD-WINNING
RENDEZVOUS MOUNTAIN MAN SERIES.

So Wild a Dream

Spirited young Sam Morgan is driven by an insatiable thirst for adventure. As he navigates uncharted territories, crosses the treacherous Rocky Mountains, and immerses himself in the ways of Native American tribes, his journey becomes a captivating tale of exploration and self-discovery.

Following in the footsteps of the legendary mountain men who blazed trails through the wilds of the American West and conquered the untamed wildernesses—forever etching their names into infamy—Sam embarks on treacherous journey, where his spirit is irresistibly drawn to the call of the wild. And thus, he is propelled into a world where the unknown beckons and the extraordinary awaits.

Beauty for Ashes

In the unforgiving wilderness of the 1820s Rocky Mountain West, trapping beavers is the perilous path to wealth—and only the strongest survive. As Sam sets out on a harrowing seven-hundred-mile odyssey from the Sweetwater River in Wyoming to Fort Atkinson on the Missouri River, he forges himself into a true mountain man.

But with his loyal coyote pup, Coy, by his side and a band of fellow trappers—including the French-Canadian Gideon Dubois, the resilient mulatto Jim Beckwourth, and the Pawnee warrior Third Wing—Sam seeks more than just fur. His heart is set on finding the love of his life. As his quest leads him through epic battles, buffalo hunts, and tribal rituals, Sam's quest becomes a heart-stopping gamble to win over love's truest affection.

Get swept up in this gripping western saga of survival, love, and self-discovery, where every twist and turn reveals the untamed spirit of the true American frontier.

AVAILABLE JANUARY 2024

A Final Note From Win's Wife, Meredith

Win finished writing *Fitz*, his last book, four months before his death in July of 2023. It is no surprise that he circled back to some of the characters he loved most, the Mountain Men.

He once wrote:

"I love the mountain man. The cowboy is a figure from pseudo-realism, but the mountain man is from romance. In one of the great adventures in a trapper tale, a man rides down a ridge on a thunderstorm bellowing Beethoven back at the gods. No cowboy ever did that!"

Win loved their adventurous spirits. The mountain men did not head into the wilds to conquer the land nor to oppress or convert the Indigenous tribes. Many of them married and had mixed-blood children; all were welcome if they lived well and audaciously. They had a strong bond with the natural world and appreciated its awesome power.

Publisher's Weekly says that Win was "known for his mastery of western lore." Whether you're a history buff, a fan of literature of the West, or simply amazed by the folks who lived, survived, and thrived with sheer will, humor, and innovation, the mountain men are a wonder. Their era covers only a slim slice of time, but oh... What a time it was.

Acknowledgments

Large gratitude goes to Mike Bray and Jake Bray for giving Win's work a final rendezvous. Thanks, also, to Patience Bramlett, an editor whose name is a perfect fit. (Any mistakes in this manuscript are mine—not theirs and not Win's.)

And thank you to all the creative and free-spirited folks Win and I met at Rendezvous over the years, including Bobby Bridger, Gil Bateman, Paul Taylor, and Cookie Murraye. The year 1998 particularly comes to mind: A pipe ceremony beneath a full moon, filling the Wyoming sky with buttery light, then huddled around a small black-and-white TV, cheering as Mark McGwire hit historic homerun #62. You are each well-loved and respected—fine folks to run the river of life with.

About the Author

Win Blevins was an award-winning author best known for his fiction and non-fiction books of Western lore and Native American leaders, lifestyle, and spirituality. He was the recipient of a lifetime achievement award from the Western Writers of America, and a member of the Western Writers Hall of Fame; a three-time winner of Wordcraft Circle Native Writers and Storytellers Book of the Year; two-time winner of a Spur Award for Best Novel of the West; and was nominated for a Pulitzer for his novel about Crazy Horse, *Stone Song*.

Blevins, whose own origins were a mix of Cherokee, Welsh-Irish, and African American, published his first novel in 1973. That book, *Give Your Heart to the Hawks, a Tribute to the Mountain Man*, is still in print fifty years later and recently returned to the *New York Times* bestseller list.

Over his long career, Blevins wrote nearly forty books, including the historical fiction Rendezvous series, a dozen screenplays, and numerous magazine articles. His *Dictionary of the American West* is held in 750 libraries.

Born in Little Rock, Arkansas, on October 21, 1938, Blevins was an honors graduate of Columbia University —where he earned a master's degree—and the Music Conservatory of the University of Southern California. He began his writing career as a music and drama critic for the *Los Angeles Times* and became the principal entertainment editor for the *The Los Angeles Herald Examiner*.

During that time, he hung out with the likes of Sam Peckinpah and Strother Martin, and began diving into the lives of Mountain Men and Native Americans of the West.

He also served as the Gaylord Family Visiting Professor of Professional Writing at the University of Oklahoma. For fifteen years, he was a book editor for Macmillan Publishing and TOR/Forge Books.

Win loved and felt a deep connection with nature. He climbed mountains on four continents and was a boat-man-guide on the Snake River. Once caught in a freak blizzard while climbing, he took shelter inside a tree for more than twenty-four hours. His feet were frozen, but he refused to have them amputated. Almost twenty years after that event, he climbed the Himalayas—despite an awkward gait.

Native Spirituality suited him. He was pierced during a Lakota ceremony and was a pipe carrier. He went on twelve vision quests and felt the pull of the red road.

Win spent the last twenty years of his life, living quietly in the Southwest among the Navajo. His passions grew with time. In the center was his wife Meredith, their children, and many grandchildren. Classical music, baseball, roaming red rock mesas, and rafting were great loves, and he considered himself blessed to create new stories about the West. He was also proud to call himself a member of the world's oldest profession—storytelling.